ARTHUR MILLER:

THE BURNING GLASS

SHEILA HUFTEL

Arthur Miller:
The Burning Glass

THE CITADEL PRESS   NEW YORK

76317

For my Mother, and in memory of my Father

Contents

INTRODUCTION

Of all modern dramatists, Arthur Miller pierces most reso-
lutely to the core of a problem. He does not flick over it or
under; he attacks its heart. Any student of his plays should
work in the same manner. Few do; but Sheila Huftel does, and
her analysis in depth is the kind of tribute Miller must value.

Genuine appreciation means understanding, not a vague
fuzz of sympathy. Miss Huftel understands and appreciates;
she has thought herself into the dramatist's imagination. It is
rare indeed to find so concentrated a scrutiny of a modern
writer's work for a theatre he respects. The phrase is important. Arthur Miller respects the theatre: he does not seek to
turn his stage into a pulpit. He is an intellectual, without
quotation marks, and his plays (though mind must meet
mind) are not pretentious—the death of a dramatist. This
study prickles with insights that explain why Miller is a man
of the living theatre and one (in my own opinion) likely to
endure longer than Tennessee Williams, that beaker full of
the warm South.

We are dealing with a man of a singular creative intensity. A playgoer told me once that he had always a lurking sense of guilt at a Miller play. There is an unsparing search for truth; from it a major dramatist has developed. *All My Sons*, *Death of a Salesman* (which Miss Huftel calls "a daily tragedy"), *A View From the Bridge:* these are three of the century's definitive plays of the American scene. The English National Theatre, as I write, is about to stage a fourth, *The Crucible*, under Sir Laurence Olivier's direction.

Here—intruding a personal note—I have to return, surprisingly, to my childhood in the south of Cornwall. Every afternoon I would take a book to a great cliff-rock that commanded an empty glitter of sea; eastward, headland upon headland stretched to the distance like a regiment of saurians fixed there since prehistory. It was then that I read a play by Longfellow, gentlest of New Englanders, about a Salem farmer and his wife falsely condemned for sorcery, their lives swept away in the hysteria of a black hour when reason tottered.

Written barely and quite without guile, the drama stayed with me through the years. With a shock, on opening a program at the Bristol Old Vic in the autumn of 1954, I realized that Arthur Miller had treated the same theme; in describing the Salem hysteria he sought a parallel with our own day. Where Longfellow's *Giles Corey* had had a certain dignified remoteness, *The Crucible* scorched. It is a strange exercise now to move from one text to the other, from simple statement to a play every line of which seems to be stamped out with a hot iron.

Miller forces us to remember. Six months, a year, ten years after one of his *premières*, the play still glows. We remember it. We may argue; we may disagree; we may rage; but we remember. Miss Huftel's book tells us why. She is, in the contemporary word, as committed a student of Miller as he is a committed dramatist: we are grateful for it.

I think now of a man very different from Miller. "Experience," said Henry James, "is never limited and it is never complete; it is an immense sensibility. . . ." For me those last three words speak for the dramatist whose work is now minutely charted before us.

J. C. TREWIN
President, The Critics' Circle (London), 1964–65.

AUTHOR'S NOTE

My special gratitude to Arthur Miller for an endless kindness: for allowing me to quote so freely from his work and for adding new insights through his letters.

Surely no new writer can have had a happier introduction than the one written by John Trewin for this book. I cannot thank him and Wendy Trewin enough for their encouragement and for sharing each enthusiasm.

S. H.

London, 1964.

ACKNOWLEDGMENTS

I should like to thank The Viking Press, Inc., New York, for permission to quote from *After the Fall, All My Sons, Death of a Salesman, A View From the Bridge, The Misfits, Incident at Vichy,* and the Preface to Arthur Miller's *Collected Plays.* For permission to quote from *The Man Who Had All the Luck* I thank The Ashley Famous Agency, Inc., New York.

Acknowledgments are due, too, to the authors and publishers of the following books which I consulted in the preparation of my book and from which, in some cases, I have quoted briefly: *The Dramatic Event* and *What Is Theatre?* by Eric Bentley (Dennis Dobson, London); *The Crucible* by Arthur Miller (Dramatists Play Service, Inc., New York); *Focus* by Arthur Miller (Victor Gollancz, Ltd., London); *Armchair Esquire,* which includes "The Misfits," a short story by Arthur Miller (William Heinemann, Ltd., London); *An Enemy of the People* by Henrik Ibsen (William Heinemann, Ltd., London); *Brecht on Theatre,* translated by John Willett (Methuen & Co., Ltd., London); *Marilyn Monroe* by Pete

Martin (Doubleday & Co., New York); *Person to Person: Introduction to "Cat on a Hot Tin Roof"* by Tennessee Williams (New Directions, New London, Conn.); *Preface to "Man and Superman"* by George Bernard Shaw (Odhams Press, Ltd., London); *The Face of the World* by Cecil Beaton (Weidenfeld and Nicolson, London); *How Not to Write a Play* by Walter Kerr (Simon and Schuster, New York); and *Eichmann in Jerusalem* by Hannah Arendt (The Viking Press, New York).

I should like also to thank the editors of the following periodicals for use I have made of materials from them: *Commentary*, *Encore*, *Esquire*, the *Manchester Guardian*, *Harper's*, *Holiday*, *Life*, the *New York Herald Tribune*, the *New York Post*, the *New York Times*, the *New York World-Telegram & Sun*, *Newsweek*, the *New Republic*, *The Observer*, the *Saturday Evening Post*, *Saturday Review*, *The Stage*, the *Sunday Times* (London), *Theatre Arts*, *Theatrical Educational Journal*, *Time*, and *The Times* (London).

For the photographs used in this book I wish to thank Inge Morath and Magnum Photos, Inc., W. Eugene Smith, Gjon Mili, and United Artists Corporation.

S. H.

ARTHUR MILLER:

THE BURNING GLASS

CHAPTER I

Arthur Miller

Arthur Miller was born in Harlem, Manhattan (New York), on October 17, 1915. His father, Isadore Miller, came to America when a small boy from a small town in Austria. He was a man of little education, and before the Depression was a well-to-do manufacturer. Miller's mother was born in America, and he went to the school in Harlem from which she had graduated. Miller had a featureless school career; he was a poor student and evidently made no impact whatever on his teachers. They simply did not remember him. Once he became known as a dramatist they did find his name in the school records, but it remained a name without a face. The boy himself escaped them entirely.

The Great Depression of the thirties both shattered and shaped Miller's life. It began when he was fourteen and in a few years reduced his family to poverty. The day before the banks closed Miller withdrew his total capital of twelve dollars to buy a bike from a friend. He was, then, momentarily untouched. "What did bother me," he wrote in "A Boy

Grew in Brooklyn" (*Holiday*, March, 1955), "was that the day after the bank closed I got hungry, left the bike in front of our house, went inside for some bread and jam, and came out to find no bike, and a block can never look as empty as it does to a boy whose bike should be on it and isn't. In that emptiness lay a new reality."

Miller has an older brother, Kermit, and a younger sister, Joan. Isadore Miller had several jobs during the Depression, including one as a salesman for a time; but Miller insists that neither his father nor his brother were drawn as characters in any of his plays. He wrote vividly of his boyhood in "Shadows of the Gods" (*Harper's*, August, 1958). The paragraphs come alive like snapshots—suddenly the past is the present. "An adolescent must feel he is on the side of justice. That is how human indignation is constantly renewed. But how hard it was to feel justly, let alone to think justly. There were people in the neighborhood saying that it had all happened because the workers had not gotten paid enough to buy what they had produced, and that the solution was to have Socialism, which would not steal their wages any more the way the bosses did and brought on this depression. It was a wonderful thought with which I nearly drove my grandfather crazy. The trouble with it was that he and my father and most of the men I loved would have to be destroyed."

Looking back on his younger self, Miller records: "I too had a religion, however unwilling I was to be so backward. A religion with no gods but with godlike powers. The powers of economic crisis and political imperatives which had twisted, torn, eroded, and marked everything and everyone I laid eyes on."

After graduating from high school he went to work—

driving trucks, unloading cargoes, waiting on tables in hotels, and in a warehouse. One rainy afternoon, by accident and mistaking it for a detective story, he picked up *The Brothers Karamazov*. "The same yearning I felt all day for some connection with a hidden logic was the yearning in this book. It gave me no answers but it showed that I was not the only one who was full of this kind of questioning, for I did not believe —and could not after 1929—in the reality I saw with my eyes. There was an invisible world of cause and effect, mysterious, full of surprises, implacable in its course." Miller's commitment is made here. The need to discover and define this particular logic is the dominant purpose of his plays, and the scars and lessons of this time persist through them. As recently as March 20, 1960, when Miller was interviewed by Henry Brandon for the *Sunday Times* (London), he stressed the need for drama to "readdress itself to the world beyond the skin," to concern itself with fate. Miller summed up memorably: "And fate is always the others—even if it is *you* that dies of it."

He read *The Brothers Karamazov* on the subway to and from the warehouse, and soon afterward began saving money to go to college. The fees at the University of Michigan were the lowest in the country; there he studied playwriting under Professor Kenneth T. Rowe. Until this time Miller had seen only one play and read Shakespeare's tragedies. Within four years he had won three drama prizes, and in 1936 he won the Theatre Guild National Award with *The Grass Still Grows*, one of his earliest plays. In *Holiday* (December, 1953), he gave some idea of what Michigan was like during the four years he spent there: "We saw a new world coming

every third morning, and some of the old residents thought
we had gone stark, raving mad."

After his graduation in 1938 he joined the Federal Theatre
Project for its brief life, and for it wrote a tragedy about the
conquest of Mexico; but this remained a desk-drawer play.
Miller then wrote radio scripts for a living. He and Mary
Slattery married in 1940 and they have two children, Robert
and Jane Ellen. Rejected by the Army on medical grounds,
Miller spent a year as a fitter in the Brooklyn Navy Yard,
until he was asked to write a film script about Army training,
The Story of G.I. Joe. He collected the material on which the
film story was based and later published it in his first book,
Situation Normal. . . .

In the Preface to his *Collected Plays* he wrote of the importance of the Group Theatre to him; *All My Sons* reflects its
influence. In those days Miller's playgoing was cut to the
minimum: Ibsen, Strindberg, and Odets. He wrote to me:
"Over a period of some ten years I wrote about as many plays
until I somehow saw that it was necessary to complete a
work. That is, to do more than express a feeling, and to press
things to the wall. The first such attempt was *All My Sons*,
which was almost two years in the making for this reason."
He described his desk-drawer plays in his Preface—plays
written with detachment on themes chosen at random. He
found no continuity between one play and the next and did
not see himself in what he had written. The first of these
aloof plays was about a family, the next about two brothers
at college, on either side of radicalism. He then wrote about a
prison psychologist, who found that the sane were joining
the mad; he wrote of a ship's officer turned pirate by his

desire for death; and many others that he himself no longer remembers.

Situation Normal . . . was published in 1944. Miller's first Broadway play was *The Man Who Had All the Luck*, 1944; it closed in a week. In 1945 his novel *Focus* was published. *All My Sons*, 1947, won the New York Drama Critics' Circle Award 1946–47. Miller had decided that if this play failed he would go into another line of work. Success, complete and carefree, came when *Death of a Salesman* broke all records in 1949 by winning the Drama Critics' Circle Award 1948–49, the Pulitzer Prize, and the Antoinette Perry Award. Miller's adaptation of *An Enemy of the People* opened in 1950, followed by *The Crucible*, which was uneasily received in 1953. The double bill of *A View From the Bridge* and *A Memory of Two Mondays* opened in 1955. In 1961 he wrote the film script for *The Misfits*. *After the Fall* was the initial production at New York's Lincoln Center in 1964, to be followed by *Incident at Vichy* in its second season the same year.

"If the reception of *All My Sons* and *Death of a Salesman* had made the world a friendly place for me, events of the early 50's quickly turned that warmth into an illusion," Miller said in his Preface. He went on to describe America at the time of McCarthy: "There was a new religiosity in the air, not merely the kind expressed by the spurt in church construction and church attendance, but an official piety which my reading of American history could not reconcile with the free-wheeling iconoclasm of the country's past. I saw forming a kind of interior mechanism of confession and forgiveness of sins which until now had not been rightly categorized as sins. New sins were being created monthly. It was very odd how quickly these were accepted into the new

orthodoxy, quite as though they had been there since the
beginning of time."

One, perhaps minor, facet of this time was the fate of
"Bridge to a Savage World," a film script on juvenile delinquency that Miller was commissioned to write by the New
York City Youth Board. The film was never made. It is
difficult at this distance to pry into reasons and motives, but
as far as I can see, the decision had nothing whatever to do
with the film script. In 1955, at the height of "McCarthyism,"
it had everything to do with Arthur Miller's having written
it. The American Legion, the Catholic War Veterans, and
AWARE, an organization whose purpose was to "expose"
Communist influence in entertainment, protested that Miller
was associating with left-wing groups. The Youth Board
stopped "Bridge to a Savage World" when they were secretly
told by the Un-American Activities Committee that Miller
was likely to be subpoenaed. Let us explore Miller's raw
material for "Bridge to a Savage World," which was published and salvaged by *Esquire* in October, 1958.

Miller began by describing the work of the Youth Board,
then about eleven years old. It was one of the first experi-
mental projects of its kind, one that broke new ground by
sending its men "into the streets, the pool rooms, the dance
halls, the homes and hangouts of the very worst gangs, prepared to spend years with them, giving them every kind of
leadership and aid in order to relate their members to the
values of civilized society."

For two months Miller worked with these men, saw the
gangs through fights and at meetings of reconciliation, and
from them collected the material for his film. At the outset,
characteristically, he defined the problem:

"There are elements in the gang codes today," he wrote, "which are more primitive than those that governed the earliest clan societies. When a Youth Board worker descends into the streets he is going back into human history a distance of thousands of years. Thus it is fruitless merely to say that the delinquent must be given love and care—or the birch rod. What is involved here is a profound conflict of man's most subtle values. The deeper into their lives the Youth Board worker goes, the more apparent it becomes that they are essentially boys who have never made contact with civilized values: boys without a concept of the father, as the father is normally conceived, boys without an inkling of the idea of social obligation, personal duty or even rudimentary honor. . . . In this picture we shall meet boys who, before they are reached, could fit comfortably into the behavior patterns of the early hordes that roamed the virgin forests."

"Before they are reached" is a persistent theme in Miller's writings: the isolated people are those cut off from society, and who are less human, if only for this reason. In the delinquent boys of "Bridge to a Savage World," Miller has a concrete image that not only illustrates his belief but also proves it. These boys are in a vacuum before the Youth Board worker reaches them, and even when he does, only some of them are able to break out of it. Miller's Jerry Bone reaches them because no other person has shown concern for them without demanding something in return.

Miller warns that his script outline is "simply a glimpse into what is at stake in this film." And for this reason alone it is of value. It is a piece of work in the making. In the raw material for such a film the values are naked and exposed instead of built into a story, expressed through people and influenced by their attitudes. In this way a situation is stripped down to its fundamental meaning, like the skeleton structure of a building before the walls go up. This is not to say that the bare structure is of greater value than the finished building. You cannot live in it, but it is reassuring and enlightening to see.

Of Jerry Bone, the Youth Board worker in the film, Miller writes: "We shall ultimately come to see on the screen a kind of love in him which most men never approach for their fellow human beings." Jerry Bone is Miller's "seeing man," who will not be confused by sentiment and who is too realistic to become an unthinking do-gooder. To say this is not to say that Miller is making over this material in his own image; it is to show how admirably suited he would have been to write that script. One can be certain that had Miller's image not jibed with the facts, the image would have been changed; he has said this more than once. In this instance, however, he seems to have been in particular sympathy with what he found: "The Youth Board worker in this picture is a faithful portrait of actual workers I have met."

Miller brings out the conflicts in the character, charting his growth almost as though Jerry Bone were new-minted in his mind. "The proud exhaustion of Jerry Bone will emblazon the fact I believe must be placed before the people: The work is hard beyond belief; it wears out people, it makes those who engage in it face every one of their own failings. . . . One must be open to knowledge, and above all one must learn how to set fear aside." This is the heroic face of Jerry Bone, but, because Miller is writing about him, this man must come to a realization of himself. "Bone will become aware as he sets forth these values . . . that what he is teaching them he must first teach himself. Thus, we shall witness the maturation of Jerry Bone."

Gradually the boys begin to respect him and later they come to identify themselves with him as though he were, in fact, their father. The story is the process of this identification as Jerry moves closer into their lives. Joe Meister turns toward him because although his own father tries to help him, he has no dignity in his son's eyes. The boy sees his father as a clown and cannot respect him. Jouncey, leader of the South Bay Rangers, is the most violent of the boys. He is illegitimate and his mother's guilt rises every time she sees him. She tries to help him, but this is "a boy looking endlessly for his father."

Miller carries this dominant theme of the film through to Jerry's private life. "Finally, Jerry's own kids, having lived a life of waiting for him, having lived, in fact, without his supervision, begin to show the dreadful signs of delinquency themselves. The thematic principle of this story, barely suggested here, is that we have time for everything but our children; but more, that sometimes it is beyond good and evil." In the end "Jerry is scarred, and he is tired, and he is no longer the thirty-year-old athlete we saw at the beginning." Victory is never total and often more weary than triumphant. Jerry Bone finds himself personally defeated, but with a public victory: he has changed a neighborhood.

The film was to follow the lives of the delinquent boys. "Their neighborhood is one of decaying brick and brownstone four-story tenements, small factories, and a few boarded-up buildings." The first time Jerry reaches them is just after he has talked the cops out of jailing them. No sooner have they been reprieved than they hear that their territory, a strip of

street, has been invaded by a hostile gang. A savage fight
follows. When Jerry tries to help them, they flare up at him.
"For he wants to know why they fought, what good it did.
. . . For a moment Jerry sees that for them this fighting
represents a kind of knighthood, an opportunity for bravery,
for conquest, for courage, against an enemy that can be seen
and felt and hurt. They want compliments on their bravery
now, not questions." Jerry sees the reasons for their fighting
—they don't. For them the answer is not known, not realized,
not understood. In Miller there is always an outside observer
to see into the situation that blinds his characters.

The film would have shown the gang in conflict with itself,
uncertain how to react to a threat that had always been
answered with a murderous fight. And always alongside the
victories will go the many reverses. It is perhaps a part of the
shell of irony that somehow encloses "Bridge to a Savage
World" that some of the material suggests a straight and
serious version of *West Side Story*.

Quoting from Miller's outline: "One of the greatest days of
their life (and mine) [was] when they finally agreed to go on
a camping trip. Throughout the picture their boredom will be
like an insistent counterpoint to every moment, every act.
They simply have nothing to do. The great city is building
and rebuilding, the traffic is endlessly flowing, the phones
by the millions are ringing, the lights are blinking on a thousand marquees, but they are afraid to leave their corner,
especially alone, and they live without an inkling that people
are supposed to occupy themselves, that their lives are supposed to be meaningful. Thus, the idea of a camping trip is
outlandish at first. What's to be gained? Girls? Free whiskey?
What?"

Miller describes the camping trip, the chaos of four boys wanting to cook at once, and the difficulty of persuading anyone to play the outfield. If the fielder missed a catch the indignity would be too much for him. "We will see the slum confronting nature. Livertrouble catching a fish, the first live one he ever saw, tying a string around it and walking along the shore with 'my fish,' which he is heartbroken to leave when they have to return home. ('I'm commutin' with nature,' he said to me.)"

The trip will also confront the Rangers with some middle-class children, whom they despise at first. Until they discover that the children can really play baseball, swim, and run—because they have learned to cooperate, had a chance to play, and did not start smoking and drinking at the age of nine. The South Bay Rangers watch them play.

Individuals emerge from this gang. One of them, Paul Martense, who began the film leading the fight, ends it as a Youth Board worker, walking into a new district. Miller writes this about Paul: "The saved boy, in a word, becomes not merely a 'good citizen' or 'just like anybody else' after having been an outlaw. Having seen society from the very bottom, the insight he gains is remorselessly honest when he does gain insight. He cannot be 'conned'; he is immune to the easy solutions that bemuse the rest of us who are less tightly bound to reality; he is pragmatic and breath-takingly idealistic at the same time." Paul is the hardheaded but aspiring person for whom Miller reserves his admiration.

In the film we would have seen the change of attitude in some of the boys, and their growth, as well as the failure of others. Rabbit Lewis, a boy without a family, was on the streets at seven when his parents died. By the time Jerry

reaches him Rabbit is a junkie; he is finally brought by Jerry
to the point where he is able to face his situation. The boy is
desperately eager to be cured. He wants help and is ready to
accept it. But there is nowhere he can get it. There are no
facilities in the prisons. Still, he gives himself up to the police
in the hope that the isolation of prison and his own will to
survive will cure him. But he is not jailed. He is paroled to his
only relative, an aunt in the country, on condition that he
never come back to the neighborhood. Looking for com-
panionship, Rabbit finds only commands and an endless
watchfulness. He is constantly suspect. "In South Bay,"
Miller writes, "he is accepted, left alone. . . . Rabbit ends a
junky, the ultimate image of the boy whom nobody gave a
damn for; a boy to whom Jerry came too late. . . .

"The overhanging question will be, quite simply, whether
and how each of these boys, with whom we shall have
sympathy, will 'make it.' " This struggle to survive a bottom-
less confusion rolls like a backwash through the film. And the
conflict is at its greatest in Jouncey—"a hoodlum, somebody
to frighten any man on any street." If Rabbit is symbolic of
the boy "nobody gave a damn for," Jouncey in himself is
symbolic of their turmoil.

When Jerry Bone appears to threaten his leadership
Jouncey fights him. Later that night Jerry comes back to
apologize and Jouncey is "brought down to a weeping hulk
. . . by his own confusions," which Jerry forces him to face.
This boy who has looked for a father all his life, wants Jerry's
love but cannot accept it. Instead, he finds an outlet in
violence and sees a way out through drugs, a habit he is
strong enough to break. The film will follow Jouncey's
career: his triumph when he persuades the Army General in

charge of recruiting to forget his police record and let him join the Army; his return without leave, lost and turned against himself, and his failure to get any psychiatric help. "And he will commit his great crime in order to bring himself over the edge of the abyss."

Wherever Jouncey looked it was Everest.

Miller's account of his film story ends characteristically with emphasis on the fundamental value of an individual's self-respect. "What they must have in exchange for peace, however, is a shred of dignity. These are children who have never known life excepting as a worthless thing. They have been told from birth that they are nothing, that their parents are nothing, that their hopes are nothing. The group in this picture will end, by and large, with a discovery of their innate worth. . . . That is what this picture is about." That is what most of Miller is about, in that his characters are invariably left aware and self-knowing.

On Thursday, June 21, 1956, Arthur Miller was summoned to appear before the House Committee on Un-American Activities, where he refused to turn informer and name people he had seen at Communist writers' meetings ten years before. Here are extracts from the "Testimony of Arthur Miller, accompanied by Counsel, Joseph L. Rauh, Jr." The chairman of the Committee was Francis E. Walter; Richard Arens was staff director. It was Part 4 of an "Investigation of the Unauthorized Use of United States passports, 84th Congress."

Early in his testimony, Miller explained his position with the Youth Board over "Bridge to a Savage World": "The

*issue there, quite clearly, was whether I was trustworthy
enough to write a screenplay on juvenile delinquency without
warping the truth about this very grave problem. Now, I
understood perfectly why they would be concerned about
this; I would be too." Miller went on to say that the Board
and their experts were enthusiastic about the outline for the
film, so there was no question of his warping the material.*
(page 4661)

*The inquiry went on; Miller was reminded of several causes
he had supported in 1947 and forgotten, and also of times
when he had been listed as a speaker at meetings, but had
made no speech. He had supported the protest against the
hearings that exposed Communists in Hollywood, and also
the movement to defend Howard Fast.*

MR. MILLER: That was my opinion at the time. It did reflect
   my opinion that in my experience I know really very little
   about anything except my work and my field, and it seemed
   to me that the then prevalent, rather ceaseless, investigating
   of artists was creating a pall of apprehension and fear
   among all kinds of people.
THE CHAIRMAN: But did you know that those very artists
   were the chief source of supply for the funds that were
   used by the Communists in the United States? Did you
   know that when you were defending these people that they
   were the people who contributed thousands of dollars
   monthly in order to assist in the organization of labor un-
   ions that were Communist-dominated? Did you know that?
MR. MILLER: Mr. Walter, I will tell you—
THE CHAIRMAN: Or did you not care?
MR. MILLER: Quite frankly, that was not the consideration

in my mind. The consideration in my mind was that, as far as I could see, there was a distinct pall of apprehension and fear. People were being put into a state of great apprehension and they were—

THE CHAIRMAN: Apprehension of what, Mr. Miller?

MR. MILLER: Well, in some cases just punishment and in some cases unjust punishment.

THE CHAIRMAN: Do you know of any artist who was prosecuted as a result of any information obtained from these hearings who was not a member of the Communist apparatus?

MR. MILLER: Quite frankly, sir, that wouldn't have been the issue in my mind, if you are asking me to tell the truth.

THE CHAIRMAN: You are talking about the issue in your mind, and, in view of the fact that you have raised this question repeatedly about your mood, your mind, may I ask if you changed your mind since the revelations concerning Mr. Stalin have been made?

MR. MILLER: My mind was, I have been in—let me put it this way: I suppose that a year has not gone by that I have not altered my opinions or beliefs or approach to life, and long before that I had shifted my views as to my relations or my attitude toward Marxism and toward Communism.

THE CHAIRMAN: When did you change your views about Marxism?

MR. MILLER: This is not—I was not a Saul of Tarsus walking down a road and struck by a bright light. It was a slow process that occurred over years . . . really through my own work and through my own efforts to understand myself and what I was trying to do in the world. (*pages 4668–4669*)

Miller went on to argue his objections to the Smith Act:

MR. MILLER: I am opposed to the Smith Act and I am still opposed to anyone being penalized for advocating anything. I say that because of a very simple reason.

I don't believe that in the history of letters there are many great books or great plays that don't advocate. That doesn't mean that a man is a propagandist. It is in the nature of life and it is in the nature of literature that the passions of an author congeal around issues.

You can go from *War and Peace* through all the great novels of time and they are all advocating something. Therefore, when I heard that the United States Government wanted to pass a law against the advocacy without any overt action, I was alarmed because I am not here defending Communists. I am here defending the right of an author to advocate, to write.

MR. SCHERER: Even to advocate the overthrow of this Government by force and violence?

MR. MILLER: I am now speaking, sir, of creative literature. There are risks and balances of risks.

THE CHAIRMAN: We will have a recess of about five minutes.

(A short recess was taken with the following committee members present: Representatives Walter, Doyle, Willis, Kearney, Jackson, and Scherer.) (Representative Velde entered the hearing room.)

THE CHAIRMAN: The committee will be in order. Proceed.

MR. SCHERER: Mr. Chairman, I was asking the witness a question which I would like to pursue. Witness, counsel asked you about your protesting the prosecution of the twelve Communists in Foley Square, and you said that you had protested that prosecution and, in explanation of that action on your part, you said, "I am opposed to the prosecution of any one for advocating anything." Do you recall that you made that statement?

MR. MILLER: Yes.

MR. SCHERER: You understood, did you not, that the twelve Communists were prosecuted for advocating, teaching, and urging the overthrow of this Government by force and violence through unlawful means? Now, my question is, do you mean that you would be opposed to the prosecution of anyone today for advocating the overthrowing of this Government by force and violence? I cannot draw any other conclusion.

MR. MILLER: Mr. Scherer, there is another conclusion which I would like to speak on for just one moment. The Smith Act, as I understood it and as I understand it now, does lay penalties upon advocacy.

MR. SCHERER: Upon what?

MR. MILLER: Upon advocacy of beliefs or opinions, and so forth. What I felt strongly about then—

MR. SCHERER: Not opinions. It does not lay any upon opinions.

MR. MILLER: I am not that close to the text of it, but my understanding of it is that advocacy is penalized or can be under this law. Now, my interest, as I tell you, is possibly too selfish, but without it I can't operate and neither can literature in this country, and I don't think anybody can question that.

MR. SCHERER: I am not asking you about advocacy generally.

MR. MILLER: Yes, sir; but, sir, I understand your point.

MR. SCHERER: I do not understand yours.

MR. MILLER: . . . If advocacy of itself becomes a crime, in my opinion, or can be penalized without overt action, we are smack in the middle of literature and I don't see how it can be avoided. That is my opinion. That is, where I can understand yours, I ask you to understand mine.

MR. SCHERER: We are not talking about literature. These twelve Communists were on trial for advocating the violent overthrow of this Government by force and violence. Does your theory or your belief carry so far as for you to sit here today and say that you are opposed to prosecution of anyone who today would advocate, teach and urge the overthrow of this Government by force and violence, limiting it to that? Let us leave literature out of that.

MR. MILLER: You see, you are limiting it to that. Let me put it quite simply. If a man were outside this building and telling people to come in and storm this building and blow it up or something of that sort, I would say, "Call out the troops." There is no question in my mind about that. That is advocacy, but in the Smith Act, as I understand it, it is applicable and can be applied, given a sufficient public backing, to literature.

Now, in my opinion, that cannot be equated with the freedom of literature without which we will be back in a situation where people as in the Soviet Union and as in Nazi Germany have not got the right to advocate.

MR. SCHERER: Let us go into literature. Let me ask you, do you believe that today a Communist who is a poet should have the right to advocate the overthrow of this Government by force and violence in his literature, in poetry or in newspapers or anything else?

(*The witness confers with his counsel.*)

MR. MILLER: I tell you frankly, sir, I think if you are talking about a poem I would say that a man should have the right to write a poem just about anything.

MR. SCHERER: All right.

MR. JACKSON: Let me ask one question. Then I understand your position is that freedom in literature is absolute?

MR. MILLER: Well, I recognize that these things, sir, are not; the absolutes are not absolute.

MR. JACKSON: My interpretation of your position is that it is absolute that a writer must have, in order to express his heart, absolute freedom of action?

MR. MILLER: That would be the most desirable state of affairs, I say; yes.

MR. SCHERER: Even to the extent of advocating the violent overthrow of the Government of the United States at this time?

MR. MILLER: Frankly, sir, I have never read such a book.

MR. SCHERER: I did not say you have read it. I am asking you what your opinion is with reference to it.

MR. MILLER: I think a work of art—my point is very simple. I think that, once you start to cut away, there is a certain common sense in mankind which makes these limits automatic. There are risks which are balanced. The Constitution is full of those risks. We have rights, which, if they are violated, are rather used in an irresponsible way, can do damage. Yet they are there and the common sense of the people of the United States has kept this in sort of a balance. I would prefer any day to say, "Yes, there should be no limit upon the literary freedom," than to say, "You can go up this far and no further," because then you are getting into an area where people are going to say, "I think that this goes over the line," and then you are in an area where there is no limit to the censorship that can take place.

MR. SCHERER: Do you consider those things that you have written in the *New Masses* as an exercise of your literary rights?

MR. MILLER: Sir, I never advocated the overthrow of the United States Government. I want that perfectly clear.

MR. SCHERER: I did not say you did. I want to get what you consider literature.

MR. MILLER: I didn't advocate that. I wouldn't call it especially an exercise in freedom. It was simply an effusion of mind. It didn't require a mandate to do it. The *Masses* was widely circulated. Writers were writing for it. Some of the greatest writers today have written for the *New Masses*.

MR. SCHERER: Then you believe that we should allow the Communists in this country to start actually physical violence in the overthrow of this Government before they are prosecuted?

MR. MILLER: No, sir, you are importing.

MR. SCHERER: I cannot draw any other conclusion from what you said.

MR. MILLER: You fail to draw a line between advocacy and essence. Our law is based upon acts, not thought. How do we know? Anybody in this room might have thoughts of various kinds that could be prosecuted if they were carried into action, but that is an entirely different story.

The Committee was reminded by Mr. Velde that Miller had the right to advocate the repeal of the Smith Act. Mr. Kearney then took up an ancient argument:

MR. KEARNEY: You are putting the artist and literature in a preferred class.

MR. MILLER: I thought we were going to get to this and it places me in a slightly impossible position, and I would be lying to you if I said that I didn't think the artist was, to a certain degree, in a special class. The reason is quite simple and may be absurd but, if you are asking me what I think, I will tell you.

MR. JACKSON: One brief question.

THE CHAIRMAN: Let him finish that question.

MR. MILLER: I would like to answer Mr. Kearney.

MR. JACKSON: Very well, sir.

MR. MILLER: Most of us are occupied most of the day in earning a living in one way or another. The artist is a peculiar man in one respect. Therefore, he has got a peculiar mandate in the history of civilization from people, and that is he has a mandate not only in his literature but in the way he behaves and the way he lives.

MR. SCHERER: He has special rights?

MR. KEARNEY: Please.

MR. MILLER: I am not speaking of rights. . . . The artist is inclined to use certain rights more than other people because of the nature of his work. Most of us may have an opinion. We sit once or twice a week or we may have a

view of life which on a rare occasion we have time to
speak of. That is the artist's line of work. That is what
he does all day long and, consequently, he is particularly
sensitive to its limitations.

MR. KEARNEY: In other words, your thought as I get it is
that the artist lives in a different world from anyone else.

MR. MILLER: No, he doesn't, but there is a conflict I admit.
I think there is an old conflict that goes back to Socrates
between the man who is involved with ideal things and
the man who has the terrible responsibility of keeping
things going as they are and protecting the state and keeping an army and getting people fed.   *(pages 4672–4676)*

*The hearing continued and during it there was another brisk
exchange with Mr. Scherer, which caused Miller to protest:
"Nothing in my life was ever written to follow a line. I will
go into that if you will." But Mr. Arens took over with
another line of questioning:*

MR. ARENS: Now, your present application for a passport
pending in the Department of State is for the purpose of
traveling to England, is that correct?

MR. MILLER: To England, yes.

MR. ARENS: What is the objective?

MR. MILLER: The objective is double. I have a production
which is in the talking stage in England of *A View From
the Bridge*, and I will be there to be with the woman who
will then be my wife. That is my aim.

MR. ARENS: Have you had any difficulty in connection with
your play *A View From the Bridge* in its presentation in
England?

MR. MILLER: It has not got that far. I have had the censor in England giving us a little trouble, yes, but that is general. A lot of American plays have that difficulty.

MR. ARENS: Do you know a person by the name of Sue Warren?

MR. MILLER: I couldn't recall at this moment.

MR. ARENS: Do you know or have you known a person by the name of Arnaud D'Usseau? D'-U-s-s-e-a-u?

MR. MILLER: I have met him.

MR. ARENS: What has been the nature of your activity in connection with Arnaud D'Usseau?

MR. MILLER: Just what is the point?

MR. ARENS: Have you been in any Communist Party sessions with Arnaud D'Usseau?

MR. MILLER: I was present at meetings of Communist Party writers in 1947, about five or six meetings.

MR. ARENS: Where were those meetings held?

MR. MILLER: They were held in someone's apartment. I don't know whose it was.

MR. ARENS: Were those closed party meetings?

MR. MILLER: I wouldn't be able to tell you that.

MR. ARENS: Was anyone there who, to your knowledge, was not a Communist?

MR. MILLER: I wouldn't know that.

MR. ARENS: Have you ever made application for membership in the Communist Party?

MR. MILLER: In 1939 I believe it was, or in 1940, I went to attend a Marxist study course in the vacant store open to the street in my neighborhood in Brooklyn. I there signed some form or another.

MR. ARENS: That was an application for membership in the Communist Party, was it not?

MR. MILLER: I would not say that. I am here to tell you what I know.

MR. ARENS: Tell us what you know.

MR. MILLER: This is now sixteen years ago. That is half a lifetime away. I don't recall and I haven't been able to recall and, if I could, I would tell you the exact nature of that application. I understood then that this was to be, as I have said, a study course. I was there for about three or four times perhaps. It was of no interest to me and I didn't return.

MR. ARENS: Who invited you to attend?

MR. MILLER: I wouldn't remember. It was a long time ago.

MR. ARENS: Tell us, if you please, sir, about these meetings with Communist Party writers you said you attended in New York City.

MR. MILLER: I was by then a well-known writer. I had written *All My Sons*, a novel, *Focus*, and a book of reportage about Ernie Pyle and my work with him on attempting to make the picture *The Story of G.I. Joe*. I did the research for that, so that by that time I was quite well known, and I attended these meetings in order to locate my ideas in relation to Marxism because I had been assailed for years by all kinds of interpretations of what Communism was, what Marxism was, and I went there to discover where I stood finally and completely, and I listened and said very little, I think, the four or five times.

MR. ARENS: Could I just interject this question so that we have it in the proper chronology? What occasioned your presence? Who invited you there?

MR. MILLER: I couldn't tell you. I don't know.

MR. ARENS: Can you tell us who was there when you walked into the room?

MR. MILLER: Mr. Chairman, I understand the philosophy behind this question and I want you to understand mine. When I say this I want you to understand that I am not protecting the Communists or the Communist Party. I am trying to and I will protect my sense of myself. I could not use the name of another person and bring trouble on him. These were writers, poets, as far as I could see, and the life of a writer, despite what it sometimes seems, is pretty tough. I wouldn't make it any tougher for anybody. I ask you not to ask me that question.

(The witness confers with his counsel.)

I will tell you anything about myself, as I have.

MR. ARENS: These were Communist Party meetings, were they not?

MR. MILLER: I will be perfectly frank with you in anything relating to my activities. I take the responsibility for everything I have ever done, but I cannot take responsibility for another human being.

MR. ARENS: This record shows, does it not, Mr. Miller, that these were Communist Party meetings?

(The witness confers with his counsel.)

MR. ARENS: Is that correct?

MR. MILLER: I understood them to be Communist writers who were meeting regularly.

Mr. Arens: Mr. Chairman, I respectfully suggest that the witness be ordered and directed to answer the question as to who it was that he saw at these meetings.

Mr. Jackson: May I say that moral scruples, however laudable, do not constitute legal reason for refusing to answer the question. I certainly endorsed the request for direction.

The Chairman: You are directed to answer the question, Mr. Miller.

Mr. Miller: May I confer with my attorney for a moment?

(The witness confers with his counsel.)

Mr. Walter, could I ask you to postpone this question until the testimony is completed and you can gauge for yourself?

The Chairman: Of course, you can do that, but I understand this is about the end of the hearing.

Mr. Arens: This is about the end of the hearing. We have only a few more questions. The record reflects that this witness has identified these meetings as meetings of the Communist writers. In the jurisdiction of this committee he has been requested to tell this committee who were in attendance at these meetings.

Mr. Doyle: If I understand the record, the record shows that he answered that he did not know whether there were any non-Communists there, or not. I think the record so shows.

Mr. Miller: I would like to add, sir, to complete this picture, that I decided in the course of these meetings that I had finally to find out what my views really were in relation to theirs, and I decided that I would write a paper in

which, for the first time in my life, I would set forth my
views on art, on the relation of art to politics, on the relation of the artist to politics, which are subjects that are
very important to me, and I did so and I read this paper
to the group and I discovered, as I read it and certainly by
the time I had finished with it, that I had no real basis in
common either philosophically or, most important to me, as
a dramatist. I can't make it too weighty a thing to tell you
that the most important thing to me in the world is my
work, and I was resolved that, if I found that I was in fact
a Marxist, I would declare it; and that, if I did not, I would
not declare it and I would say that I was not; and I wrote
a paper and I would like to give you the brunt of it so
that you may know me.

THE CHAIRMAN: Have you got the paper?

MR. MILLER: I am sorry, sir. I think it is the best essay I
ever wrote, and I have never been able to find it in the
last two or three years. I wish I could. I would publish it,
as I recall it, because it meant so much to me. It was this:
That great art like science attempts to see the present remorselessly and truthfully; that, if Marxism is what it claims
to be, a science of society, that it must be devoted to the
objective facts more than all the philosophies that it attacks
as being untruthful; therefore, the first job of a Marxist
writer is to tell the truth, and, if the truth is opposed to
what he thinks it ought to be, he must still tell it because
that is the stretching and the straining that every science
and every art that is worth its salt must go through.

I found that there was a dumb silence because it seemed
not only that it was non-Marxist, which it was, but that
it was a perfectly idealistic position, namely, that, first of

all, the artist is capable of seeing the facts, and, secondly, what are you going to do when you see the facts and they are really opposed to the line? The real Marxist writer has to turn those facts around to fit that line. I could never do that. I have not done it.

I want to raise another point here. I wrote a play called *All My Sons* which was attacked as a Communist play. This is an example of something you raised just a little while earlier about the use of my play in the Communist meeting, of a different sketch that I had written. I started that play when the war was on. The Communist line during the war was that capitalists were the salt of the earth just like workers, that there would never be a strike again, that we were going to go hand in hand down the road in the future. I wrote my play called *All My Sons* in the midst of this period, and you probably aren't familiar with it— maybe you are—that the story is the story of an airplane manufacturer, an airplane parts manufacturer, who sends out faulty parts to the Air Force.

Therefore, what happened was that the war ended before I could get the play produced. The play was produced. The Communist line changed back to an attack on capitalists and here I am being praised by the Communist press as having written a perfectly fine Communist play. Had the play opened when it was supposed to have opened; that is, if I could have sold it that fast, it would have been attacked as an anti-Communist play.

The same thing has happened with *Salesman. Death of a Salesman* in New York was condemned by the Communist press.

THE CHAIRMAN: Mr. Miller, what has this to do—

MR. MILLER: I am trying to elucidate my position on the relation of art.

MR. ARENS: Was Arnaud D'Usseau chairman?

MR. SCHERER: Just a minute, Mr. Chairman, may I interrupt?

THE CHAIRMAN: Yes.

MR. SCHERER: There is a question before the witness; namely, to give the names of those individuals who were present at this Communist Party meeting of Communist writers. There is a direction on the part of the chairman to answer that question.

Now, so that the record may be clear, I think we should say to the witness— Witness, would you listen?

MR. MILLER: Yes.

MR. SCHERER: We do not accept the reasons you gave for refusing to answer the question and that it is the opinion of the committee that, if you do not answer the question, that you are placing yourself in contempt.

(*The witness confers with his counsel.*)

MR. SCHERER: That is an admonition that this committee must give you in compliance with the decisions of the Supreme Court.

Now, Mr. Chairman, I ask that you again direct the witness to answer the question.

During the questioning that followed, Miller insisted that he had given the answer that he felt he must give, and denied that he had ever applied for membership in the Communist Party. Among the questions put to Mr. Miller, after the staff interrogation, was one from Mr. Doyle.

MR. DOYLE: I have no questions, but I want to make this
brief observation: With your recognized ability in your
specialized field, based on your testimony here that I have
heard, let me ask you one question. Why do you not direct some of that magnificent ability you have to fighting
against well-known Communist subversive conspiracies in
our country and in the world? Why do you not direct
your magnificent talents to that, in part? I mean more
positively?

MR. MILLER: Yes, I understand what you mean. I think it
would be a disaster and a calamity if the Communist Party
ever took over this country. That is an opinion that has
come to me not out of the blue sky but out of long thought.
I tell you further that I have been trying for years now. I
am not a fictionalist. I reflect what my heart tells me from
the society around me. We are living in a time when there
is great uncertainty in this country. It is not a Communist
idea. You just pick up a book-review section and you will
see everybody selling books on peace of mind because
there isn't any....

I believe in democracy. I believe it is the only way for
myself and for anybody that I care about; it is the only
way to live; but my criticism, such as it has been, is not
to be confused with a hatred. I love this country, I think,
as much as any man, and it is because I see things that I
think traduce certainly the values that have been in this
country that I speak. I would like more than anything
else in the world to make positive my plays, and I intend
to do so before I finish. It has to be on the basis of
reality....

MR. KEARNEY: Do I get from your answer now that you

consider yourself more or less of a dupe in joining these Communist organizations?

MR. MILLER: I wouldn't say so because I was an adult. I wasn't a child. I was looking for the world that would be perfect. I think it necessary that I do that if I were to develop myself as a writer. I am not ashamed of this. I accept my life. That is what I have done. I learned a great deal. (*pages 4684–4690*)

Throughout the testimony Miller's mind flies back to his work. Everything relates back to it; it is the determining factor. "I can't make it too weighty a thing to tell you that the most important thing to me in the world is my work." The Congressional committee members evidently took what followed to be a literary digression. They were wrong. It was the Marxist writer's truth—or lack of it, as Miller found —that concerned him and helped determine his belief. He thought that this clinched and proved his argument as, by his standards, it does.

The House voted 373 to 9 to cite Miller for contempt. He was convicted. A fine of $500 was imposed and he was given a thirty-day suspended jail sentence. He appealed, and on August 7, 1958, won his case. The *New York Times* (August 8) reported:

> The full nine-man court held unanimously that the House Committee on Un-American Activities had not sufficiently warned the playwright of the risk of contempt if he refused to answer its questions. The court ordered him acquitted.
>
> Mr. Miller issued a statement through his lawyer here, Joseph L. Rauh, Jr., that the decision made "the long struggle of the

past few years fully worth while." "I can only hope," the statement said, "that the decision will make some small contribution
toward eliminating the excesses of Congressional committees,
and particularly toward stopping the inhuman practice of making witnesses inform on long past friends and acquaintances."

According to the London *Times* (August 8, 1958), "The
Appeal Court, however, virtually ignored arguments of per-
tinency invoked at the trial by defense counsel, Mr. Joseph
Rauh, and found instead that the questions had been put to
Mr. Miller in such a way as to make contempt charges un-
tenable." The *Manchester Guardian* (August 8) summed up
by seeing the Miller case as the end of a "ritual which marred
recent American history."

Miller is now able to look back on that time and assess it.
He wrote to me: "I was not up to date—I could not forget
that the hunt was being led by people who hated culture
altogether."

In his interview with Miller for the London *Sunday Times*
(March 20, 1960), Henry Brandon said, as if seeking assurance: "Still, McCarthy stands exposed in most American eyes
as a bad influence." Miller replied: "*He* does, but what he
did doesn't. Guilt-by-association, for instance. I would say
quite as many people believe that as believed it before. I don't
think they'd recognize it as McCarthyism if it were presented
in another form. When you don't defeat somebody on the
basis of principle, he is only personally defeated, that's all. His
ghost goes marching on so long as the lesson has not been
learned in terms of the principles that he was violating. And
the defeat of McCarthy was never on that basis for the
majority."

"Marilyn Monroe," wrote Cecil Beaton with unflawed truth, "calls to mind the bouquet of a fireworks display, eliciting from her awed spectators an openmouthed chorus of wondrous 'Ohs' and 'Ahs!' "[1] She was one of the most touching legends of her time; in human terms, a butterfly on a wheel. She seemed to be in a constant struggle with her myth —a monolithic figure twenty feet tall, solid as concrete, but made of newsprint. At the end of June, 1956, she and Arthur Miller were married, and he, in particular, kept trying to introduce the person behind the legend. He tried to explain her to Henry Brandon in the *Sunday Times* interview:

> I don't regard my wife as a symbol. I know she certainly doesn't regard herself in that way. She is the most direct human being I ever knew. I don't know what explains it, if anything does, except that she has had a life as an orphan that left her unprotected from danger, and from others around her, in a way that people who have lived in secure families never know. From way back she's had to estimate her situation in life on the basis of sternest realities, and not allow sentiment to mislead her.

She lives in her films, in photographs, and in books about her when she is talking rather than being talked about; in Pete Martin's book *Marilyn Monroe*, published in 1956, she said: "I'd like to think of my life as having started right now. Somebody asked me when I was born and I said, 'Just recently in New York!' "

She lives in accounts of her spontaneity. Bill Weatherby, covering the making of *The Misfits* for the *Manchester Guardian*, went on to speak of her with a kind of incredulity:

[1] *The Face of the World* by Cecil Beaton.

"Someone who could enjoy things so much that she made you enjoy them. Even a journalist round the set of *The Misfits* was human to her." And the other side of that coin—the bad days on that same film.

But she will be known through Miller's insights about her, and through those insights she inspired in him. "Please Don't Kill Anything"[2] is a delicate pencil sketch for Roslyn in *The Misfits*. It describes an ebbing afternoon on a beach; a couple watch fishermen haul in their catch, and Marilyn Monroe glows to life. Roslyn is the full drawing of that girl on the beach, acutely observed, with a miniaturist's eye for detail. Marilyn Monroe also had a share in the depth of insight that illumines Maggie in *After the Fall*.

It was a wet late afternoon in November, 1960, when headlines, pictures, and placards announced that the Miller marriage was broken. "It's all over. There's no possibility of reconciliation."

In February, 1962, quietly, Miller's marriage to Inge Morath was announced, and the papers, with great industry but little effect, printed what they knew. They told of a free-lance photographer who came from Vienna to Paris, where she did research for Cartier-Bresson and Ernst Haas before branching out on her own; it was recorded that she was associated with Magnum.

Inge Morath has that warmth that makes it possible for her to greet a stranger as though picking up an old and lifelong friendship. To try and know her better, I paged through her photographic book *From Persia to Iran* (text by Edouard Sablier) and found delicate, almost luminous photographs in soft blue-greys and yellows heightened by the sun. Wide

[2] *The Noble Savage*, February, 1960.

landscapes end in rolling, cloudlike hills; a cobbler in black
and white against a crumbling wall takes on the timelessness of
an ancient print; Percepolis rises, a graceful ruin of columns
against a grey sky—and everywhere the balance of fair proportion. In time that can be spent away from their daughter
Rebecca, Inge is compiling a new book of pictures taken
during the production of *After the Fall*.

CHAPTER II

Focus

Luridly covered, Miller's novel *Focus* was reprinted in a paperback edition by Ace Books. The foreground shows a tough, young Paul Muni character; the background, a half-dressed woman before an exotic-looking house—a New York private eye straightening out the drug traffic in the Far East, perhaps? Nevertheless, this cover, which seems to throw a surprising light on Miller's earlier career, does have a vital connection with his book and highlights its purpose more surely than the most painstaking accuracy. It is true that *Focus* is set no farther east than Brooklyn and Manhattan. It is not about the drug traffic, but about anti-Semitism. Nor is its hero a head-bashing cop, but Lawrence Newman, a small, immaculate man turned forty. The mainspring of the book, however, is Miller's protest against other-directed mass feeling, later to be explored in *The Crucible;* and the prejudgment and prejudice invited by categories. And there is no quicker proof of his point than this particular cover. The facts of *Focus* are unshakable, regardless of the face the cover puts on the book.

Focus is a dramatist's novel: tense in construction and dynamic in climax. The reader is driven by it as tragedy commands an audience, partly by technique but mainly by intensity. The book is built on the petty day-to-day humilia-tions suffered by Lawrence Newman after he loses his security and prestige with his job, and is mistaken for the Jew he despises. Miller's insight into people and his acute feeling for their reactions to each other does not prevent his having a finger-drumming impatience with Mr. Newman. He takes over from the character and drives him, so that by the end of the book it is Miller's mind you are meeting rather than the character's. The man who began the book could never have grown into the man who ends it—it is like expecting a plump canary to grow into a hawk.

Mr. Newman's body is the outward form of his mind. See him on the subway as the train takes him to Manhattan: "He was dressed in his newest suit, a Palm Beach gray. His Panama hat curved quite handsomely over his erect, rather stubborn head. He wore a starched collar and a meticulously-tied blue cravat that he had been saving for some special occasion. His fingernails were roundly pared and shone a baby pink. There was hardly a crease in his soul."

The progress of *Focus* is the humanizing of Mr. Newman. He begins the book unknowing almost to blankness; awareness is forced on him through experience. At the outset he can convince himself that there is no need to go out and prevent a Puerto Rican woman from being beaten up. "Her accent satisfied Mr. Newman that she was abroad at night for no good purpose, and it somehow convinced him that she could take care of herself because she was used to that sort of treat-ment. Puerto Ricans were, he knew." But by the end of the book, when Miller is thinking for him, he realizes: "She could have been murdered, clubbed to death out there that night. No one would have dared outdoors to help, to even say she was a human being. Because all of them watching from their windows knew she was not white."

Mr. Newman is a born insider, one who lives in the conventional approval of his boss and his neighbors—at home in the world. He is the last man to be lonely. He works as personnel manager for one of the largest and most anti-Semitic corporations in America, and his very consciousness of its power exposes a fear in him. But this, he felt, "could not rise and take shape so long as he kept doing what he was told." This is the archconformist: not one man thinking, but one man letting all men think for him. He finds himself, for instance, drawn to the anti-Semitic slogans scrawled on the pillars in the subway, and attracted by an ideal of violence that in practice repels him.

Then, with the suddenness of a landslide, Mr. Newman is stripped of everything that holds him together: his job, his view of himself, and other people's view of him—since he essentially lives through their image. And his struggle is desperate to find himself—an outsider.

His nightmare begins when he has to confront the alarming authority of his boss. Due to failing sight, he has unwittingly hired a Jewish girl. His boss orders him to get glasses. But those glasses, to Mr. Newman's shame, turn his face into the face of a Jew and he is fired. Even then, nothing desperate need have happened to him had it not been for the pressures of his neighbors. While he worked for the Company he could meet them on his terms: a height above the brutalized Fred and the gray, self-righteous Carlson. Now he finds his life among them becoming a planned strategy, which bewilders

him because he has not changed. The neighbors are watching
and he finds himself unable to buy a paper from Finkelstein,
the only Jew on the block. The neighbors are watching and,
in self-defense, he reacts with them when Finkelstein's relations move into the block. Still he is rejected and there is no
way of proving to them that he is what he is. The intangibility
of this pressure is summed up in a visit to Fred whose company, almost protection, he needs. But this evening Carlson
is with him. "They had not even said hello. Ten minutes
passed."

So mysteriously separated from his world, Mr. Newman
moves painfully toward his individuality. Like Miller's other
heroes he is afraid of losing his sense of himself, more particularly because until now he has never had to question what
that self was. But the fear that they are making him into
something he is not stays with him. It is because of his face,
and he cannot prevent this happening. It becomes something
masklike, something alien that he is forced to live behind.
"Nobody had a right to dismiss him like that because of his
face. Nobody! He was *Him*, a human being with a certain
definite history and he was not this face which looked like it
had grown out of another alien and dirty history." He is as
ashamed of his face as if it were a deformity.

Prompted by humiliation and rejection he grows in astute-
ness. A kind of courage develops in him and a conflict begins
between his new doubts and his old knowledge of his rights.
He is not a Jew. But neither will he stay in an hotel where he
feels himself on trial. It needs more than an explanation.
"Why didn't you tell him what you are? *Tell* him." "What?
What am I going to tell him? If a man takes that attitude you
know you can't tell him anything."

It is a new realization, and he still goes all ways around it to try to escape. He attends an anti-Semitic meeting in a final bid for public recognition. Revivalist in fervor, heat and hysteria mount in the hall. The speaker is an important priest from Boston and Mr. Newman sees that this "was a man who said things as they occurred to him and he was curious as to what would come out next because he was afraid that anything in the world could come out." His attention wanders over the audience, attracted from time to time by his hysterical neighbor, and he is conscious of the heat. When he listens again, a mindless frenzy has broken out and the priest is conducting the crowd as though it were an orchestra. ". . . byword from now on. Action! Action! Action!" The floor was shaking with the stamping of the people. The priest's face was wine-red as he called over their heads, his arms stretched out stiff, his fists clenched." On this climax of hatred Mr. Newman is accused of being a Jew and thrown out of the hall.

Consciousness having been forced on him, Mr. Newman gropes toward Miller's inevitable solution: "We're going to have to stand and fight it out here." But this resolution has not yet hardened in him as it has in Finkelstein, whose sense of history makes him wonder whether the persecutions his family fled in Europe will spread to America—after the war. To Finkelstein's indignation Mr. Newman tries to persuade him to move. He tries to discover what Mr. Newman has against him, and the only conclusion the Jew can come to is, "When you look at me you don't see me. What do you see?" At last the two men are parallel; for some time the problem has been Mr. Newman's as well, and Miller sums up for them both: "People were in asylums for being afraid that the sky would

fall, and here were millions walking around as insane as anyone could be who feared the shape of a human face."

Miller has almost done with Mr. Newman, and gives him a
conclusion that marks his growth: "I'm only going to do one
thing. . . . I'm going to live like I always lived. I'm not going
to change a jot." After being beaten up alongside Finkelstein
he rejects an offered conformity, and at the end of all denial
accepts an alien identity when reporting the fight to the
police: "As he stood there about to reply, he longed
deeply for a swift charge of lightning that would with a
fiery stroke break away the categories of people and change
them so that it would not matter to them what tribe they
sprang from. It must not be important any more, he swore,
even though in his life it had been of highest importance."

CHAPTER III

Miller on Playwriting

After the Fall, when it opened in New York, was taken to be a divergence almost amounting to a revolution in Miller's work. Any category that he had been supposed to fit was burst apart, particularly that of didactic social dramatist, and all that was familiar in Miller to many eyes turned strange. But the synthesis of social and psychological in *After the Fall* has always been with him, the cornerstone on which his plays are built. This play is no great departure in a steady progression. The two sides of Miller's work are open in it and the questions it raises move through all the plays.

In defining his view Arthur Miller said: "I have tried in my plays, and *After the Fall* in this sense is no different from the others, to apply common sense to my own vision of inevitability—the questions, in short, which a hardheaded citizen might put to the characters in life. It is in this sense that I hope my plays apply to and might affect changes in the people who watch them—simply by applying overt or implied values of humanity to what is transpiring on the stage."

Miller never loses this objective viewpoint. In all his plays there is this balance held by Miller's logic between the subjective truth of the character and the objective truth of the dramatist. It begins simply in *All My Sons* in the confrontation between Keller and Chris, but grows in depth and complexity with each play. *Death of a Salesman* seems to divide this objective truth among the people around Willy; whether sympathetically in Linda, factually in Biff, or practically in Charley. In *The Crucible* the two sides fuse simply in John Proctor, in this sense making him the beginning of Quentin. In earlier plays, Miller gave detachment to someone outside the hero, who falls, usually, because he cannot reach it. Had Maggie, or Keller, or Willy been able to break through their subjectivism and bear what they saw . . . ? Alfieri's logic might have saved Eddie Carbone, in *A View From the Bridge,* had Eddie been able to accept it. In *After the Fall* both these truths merge in Quentin. Ironically, in the face of his reception, he seems to be the conscious hero that Miller was asked to create.

Miller explains his own ability to relate the two truths as a result of his experience in the Depression, which transformed the psychology of people. He spoke of the need for a person to see his position in some objective way: "In *All My Sons* Joe Keller is a father and a citizen, but because he could not take the citizen side seriously he became less of a father and destroyed his own children. You literally have to survive with this wholeness because you can't survive without it."

Alongside Miller's towering respect for the individual goes a disconcerting awareness of his limitations. He spoke of Charley, in *Death of a Salesman,* who does understand the limitations of his own person and who counters Willy's belief

that you must be liked with: "Why must everybody like
you?" Willy was a salesman and that role had to be performed. "There is a split in the personality which a person
must accept and Willy cannot. A wholeness and an objec-
tivity would have brought peace to him," Miller ended re-
gretfully, as though Willy's inability still lived with him.

Miller has an intimate understanding both of how his
people can be saved and of what destroys them. His heroes,
like Willy, are driven by their own commitment, which in
Miller's wide definition is "a particular thing that can neither
be evaded nor ignored." The uniqueness, the split balance in
the plays that is also their wholeness, probably comes from a
division in Miller himself. Not that this book is meant to be
written by guess, but it is hard to imagine anyone more deeply
committed than Miller, or with a wider understanding of
what this means; yet at the same time his thinking is practical
and sharply logical. It enables him both to understand Brand's
"all or nothing" and to show, in effect, how he need not have
been killed by an avalanche.

The committed man without that commitment "dies."
Miller would rightly point out that this is merely another
fact to be recognized, and he explains in his Preface to his
Collected Plays why his heroes are so drawn. "It is necessary,
if one is to reflect reality, not only to depict why a man does
what he does, or why he nearly didn't do it, but why he cannot simply walk away and say to hell with it. To ask this
last question of a play is a cruel thing, for evasion is probably
the most developed technique most men have, and in truth
there is an extraordinarily small number of conflicts which we
must, at any cost, live out to their conclusions. To ask this
question is immediately to impose on oneself not, perhaps, a

style of writing but at least a kind of dramatic construction. For I understand the symbolic meaning of a character and his career to consist of the kind of commitment he makes to life or refuses to make, the kind of challenge he accepts and the kind he can pass by."

As early as *All My Sons*, in Chris, there is the beginning of the Miller character who cannot settle for half. His people live by the absolutes they themselves set up. The same temperamental drive is in Willy Loman, John Proctor, Eddie Carbone, and in Quentin.

"I take it that if one could know enough about a human being one could discover some conflict, some value, some challenge, however minor or major, which he cannot find it in himself to walk away from or turn his back on. . . . Time, characterizations, and other elements are treated differently from play to play, but all to the end that that moment of commitment be brought forth. . . . I take it, as well, that the less capable a man is of walking away from the central conflict of the play, the closer he approaches a tragic existence. In turn this implies that the closer a man approaches tragedy the more intense is his concentration of emotion upon the fixed point of his commitment, which is to say, the closer he approaches what in life we call fanaticism." This remains true of all Miller's heroes, and Eddie Carbone is as committed as John Proctor, although Eddie has no "cause."

Miller's approach to social drama is human rather than heroic. Shaw spoke trumpet-tongued for the heroic in his Preface to *Man and Superman*: "This is the true joy of living, the being used for a purpose recognized by yourself as a mighty one, the being thoroughly worn out before you are thrown on a scrap-heap; the being a force of nature instead

of a feverish selfish little clod of ailments and grievances complaining that the world will not devote itself to making you
happy." So might Milton have spoken in dedication to his
God. It is tremendous.

It is a step from the titanic debate of Shaw to the argument
of Brecht. Both dramatists think in concepts before they think
in people. In Miller's hands any abstract becomes human and
real; his characters cannot get lost in abstractions because the
dramatist's sense of community is too personal—the people
on the block rather than in the universe.

Brecht's Epic Theatre carried the Drama of Concept to its
limit by establishing an anti-individual, anti-emotional, anti-
illusory theatre of fact. He freed the didactic dramatist from
his two main hurdles; the creation of characters and the communication of emotion—from the need for felt life to move
through a play. Brecht's theatre is cerebral, geared to the
argument, and the audience is encouraged to reach a verdict.

He described his theatre in an essay, "Theatre for Pleasure
or Theatre for Instruction":[1] "The stage began to tell a story.
The Narrator was no longer missing, along with the fourth
wall. Not only did the background adopt an attitude to the
events on the stage—by big screens recalling other simultaneous events somewhere, by projecting documents which
confirmed or contradicted what the characters said, by concrete and intelligible figures to accompany abstract conversations, by figures and sentences to support mimed translations
whose sense was unclear—but the actors, too, refrained from
going over wholly to their role, remaining detached from the

---

[1] *Brecht on Theatre*, translated by John Willett (London: Methuen
& Co., 1964).

character they were playing and clearly inviting criticism of him."

The story was the heart of theatre for Brecht, because it provides the audience with all the material for discussion, criticism, and alteration. In "A Short Organum for the Theatre,"[2] he explained how it was to be told. "The parts of the story have to be carefully set off one against the other by giving each its own structure as a play within the play. To this end it is best to agree to use titles; e.g.: 'Richard Gloster courts his victim's widow.' The titles must include the social point, saying at the same time something about the kind of portrayal wanted."

This theatre is, by design, repetitive. It is hard to imagine a single point being made with a greater diversity; it is captioned; it is shown in action and through dialogue; it is mimed; it is filmed; it is sung; it is narrated—it is inescapable. In spite of Brecht's aim to subject his characters to the audiences' criticism, his hand is heavy and the drawing tends to be black or white. Later, in "Letter to an Actor,"[3] he modified some of his theories, but meanwhile he had created a moralists' playhouse. Any reformer would, naturally, prefer "a detached audience who could reach a verdict." "Plays should be convincing, like court pleas" would have won applause from Shaw; and Miller has written of "a great drama being a great jurisprudence,"[4] but has no wish to exchange the stage for a pulpit.

Epic Theatre did not actually create distance—it made it dramatic currency. Until then most didactic dramatists created

[2] Ibid.
[3] Ibid.
[4] "Shadows of the Gods," by Arthur Miller, Harper's, August, 1958.

distance, an unavoidable happening due to the inability to turn genuine mouthpieces into genuine people. Shaw's plays are a triumph of observation. Every fact that will lead you to the character is recorded, in perhaps the most flawless stage directions ever written. But his interest in his characters ended with the ideas they had in their heads. Then, Shaw's versatility of intellect and delight in contradiction enabled the audience genuinely to make up its own mind. The Inquisitor has freedom of speech. There is always a case to be made for the other side, and the colliding of logics seemed to him a gift from God. As Shaw could argue for a character, so he warmed toward him, and his plays remain literally play of mind.

Max Beerbohm used to enjoy Shaw's bobbing up from time to time between his characters, and the same enjoyment can be felt at the dramatist showing through the theorist in Brecht. In attempting a straight narrative of events, in which all feeling is incidental and immaterial, Mother Courage is forced to deny recognition of her son who has been shot because she haggled over a bribe. Had Helene Weigel's scream been vocal instead of silent, the whole situation would have plunged into melodrama.

For Brecht, the price of doing away with emotional involvement has been the creation of a complex, highly technical art form that fuses narrative, lyrics, and music. In *The Caucasian Chalk Circle* it is the exchange of one dramatic value for another. He crystallized the aims of the didactic dramatist, defined them in a theory and wrote plays around it. But he remains the traditional, almost archetypal, didactic dramatist in that he does not solve the old difficulties; he repudiates them. In his synthesis of social and psychological drama Arthur Miller solves them, and seizes the best of both worlds.

Where Brecht begins with the argument, Miller begins with the questions the actor brings onto the stage with him, among them: "What does he think of himself? What do other people think of him, and why? What are his hopes and fears; and what does he say they are? What does he claim to want; and what does he really want?"[5] These last distinctions are characteristic, and the man's appearance gives way to his reality.

The questions a play chooses to answer dictate its style, and that choice is organic rather than temperamental. The more personal the questions answered, the more involved with the hero's private life, the closer the play will move to realism. Where the questions raised are thematic—an exploration of the hero's career or his position in society—the play in turn moves toward nonrealism and stylization. Miller overthrows the stylistic criterion of realism and nonrealism in that for him it depends on the questions the play answers, rather than on the language used. The definition is altogether more fundamental. He says in his Preface that the Greek dramatist was interested in "the fate and career of the hero rather than his private characteristics, or, to put it another way, his social and symbolic side rather than his family role." Miller is equally interested in both.

He walks a knife-edge and finds it a plateau. In an interview with John Wain for *The Observer* in 1957, Miller was asked whether the individual still had significance in spite of the tremendous pressures of circumstance. He replied that he had. "And I think a writer has got to show both these things in operation: both the enormous pressure of circumstances

[5] Preface to the *Collected Plays*.

and the individual act of choice. In the nineteenth century you got the rise of a phenomenon called the 'social play,' in which characters were shown as being in the grip of the economic and social system they happened to live under. And in any age a playwright might deal with a personal emotional situation, arising from the individual psychology of his characters. But I think the two have to be put back together." All Miller's plays reflect this reconciliation.

Miller is as passionately interested in ideas as Shaw or Brecht, but again with certain practical reservations. He says in his Preface: "The idea of a play is its measure of value and importance and beauty, and a play which appears merely to exist to one side of ideas is an aesthetic nullity." Deflatingly he adds that it is time someone said that no playwright ever created an original idea in his play. Shaw's social concepts were no news to the Webbs or to other socialists of his time. But the playwright can voice not-yet-popular ideas that are already in the air: "Once an idea is 'in the air' it is no longer an idea but a feeling, a sensation, an emotion, and with these the drama can deal. For one thing, where no doubt exists in the hearts of the people, a play cannot create doubt; where no desire to believe exists, a play cannot create belief."

Miller thinks that the launching of a genuinely new idea through a play would be unlikely for many practical reasons. The theatre is the here-and-now of the arts. It is a stopwatch medium and there is scant time for argument. A play must make its impact while the curtain is up. Due to this now-or-never aspect, the dramatic form would break under the weight of proof needed to convince an audience. In passing, Miller casually kicks over Shaw's dream of an ideal audience

—a pit of philosophers—by pointing out that they would require proof greater than all the rest.

The highest hurdle remains the people themselves. "An idea, if it is really new, is a genuine humiliation for the majority of the people; it is an affront not only to their sensibilities but to their deepest convictions. It offends against the things they worship, whether God or science or money." Then, a play is performed before an audience and people tend to react with a surrounding crowd rather than against it; we are at the mercy, Miller points out, of that surrounding reaction. Our standards come into conflict or agreement with it, and a truth is no longer only itself, but itself plus that reaction. By definition, conventional reaction kills an idea that is genuinely new.

Miller's humanity and his sense of community protect him from the pitfalls of the earlier didactic dramatist who tirelessly protests his humanity but cannot project it in dramatic terms. Miller can. His prose is evocative, emphatic, and he writes in a loud voice. His sympathy for people makes it impossible for him to stop short at an argument and turn the theatre into a meeting of Hyde Park orators. He cannot; it is as contrary to his approach as it is alien to the characters he creates. The person, not the platform, is paramount in Miller, and this further removes him from Shaw and Brecht. Miller does not believe that a play can be equated with a political philosophy. *Death of a Salesman* provoked an argument about whether it was a left-wing play or a right-wing manifestation of decadence. Miller takes up the question in his Preface: "The presumption underlying both views is that a work of art is the sum of its author's political outlook, real or alleged, and more, that its political implications are valid elements in its aesthetic evaluation. I do not believe this, either for my own or other writers' works. . . . A writer of any worth creates out of his total perception, the vaster part of which is subjective and not within his intellectual control. For myself, it has never been possible to generate the energy to write and complete a play if I know in advance everything it signifies and all it will contain. The very impulse to write, I think, springs from an inner chaos crying for order, for meaning, and that meaning must be discovered in the process of writing or the work lies dead as it is finished. To speak, therefore, of a play as though it were the objective work of a propagandist is an almost biological kind of nonsense, provided, of course, that it is a play, which is to say, a work of art."

Just as Miller's concern for the individual humanizes social drama, his refusal to see man in isolation breaks the subjective circle in psychological drama. In Miller, traps and doors are open and the view is wide. At *Cat on a Hot Tin Roof*, for instance, he was less concerned with Brick than with the world around him and with the questions the play raised: "We are persuaded as we watch this play that the world around Brick is, in fact, an unworthy collection of unworthy motives and greedy actions. Brick refuses to participate in this world, but he cannot destroy it either or reform it and he turns against himself. The question here, it seems to me, the ultimate question, is the right of society to renew itself when it is, in fact, unworthy. There is, after all, a highly articulated struggle for power going on here. There is literally and symbolically a world to win or a world to forsake and damn. A viewpoint is necessary if one is to raise such a tremendous issue, a viewpoint capable of encompassing it. . . . There is a moral judgment hanging over this play that never quite comes down."[6]

Where Aldous Huxley anatomized the warped intellectual —a Philip Quarles, who needed a dragoman, Tennessee Williams explores the warped romantic, who needs an interpreter. "Personal lyricism is the outcry of prisoner to prisoner from the cell in solitary where each is confined for the duration of life."[7] One catches one's breath at his lyricism—and then realizes that the man is describing a trap. As an interpreter for the walled-in people for whom society has no place Williams is unrivalled. At his best—*The Glass Menagerie* or *A Streetcar Named Desire*—he is the dramatist of the lost society, for his people are as securely isolated as if they were trapped above the snow line of the Himalayas. At his worst, he is a sensationalist. It seemed to me that *Suddenly Last Summer* was used as a battering-ram against the audience, who were emotionally clubbed into submission.

Through Williams' plays the conflict of personalities breaks personal myths. This is primarily a victim drama. His characters are committed to nothing but their own emotions and crippled by a vulnerability that they flaunt like a banner. His characters all have the pathos of the fragile. Williams draws their hysteria, the pulled and straining nerves, the vacant eyes and trembling hands; the silently screaming people.

I am haunted by a pair of caricatures Max Beerbohm might have drawn: Williams, encircled by his characters, in a pool of tears, and more dejected than they; and Miller gazing calmly at his—"Don't come and tell me about all you can't

6 "Shadows of the Gods," *Harper's*, August, 1958.
7 Tennessee Williams, introduction to *Cat on a Hot Tin Roof* (New London, Conn.: New Directions, 1955).

do. Why can't you?" Where Williams sympathizes, Miller
more restlessly looks for a cure. It is the difference between
"How pitiful!" and "What can be done about it?" The
nearest Miller can come to a "Tennessee Williams' character"
is Maggie in *After the Fall* and, lost as she is, Quentin's insight might have saved her had she been able to take it for
her own. There is always this outside voice in Miller, an al-
ternative truth that in no way lessens the character's subjective truth.

The affirmation in Miller's plays stems from his belief in
man's freedom of will. For Miller, man's failure is "his failure
to assert his sense of civilized life."[8] In the plays his committed
man tries to transcend his apparent powers and find his selfhood. Miller counterbalances acceptance by exploring the
reasons behind a situation, socially and psychologically, with
the energy of a bankrupt prospecting for gold. It is part of
the passionate search for meaning and relatedness going on in
his plays. A man's life must be meaningful, and if it is not,
why? The struggle is never abandoned. Against a fully
realized determinism, Miller's hero protests Miller's refusal to
believe in man's helplessness and predestined defeat. His
recognition that a situation is not ideal is coupled with the
realization that it does not have to be accepted. Even Willy
Loman does not have to accept the fact that there is nothing
he can do for his son. Chris Keller does not have to live
with his father's guilt; John Proctor need not compromise nor
Eddie Carbone settle for half.

"The history of man is a ceaseless process of overthrowing
one determinism to make way for another more faithful to
life's changing relationships. And it is a process inconceivable

8 *Theatrical Educational Journal,* October, 1958.

without the existence of the will of man," says Miller in his Preface. "His will is as much a fact as his defeat. Any determinism, even the most scientific, is only that stasis, that seemingly endless pause, before the application of man's will administering a new insight into causation."

Williams' belief is altogether more private: "Every artist has a basic premise pervading his whole life, and that premise can provide the impulse in everything he creates. For me the dominating premise has been the need for understanding and tenderness and fortitude among individuals trapped by circumstances." Concerned as he is with psychological truth, Williams' aim is to encourage in the audience the sympathy he feels for his characters. Form in these plays is the orchestration of an emotional effect—his end, its impact. Nothing checks the raw pity, terror, and compassion on which these plays are built. In them Williams achieves a particular brand of gothic romanticism that falls apart in the hands of disciples. It is a strange dualism of offsetting the ugly by the lyrical, perhaps seen at its most complete in Blanche.

Miller shares none of Williams' half-light romanticism, and mood drama breeds mistrust in him. He was appalled by the inconsolable audience at *Death of a Salesman:* "I was forced to wonder whether I knew myself at all if this play, which I had written half in laughter and joy, was as morose and as utterly sad as its audiences found it," he writes in his Preface. Deliberately, his are daylight plays. You are intended to see and know where you are going. *All My Sons* was first called "The Sign of the Archer" and early drafts made much of Kate Keller's belief in astrology. But as the play progressed, the conflict between Joe and his son took over and mysticism gave place to psychology. Miller found the temptation to mysticism perfectly resistible: "There was also the impulse to regard the mystical with suspicion, since it had in the past given me only turgid works that could never develop a true climax based upon revealed psychological truths. Where in the past I might well have been satisfied to create only an astrologically obsessed woman, the obsession had to be opened up to reveal its core of self-interest on the character's part. Wonder must have feet with which to walk the earth." Mysticism and obsession, however dramatic, melodramatic— Miller might add "theatrical"—blur understanding. The audience must know how the character's life came to be broken; otherwise it is like beginning a performance of *King Lear* with the scene on the heath, leaving out his vanity and his daughters' goading.

Miller and Williams are opposed in attitude, opposed in outlook, and opposed in their approach to an audience. Miller enters into a hesitant, tactful relationship, like someone unsure whether or not to shake hands. "My concept of the audience is of a public each member of which is carrying about with him what he thinks is an anxiety, or a hope, or a preoccupation which is his alone and isolates him from mankind; and in this respect at least the function of a play is to reveal him to himself so that he may touch others by virtue of the revelation of his mutuality with them. If only for this reason I regard the theatre as a serious business, one that makes or should make man more human, which is to say, less alone."[9]

To Williams the audience is his confidant. It is a personal relationship, like the one struck by Gide with his reader, and from the outset you are to be involved inescapably. "I want to go on talking to you as freely and intimately about what

[9] Preface to the *Collected Plays*.

we live and die for as if I knew you better than anyone else whom you know."[10]

For Williams the theatre is the forcing ground of feeling— the "emotional jag" complained of by Brecht, his direct opposite. To move from one to the other is to step down from a high, high rostrum into a cloistered confessional; from archpropagandist to archpenitent; from State to Self; from categories to chaos; from *I know* to *I feel;* from *I'll tell you* to *I'll show you;* from alienation to involvement; from detachment to self-laceration; from reasoned logic to near-madness and from solution to confusion. Williams' is the drama of subjective feeling, a form as extreme as Brecht's, which is perhaps why complete fulfillment can come from neither of them. They flourish as the most perfect of their kind, and part of our pleasure comes from seeing a particular form of playwriting taken to its limit—so *this* is how it works! It is like catching up with the horizon.

[10] Introduction to *Cat on a Hot Tin Roof.*

CHAPTER IV

The Man Who Had All the Luck

The Man Who Had All the Luck is early Miller, the play nearest to his desk-drawer plays and his first to reach Broadway (in 1944) for its less than a week's run. Like *Situation Normal . . .*, it leaves some impression of the young Miller and of the beginning of ideas that stay with him and grow through the later plays. It has to be said that it is not a good play, faulty in many ways, but it holds an indisputable place in Miller's work. Page after page of dialogue is conventional: the solid inflexible dialogue of any number of American plays in the forties. Suddenly Miller speaks through it.

J. B. FELLER Yeh, no kids. Too old. Big, nice store with thirty-one different departments. Beautiful house. No kids. Isn't that something? You die, and they wipe your name off the mailbox and . . . and you never lived.

The play flares into life. Miller's dialogue and one of Miller's themes—a person's need to achieve something in the world and to leave some imprint after him. Then again, here is the

76

beginning of Miller's definitive comment on his characters. J.B. says of David, "He's got his whole life laid out like a piece of linoleum." It is not unlike Kenneth's description of Bert, the young boy working in the warehouse in *A Memory of Two Mondays.*

Perhaps the key for *The Man Who Had All the Luck* can be taken from Miller's play description of David. He "has the earnest manner of the young small town businessman until he forgets it, which is most of the time. Then he becomes what he is—wondrous, funny, naive, and always searching." Everything David Beeves wanted came to him. It seemed that he could not lose. He married the girl he'd always loved; they had the son he wanted; his businesses thrived and his mink ranch prospered. There was no reason for his luck and this, above all else, unnerved him. All around him people were losing. It seemed an unwritten and universal law that every man was frustrated in something: everybody paid, everybody —except David. His brother Amos trained twelve years to be a baseball pitcher, only to find that he could never play in the big leagues. Through a mistake he had been wrongly trained. David, uneasy at his good fortune, expects retribution. He tries to bring on his own disaster, so that he can survive it. He talks himself into believing that his child will be born dead or maimed; when it is born perfect he can face neither his wife nor himself because, secretly, he wanted it his way. He tries to bankrupt himself by sinking all his capital in a mink ranch, expensive animals that die easily, but disaster still evades him. It never comes. At the last he can only accept his ability to succeed.

The young man in the factual story on which the play was

based killed himself less than a year after the beginning of his obsession.

The play is theatricality streaked with insight. It has the obvious kind of drama that Miller is to reject, and its characters seem to be created by the book. They have all the outward characteristics of the people they are supposed to be— and yet are not that person. Shory is a "character" in a wheelchair and Belle is a "character" aunt. But with J.B., with Pat, and with Amos, Miller has thrown the book out of the window. They are his, drawn to no pattern. The play clicks tidily into place. A careful exposition explains how people make their own luck, and the clues for their collapse are well laid: in the first scene, for example, Amos has difficulty playing the bases. But the cost of this precision is subtlety.

Pat excepted, Miller is not really feeling *with* these people yet, or is with them only momentarily. David is Miller's first hero to insist on making sense of his situation, but he does not come alive. He is like a polite guest and says the right thing to carry forward his point of view: "Yeh, but is a thing really yours because your name is on it? Don't you have to feel you're smart enough, or strong enough, or something enough to have won it before it's really yours?" Perhaps David is too consistent, and therefore predictable, to be desperate. He is always in character and in this is nearer an ideal than a person, losing his life in this abstraction. He is there to speak Miller's mind on this subject, and Miller's interest is on his theme. It is something like trying to create a person from what he says in public. The difference between *The Man Who Had All the Luck* and the later plays is that you are drawn into the later plays but are merely looking at *The Man Who Had All the*

Luck. It is a difference of depth and color, something like the difference between, say, a Munnings and a Van Gogh.

Just as Miller's own voice breaks into the conventional dialogue, making it individual, his own sense of character and relationship disrupts the stereotype from time to time, making it personal. This was the first play in which Miller found himself: "Had I known then what I know now I could have saved myself a lot of trouble," he writes. "The play was impossible to fix because the overt story was only tangential to the secret drama its author was quite unconsciously trying to write. But in writing of the father-son relationship and of the son's search for his relatedness there was a fullness of feeling I had never known before."[1] While David argues Miller's theme, Pat and Amos explore the father-son relationship, and it is as much their play as his. Miller's dualism is early apparent, and with it the bafflement of some critics as to what his play is about.

Amos is older than his brother David by two years, and his father is totally preoccupied with him. He is the adored son for whom all Pat's plans are made, rather in the position of Biff in *Death of a Salesman*. Pat has a certain dignity when he asserts himself as David's father, a thing he tends to forget. This is painful for David, who grows and thrives much the way Bernard does in *Salesman*—through being left alone. This is not to compare the two plays, but merely to suggest that *The Man Who Had All the Luck* seems an indispensable first draft, both for *Salesman* and *All My Sons*.

Pat's dream for Amos is the dream of making him a great athlete. Pat has the overblown values that all fanatics share,

[1] Preface to the *Collected Plays*.

whether they are fathers or freedom fighters, athletes or
actors, doctors or dons, playwrights or Brand-like prelates. In
short, Pat is committed to molding his son's life the way Pat
wants it to be. His passionate conviction both makes him a
laughing stock and gives him tragedy.

Pat's and Amos' lives are destroyed when the scout for the
Detroit Tigers explains that Pat has trained Amos badly, re-
peating the same mistake for twelve years. Miller finds his
voice in the showdown between Amos and Pat:

AMOS (*amid his own, and Pat's weeping. To Pat*) You liar! I'll
kill you, you little liar, you liar! ...

PAT Come on, boy, please, boy, stop now, stop, Amos; look
Ame, look, I'll get Cleveland down here, I'll go myself, I'll
bring a man. Ame, listen, I did what I could, a man makes
mistakes, he can't figure on everything. (*He begins shaking
Amos who continues sobbing.*) Ame, stop it! I admit it, I
admit it, Ame, I lie, I talk too much, I'm a fool, I admit it,
but look how you pitch, give me credit for that, give me
credit for something! Stop that crying! God Almighty,
what do you want me to do! I'm a fool, what can I do?

DAVID Listen, you! He made a mistake. That's over with.
You're going to drill on base play. You got a whole life. One
mistake can't ruin a life. He'll go to Cleveland. I'll send him
to New York ... The man can be wrong. Look at me! The
man can be wrong, you understand!

AMOS He's right. He's right. I always knew I couldn't play the
bases. Everything the man said was right. I'm dumb, that's
why. I can't figure nothin'. There wasn't no time, he said,
no time for nothin' but throwin' that ball. Let 'em laugh, he
said, you don't need to know how to figure. He knew it all.
He knows everything! Well, this is one time I know something. I ain't gonna touch a baseball as long as I live!

And the tragic thing about these scenes is not that Pat guessed wrong about the way a baseball pitcher is trained but, in effect, the puppet he made of his adored son. Amos is batted from the scout to Pat to David, and has no dignity left as a person. It's his life but, as though he were five years old, the scout talks to Pat or to David. When Amos realizes that he has nothing he blames Pat, who is not wholly responsible. In line with Miller's belief that you make your own life, Pat did not singlehandedly ruin Amos; Amos had some share in it through refusing to take responsibility for himself. He allowed Pat to take him over. When this was not working out too well, he appealed to David:

AMOS You're movin' like a daisy cutter, Dave, you know how to *do*. Take me over. . . .

DAVID But I only know what I picked up. I ain't a trained man. You are. You *got* something . . . and you're going to be great. You are, Ame, because you deserve it. You *got* something, you know, something perfect.

David reminds him that he is Pat's whole life. So Amos lives with the commitment Pat chose for him. Amos does not choose a single thing. It is perhaps significant that he is the only character in these plays to accept his defeat, and struggle no further.

Another aspect of this play links with *Death of a Salesman:* Pat wills Amos to succeed but has an insufficient understanding of reality; he does not know the way a pitcher is trained. This is not the same thing as a father destroying his son because he has unrealistic aims for him. As long as there are baseball players as well as bank clerks, Pat's aim is realistic.

"The play was an investigation to discover what exact part

a man played in his own fate."[2] The question rises automatically: And what conclusions did you come to? You are
confident that there will be an answer, that the problem will
be defined. It's as axiomatic as What did they say then? at a
play by Shaw. Miller's answer is that luck is man-made. Your
life is yours to make or break. Willy tries to persuade Biff
of this in *Death of a Salesman*. And what else is Quentin's
battle with Maggie in *After the Fall* if it isn't to rouse in her
a sense of responsibility for her own life?

A clear line of argument—determinism or free will?—runs
through *The Man Who Had All the Luck*. Does a man make
his own life, or is it made for him by forces over which he
has no control? David (like Miller) believes that there must
be a reason for things happening the way they do. The fact
that he can find no valid cause for his luck is driving him mad.
"Damn it all, if everything drops on you like fruit from a
tree, for no reason, why can't it break away for no reason?
Everything you have . . . suddenly." Characteristically David
must know why. An explanation is given him when his wife
persuades him that just as surely as he made his own life, he
is destroying it. She finally convinces him: "You made it all
yourself! It was always you!" But the reasons Hester gives are
superficial. The later plays explore the present situation and
the reasons behind it more faithfully. In them, the man who
makes his own luck becomes the man whose situation can be
explained. He still makes his own life in that he does not have
to accept his situation; he struggles against it to find some
meaning that will define him.

The Man Who Had All the Luck is a kind of simple
alphabet of ideas that will be developed later. Shory is Miller's

[2] *Ibid.*

devil's advocate and the argument is imaginatively expressed. He warns David: "You can't make anything happen any more than a jellyfish makes the tides, David. . . . The tide goes in and the tide goes out. About what happens to him, a man has very little say. . . . Amos' walls happened to blow out. And you happen to be a lucky boy, brother David. A man is a jellyfish, and a jellyfish can't swim no matter how hard he tries; it's the tide that pushes him every time. So just keep feeding, and enjoy the water till you're thrown up on the beach."

Shory's belief in a reasonless chance has the same effect as a fully operating determinism. In both cases a man is never guilty or innocent in what he does. His action is never his responsibility, or even his concern. In both cases, "I could not help it" is a complete defense. The blame is always elsewhere —fate, chance, God, psychology or economics. A man does not see himself in his own life.

In Miller nothing is written in the clouds, and you *can* help it. A man is totally responsible, responsible for his "luck." Gus speaks for him with towering conviction:

"Here you are not a worm, a louse in the earth; here you are a man. A man deserves everything here! . . . A man must believe that on this earth he is the boss of his life, not the leafs in the teacup, not the stars. In Europe I already seen millions of Davids walking around, millions. They gave up already to know that they are the boss. They gave up to know that they deserve this world. . . . A man must understand the presence of the god in his hands. And when he doesn't understand it he is trapped."

CHAPTER V

All My Sons

"You have such a talent for ignoring things." This exasperated accusation is made by Chris in *All My Sons*, which, like Miller's adaptation of *An Enemy of the People*, deals with the clash between people who can and people who can not walk away from things. Both plays are about evasion and commitment, a wilful blindness and a need to see. Joe Keller and Peter Stockmann can settle for an unprincipled practicality; Chris and Dr. Stockmann cannot.

Keller protests, in excuse, "Chris, a man can't be a Jesus in this world!" It is meaningless to Chris: without his commitment there would be no person left. Through Jim Bayliss, Miller shows what would have become of Chris had he followed the "practicality" urged on him. Jim was a doctor committed to research who imagined that he could give it up, accept a small-town practice, and not be lost. He is, in fact, destroyed far more deeply than Keller. "These private little revolutions always die. The compromise is always made . . . and now I live in the usual darkness; I can't find myself; and

84

it is even hard sometimes to remember the kind of man I wanted to be." But for Miller compromise is not obligatory, and in these plays it is rarely made. Chris, Willy Loman, John Proctor, the helplessly driven Eddie Carbone, all preserve their selfhood by standing out against Jim's assumption; it is the compromises made in *After the Fall* that cripple Quentin.

The time of the play is just after the war and Chris embodies Miller's argument: "Everything was being destroyed, see, but it seemed to me that one new thing was being made. A kind of responsibility. Man for man. You understand me? To show that, to bring that onto the earth again like some kind of monument and everyone would feel it standing there, behind him, and it would make a difference to him. And then I came home and it was incredible. I—there was no meaning in it here; the whole thing to them was some kind of bus accident. I went to work for Dad and that rat-race again. I felt—what you said—ashamed somehow. Because nobody was changed at all. It seemed to make suckers out of a lot of guys. I felt all wrong to be alive, to open a bankbook, to drive the new car, to see the new refrigerator. I mean you can take those things out of a war, but when you drive that car you've got to know that it came out of the love a man can have for a man. You've got to be a little better because of that. Otherwise what you have is really loot, and there's blood on it."

Chris's belief seems to have grown out of a long line of experience. During the war Miller was asked to go round the camps and training centers of America to find the material for a true war film—only the facts, shorn of all fiction. Miller did not complete the script for *The Story of G.I. Joe*, but published what he had found in *Situation Normal*. . . . It is a sensitive book and through it Miller is driven by the need to define a belief that will make sense of the war. "Something besides horror must be proved, or only horror will remain." He was concerned with the individual behind the uniform, with the kind of world the soldier would be coming back to and what would happen if he was disappointed.

Some aspects of the book seem to influence *All My Sons* and especially the full drawing of Watson. Through his heroism in the Pacific Watson had been chosen for officers' training and sent home. He had found it hard to leave the island because he knew that "everybody had a right to go and wanted to."

His home town gave him a big demonstration and made him a hero. He talked with Miller mainly to ensure that there would be no mistakes in the film. "I liked it at the beginning," he told him, "but Jesus Christ, the real heroes never come back. They're the real ones. They're the only ones. Nobody's a hero if he can still breathe. . . . I mean I don't want to cheat so many dead men."

Watson spoke of the friendship out there, and his loyalty is reflected in Chris. When he tells Ann about the company he lost, he says in effect: "Friendship is the greatest thing out there. I mean real friendship, not because a guy can give you what you want. I tell you the truth: I would die for any one of the thirty or forty men out there just as easy as I'd flick out this match. I swear this is the truth. I don't expect you to believe it, but I swear it."

By contrast, Watson was alone in America. He was not doing well at the training camp and seemed not to have the intellectual ability for the courses. His dread was that if he

failed he could not go home or back to the front. He did not
know what he was going to do.

Miller understood the debt Watson felt, and in explaining
him wondered what would become of the countless Watsons
coming home to an America not conscious of nor fighting for
its belief. "Half of him, in a sense, must die." He would have
had a place in the struggle for a belief. "It would demand
that part of his character which requires sharing. As it is, the
company is gone and all that the company meant. He must
wall himself from his fellow man, he must live only his own
little life and do his own unimportant, unsatisfying job when
he gets out of the Army. He must begin again the stale and
deadly competition with his fellow men for rewards which
now seem colorless, even if necessary for his survival. He is
alone. Cut off from mankind and the great movement of mankind he was once part of. And the world is alien. . . ." Miller
predicted that Watson "will be wondering why he went and
why he is alive for the rest of his days. . . ." And this is the
position Chris holds in the play. The difference is that through
Chris, Miller defines the "idea" growing among the soldiers.

Miller wrote *Situation Normal* . . . when he was twenty-
seven, and the book is rather like a young photograph. He
remains concerned with how the world can be made less
alien; we will meet this concern again over Willy Loman. In
After the Fall Quentin, outside the concentration camp, nails
the idea behind *Situation Normal* . . . to one line: "And I
without belief stand here disarmed."

The idea of *All My Sons* was in the air—almost, it must
have seemed, tangible. The details of the plot were fact.
Miller was told of a family in which the daughter discovered
that her father had sold defective machinery to the Army,

and she handed him over to the authorities. All Miller's plays
are rooted in reality. It is part of his ambition to write plays
for common-sense people, and ensures that his ideas will not
float about like ghosts who have permanently lost their haunt-
ing-ground. His plays are built as though he were construct-
ing skyscrapers, not scenes. He says in his Preface that he
desired above all to write rationally, and adds: "I have always
been in love with wonder, the wonder of how people got to
be the way they are." Wonder, for Miller, is something
essentially explicable, a logic of people and events caused by
"the gradual and remorseless crush of factual and psychological conflict."

This is the basis of *All My Sons* and of all Miller's flesh-
and-blood social drama. Keller killed twenty-one pilots during
the war by shipping defective airplane parts, for which his
partner was jailed. Nothing could be more clear cut; so far
it is cardboard drama. But these people are involved in a
forest of mutual and parallel relationships, and the play is so
balanced that if Chris's relationship with his father is not fully
established, half the play is lost. The relationships in *All My
Sons* make it the dramatic equivalent of the plot of *Bleak
House*. Chris loves his parents and, although haunted by his
brother's death, plans to marry Larry's fiancée, who is also
the daughter of the jailed partner. The marriage is guaranteed
to upset his mother because it confirms her son's death, something she cannot accept, sensing that if Larry is dead Keller
is responsible. Chris is parallel to Frank, a practical oppor-
tunist, to George, the jailed man's son, and to Jim. He relates
to every character in the play.

Miller carries this relatedness through from people to
events; it is the foundation on which *All My Sons* is built.

"Joe Keller's trouble . . . is not that he cannot tell right from wrong but that his cast of mind cannot admit that he, personally, has any viable connection with his world, his universe, or his society."[1] Miller shies away from the obvious "crime" element in the play, the selling of defective airplane parts. That is too simple. It does not say enough. To Miller that would be the plot of a thriller, a meaningless kill-time. Having generously bequeathed the plot to the American counterpart of Agatha Christie, in his Preface he defines what his play is about: "The fortress which *All My Sons* lays siege to is the fortress of unrelatedness. It is an assertion not so much of a morality in terms of right and wrong, but of the moral world's being such because men cannot walk away from certain of their deeds." Relatedness and responsibility. The central problem of the play is to bring the fact home to Joe Keller, to batter down the opaque-glass walls of his isolation. Miller is concerned with consciousness, not crime, and with bringing a man face to face with the consequences he has caused, forcing him to share in the results of his creation.

He is not a chess-playing dramatist, a manipulator of black and white pieces of wood hierarchically designed. Keller literally stands for the world that Chris has come back to, self-centered and unseeing. But Miller cares too much for his people to reduce them to ciphers; with Keller he wins his argument, but without crucifying the man. Keller is committed only to his family, and can see no further—nothing beyond that. Miller's drawing is always compassionate, and the man is so drawn that the general concepts of his son are outside the range of his understanding. His limitation is explained: "A heavy man of stolid mind and build . . . but the

[1] Preface to the *Collected Plays*.

imprint of the machine-shop worker and boss still upon him.
When he reads, when he speaks, when he listens, it is with the
terrible concentration of the uneducated man for whom there
is still wonder in many commonly known things, a man whose
judgments must be dredged out of experience and a peasant-
like common sense."

Keller illustrates Miller's belief that an idea is no guide to
the man holding it until you know why he believes as he
does. Keller's vulnerable position makes him appear more
liberal than Ann when he, naturally, protests against her attack on her father: "I never believed in crucifying people." It
is himself he is defending. Chris sees the facts; the man killed
twenty-one pilots. There is nothing to add, and he drives
Keller to his only defense: "A father is a father!" Miller adds
a stage direction to deepen understanding of Keller; he has
been particularly careful over him: "As though the outburst
revealed him, he looks about, wanting to retract it."

The insights Keller does have are nervelessly bludgeoning
and accurate. His partner was "a little man . . . always scared
of loud voices." Finally, this rock-solid egocentric is desperate
and alone, alone in his version of what he has done. Baffled
in the extreme, he still tries to blink facts by reaching for his
family. His plea is a general one: "Then what do I do? Tell
me, talk to me, what do I do?" Kate cannot help him, except
to warn: "You want to live? You better figure out your life."
Unrepentant, he argues that nothing is bigger than the family:
"There's nothing he could do that I wouldn't forgive. Because
he's my son. Because I'm his father and he's my son . . . and if
there's something bigger than that I'll put a bullet in my
head." In spite of the family, in spite of the generally accepted
code of practicality—"Who worked for nothin' in that war?"

—his self-justification breaks. It breaks on the realization that Larry deliberately crashed his plane, so making his father directly responsible for his death. And with final realization, Keller kills himself.

Miller draws his minor characters with a precision that tells you only what you need to know. This can make them appear underdrawn until you notice how meticulously they reveal themselves. Frank, who believes in fortunetelling by the stars, accuses Jim: "The trouble with you is, you don't *believe* in anything." Sue resents "living next door to the Holy Family. It makes me look like a bum, you understand?" George, Ann's brother, has a deeply felt sense of relationships: "I wanted to go to Dad and tell him you were going to be married. It seemed impossible not to tell him. He loved you so much . . . Annie, you don't know what was done to that man. You don't know what happened." This passionate concern for the individual is expressed in all Miller's plays.

Miller's realism is the strength of his characters. The Kellers live on and are consoled by the heroism of their dead son, particularly the mother. Miller describes her as "a woman of uncontrolled inspirations and an overwhelming capacity for love." Kate is too sensitive to stare past facts like Keller. She wraps herself in dreams and from this phantom comfort tries to will Larry back to life by faith. Miller explores the reasons for Kate's delusion—her sickness, her being driven to clutch at mysticism and astrology—and at bottom discovers a genuine faith in a moral order. "Your brother's alive, darling, because if he's dead, your father killed him. Do you understand now? . . . God does not let a son be killed by his father."

Kate has to believe it. But when the dream breaks she protects Keller. Most often there is resilience in Miller's dreamers. The person comes through and they are not allowed to wander far from reality. (Willy Loman's tragedy is that he is over-aware of things as they are, and that they contradict his longing.) Look at the ghost-haunted Kellers: "We're like at a railroad station waiting for a train that never comes in." And yet they are not pseudo-Hamlets, nor do they search for their egos in a mental looking glass. Everyday things crowd in upon them and in this welter of triviality there is no time for tragic grief. Day-to-day living never leaves Miller's characters alone. Choosing between Aldous Huxley's "Tragedy and the Whole Truth," he chooses the whole truth. The whole truth admits all the facts and irrelevancies that in life temper situations and characters; tragedy excludes them because they diminish its height and purity. The whole truth forbids Kate to languish in grief. She comes out into daylight and tries to prevent Chris from jailing Keller: "The war is over! Didn't you hear? It's over!" However moving, because coming from her, Chris reminds her that Larry didn't kill himself so that she and Keller could be "sorry."

KATE What more can we be?

CHRIS You can be better! Once and for all you can know there's a universe of people outside and you're responsible to it, and unless you know that, you threw away your son because that's why he died.

As often happens with Miller's plays, his intention was contradicted by its reception in New York. In the face of Miller's denial the press insisted that the play was theatrical and praised it accordingly (all but Robert Coleman, of the *Daily Mirror*, who lived up to the tough New York critic's reputation by complaining that the play was underwritten and the people placid. I have visions of him living on a steady diet of pale playwrights and drinking molten lead.) Miller stressed that the play was intended to be as untheatrical and artless as possible; but his natural talent cheated him. To Miller, it appears, "theatrical" is suspect praise. In his Preface he said: "It began to seem to me that what I had written until then, as well as almost all the plays I had ever seen, had been written for a theatrical performance, when they should have been written as a kind of testimony whose relevance far surpassed theatrics."

In writing about Miller, people seem impelled to over-simplify him, arriving at a clear-cut half-man, half-truth. He denies the role thrust upon him of abstract moralist—talkative upon a peak in Darien. "*All My Sons* has often been called a moral play, but the concept of morality is not quite as purely ethical as it has been made to appear, nor is it so in the plays that follow."[2] Put it this way: Miller is concerned with why people live the way they do; he is a builder with available materials rather than an architect hawking blueprints for an ideal house.

All My Sons is fervent early Miller, a step away from *Situation Normal*. . . . The voice is authentic and arresting, the technique still stiff with its newness—for instance in the contrived discovery of the letter—and from time to time the key is too high, like a singer uncertain of pitch. The dialogue is alternately collar-gripping or wryly ironic. A new light was thrown on the ending by a friend who knew nothing of the play, but arrived in time to catch the last few minutes of it on television. A shot is heard from the house, and in the final

[2] *Ibid.*

scene Chris is being comforted by Kate. Without even asking what the play was about, he said: "It looks like something straight out of Dostoevsky." Perhaps he was more right than he knew. Miller was steeped in Dostoevsky at that time.

Miller in *All My Sons* has been carelessly labeled "Ibsenite" and an immutable pattern has been set up. People who use labels are like a man capable of seeing ten miles, swearing that he can see only five because that is as far as he expects to see. Let us ignore "Ibsenite" as a short cut to defining Miller and concentrate on Ibsen's influence upon him, which is not the same thing. One writer's influence on another does not create a blood-discipleship, and should not, unless the second is to become a carbon copy of the first. The differences between the two writers are too obvious to need retelling, but let us trace their connection.

There is a certain like-mindedness between them. Some lines in Ibsen's letters could well have come from Miller, and I suspect they would find common ground in Ibsen's speech to the Norwegian students on September 10th, 1874: "It was a long time before I realized that to be a poet means essentially to see; but mark well, to see in such a way that whatever is seen is perceived by his audience just as the poet saw it. But only what has been lived through can be seen in that way and accepted in that way. And the secret of modern literature lies precisely in this matter of experiences that have been personally lived through. All that I have written these last ten years I have lived through in spirit. But no poet lives through anything in isolation. What he lives through, all his country-men live through with him. If that were not so, what would bridge the gap between the creating and the receiving mind?"[3]

Miller would probably agree with this definition of insight as the importance of seeing and truth of reporting. His plays reflect his experience, always in relation to his time, and that time to a general truth. The "Now" of the plays is like a stone flung into water that rings around it. Miller's concern is as much with the rings as with the stone; with its effect as well as its impact. His concern is with causes, actions, and the consequences of actions. He sees beyond the present fact which often blinds his audience, with the result that appreciation of his plays grows as time distances them. This happened with *The Crucible* and will happen with *After the Fall*. Then his relationship with his audience proves that he, too, believes that nothing is lived through in isolation.

Miller admits turning to Ibsen with a sense of homecoming. Here was an organic drama of fact, a synthesis of person and action, of fact with feeling, instead of their isolation. Miller had been immersed in drama of feeling at that time and had come to distrust it. It is possible that Ibsen helped make some of his ideas articulate for him. There is, somehow, excitement and elation in the recognition he felt: "I saw . . . his ability to forge a play upon a factual bedrock. A situation in his plays is never stated but revealed in terms of hard actions, irrevocable deeds; and sentiment is never confused with the action it conceals."[4] Miller holds this same balance in *All My Sons* and through all his plays.

When Arthur Miller adapted *An Enemy of the People* in 1950, he wrote in his Introduction: "Ibsen's profound source

[3] Sprinchorn, Evert (ed.), *Ibsen, Letters and Speeches* (New York: Hill & Wang, 1964).
[4] Preface to the *Collected Plays*.

of strength . . . is his insistence, his utter conviction, that he is going to say what he has to say, and the audience, by God, is going to listen. It is the very same quality that makes a star actor, a great public speaker and a lunatic."

It is certain that Miller found Ibsen's outlook an inspiration. Miller also wrote in his Introduction that "Now listen here!" gave him a way out and went on to deplore the state of neon-lit fiction which must have appealed to him like spun sugar to a diabetic. "It has become the fashion for plays to reduce the thickness of life to a fragile facsimile, to avoid portraying the complexities of life, the contradictions of character, the fascinating interplay of cause and effect that have long been part of the novel." His interpretation is wide as the world; and we are in fact planets away from "Now listen here," which usually means that an argument is to be heard, and "thickness" can be fragile to transparency. Again, this is the wholeness in Miller, that wholeness he admired in Ibsen.

Miller took this up again in his Preface, and Ibsen's technique seemed specially designed to fit Miller's ambition to bring to the stage the density of the novel. To achieve this a play must accept and reflect change and development; otherwise it suggests that people and situations are static. Then once characters are mutilated to fit the present, the all-important explanation is left unmade. So concerned was Ibsen with documenting and dramatizing the past that it is the past that is alive. In *The Master Builder* Solness is only half burnt out, but in *John Gabriel Borkman* the past takes total possession and the characters really "died" twenty years before. This is Ibsen at his most surrealist—the dead are talking with the dead. "I think too many modern plays assume," said Miller, "that their duty is merely to show the present countenance rather than to account for what happens."

Miller believes that drama can never attain full consciousness until the past can be contrasted with the present and the audience made aware of how the present has become what it is. Simply and directly, *All My Sons* accounts for what happens; but both *Death of a Salesman* and *After the Fall* are built toward full consciousness, with a living contrast between past and present. This grows out of Miller's definition of the value of Ibsen to him: "What is precious in the Ibsen method is its insistence upon valid causation. . . . This is the 'real' in Ibsen's realism for me, for he was . . . as much a mystic as a realist, which is simply to say that while there are mysteries in life which no amount of analyzing will reduce to reason, it is perfectly realistic to admit and even to proclaim that hiatus as a truth. But the problem is not to make complex what is essentially explainable; it is to make understandable what is complex without distorting and oversimplifying what cannot be explained."[5] On that the balance of Miller's plays rest.

"No, don't walk around it" sets the mood for the adaptation of *An Enemy of the People*, as it did for *All My Sons*. Both plays are essentially about evasion. Miller sums up definitively by adding a line not in the Archer translation. Stockmann's two boys have been sent home from school after one of them was hurt in a fight.

EJLIF They started calling you names, so he got sore and began to fight with one kid, and all of a sudden a whole bunch of them—

MRS. STOCKMANN Why did you answer?

[5] Preface to the *Collected Plays*.

MORTEN They called him a traitor! My father is no traitor!

EJLIF *But you didn't have to answer!* [my italics]

The whole play turns on the fact that you do have to answer.

"The whole cast of his [Ibsen's] thinking was such that he could not have lived a day under an authoritarian regime of any kind."[6] And neither could Miller. The main conflict of the play is between the individual and authority. "Simply, it is a question of whether the democratic guarantees protecting political minorities ought to be set aside in time of crisis. More personally, it is a question of whether one's vision of the truth ought to be a source of guilt at a time when the mass of men condemn it as a dangerous and devilish lie . . . because there never was, nor will there ever be, an organized society able to countenance calmly the individual who insists that he is right while the vast majority is absolutely wrong."[7]

Stockmann is just such an individual. He insists that the water at the newly built health springs is poisoned; this has been scientifically proved. It is the truth. All at once he is made the figurehead of a progressive revolution, with the backing of the liberal majority—until his discovery affects the town's pocket. The Mayor, his brother, threatens a new tax to pay for the rebuilding, which will take two years. In the face of the new tax and lean years, it is convenient to believe Peter that Stockmann's report ". . . is based on vindictiveness, on his hatred of authority and nothing else. This is the mad dream of a man who is trying to blow up your way of life! It has nothing to do with reform or science or anything else, but pure and simple destruction." In mob vs. man Stockmann

[6] Miller's Introduction to *An Enemy of the People.*
[7] *Ibid.*

is branded a traitor. Truth is made irrelevant and shied away from as if it were a disease.

The play reflects Ibsen's anger over the Norwegian reaction to *Ghosts*.[8] He wrote to Georg Brandes, January 3, 1882: "And what can be said of the attitude assumed by the so-called liberal press—of those leaders of the people who speak and write of freedom of action and thought but at the same time make themselves slaves to the supposed opinions of their subscribers. . . ?"[9]

It must have seemed to Ibsen that there was always a stupid, savage crowd somewhere, ready to tear a man apart, and Stockmann stands out against that crowd in the most resounding defense of individualism in all drama. His meeting has been taken away from him, but at least he is given permission to speak, provided he does not mention the poisoned springs. But by now he has found a new truth: ". . . don't think you can fog up my brain with that magic word—the People! Not any more! Just because there is a mass of organisms with the human shape, they do not automatically become a people. That honor has to be earned! Nor does one automatically become a Man by having human shape, and living in a house, and feeding one's face—and agreeing with one's neighbors. That name *also* has to be earned. . . . Before many can know something, *one* must know it! It's always the same. Rights are sacred until it hurts for somebody to use them." F. L. Lucas, in his book *Ibsen and Strindberg*, suggested that a national theatre could best educate its public by performing *An Enemy of the People* every year.

Ibsen's anger carried his Stockmann toward fascism: and

[8] Sprinchorn, *op. cit.*
[9] *Ibid.*

here, Miller thought, had come the time to cut. The play lies somewhere between the ring and the circus. Anger inspires it and the dialogue is flung down like a challenge—"What am I not going to do?" It is the dramatist's equivalent of the circus high wire; a man is about to get his life broken. The words presage personal disasters; a variation of them led to the blinding of Oedipus and the stoning of Brand.

Basically, Stockmann is Miller's committed man, who cannot compromise. He is told that he could have everything—except the truth. That "everything" he sees as nothing, and he confirms his isolation and suffers the social and economic consequences for himself and his family. Not all Ibsen's fighters are seen from this angle and found right. *The Wild Duck* was written as a warning against absolute truth when the price is inflated. Gregers Werle's progress is reflected in lives breaking like egg shells around him, and Brand remains a warning against total commitment to an abstract ideal, however high.

Stockmann has been carefully drawn to avoid a voice-through-a-megaphone reformer. There is an uncertainty about him, his manner is confused, and even, on occasion, lost. He has doubts, enthusiasms, and nerves. He is impractical to the verge of innocence. Chaplinesque is the situation as he visits the editor who is about to print his report on the Springs. Hot-foot with excitement, he has come to see the proofs, and—

STOCKMANN Just walking down the street now, I looked at the people, in the stores, driving the wagons, and suddenly I was —well, touched, you know? By their innocence, I mean. What I'm driving at is, when this exposé breaks, they're

liable to start making a saint out of me or something, and I—
Aslaksen, I want you to promise me that you're not going to
try to get up any dinner for me or—

ASLAKSEN Doctor, there's no use concealing—

STOCKMANN I knew it. Now look, I will simply not attend a
dinner in my honor.

What there was no use concealing was that Peter had talked
them out of printing the report, and that Stockmann was to
be broken by his former friends.

In an interesting production of the play at Lincoln by
John Hale, George Coulouris played Stockmann as bovine
and avuncular. He was a man capable of being converted to
any cause, a sleep-writing pamphleteer. Certainly this is a
possible interpretation that underlines the fact that Stockmann
is not necessarily always right. There is an element of "good
fellow" in Stockmann that Miller has preserved and even
accentuated, and it is this that Mr. Coulouris stressed. He was
a bewildered man who obstinately knew he was right, and
was holding firmly to that knowledge. His interpretation gave
Peter grounds for impatience. But, for me, he was the wrong
kind of man with the wrong kind of enthusiasm.

The fact of the matter is, regardless of how intelligent Miller makes Stockmann and of any personal preference, George
Coulouris did play the Stockmann Ibsen intended. In the
Preface to the Archer edition (1907), you will find this ex-
tract from Ibsen's letter to Hegel: "But the Doctor is a more
muddleheaded person than I am, and he has, moreover, several other characteristics because of which people will stand
hearing a good many things from him which they might
perhaps not have taken in such very good part had they
been said by me." Ibsen, of all people, choosing the screen

of stupidity! Mr. Coulouris is content with Ibsen's Stock-mann; Machiavelli aside, I prefer Miller's. He is a man of greater mind, of more dynamic intelligence, who has ideas going off in his head like firecrackers. He is altogether less fussy and more colorfully self-dramatizing. With him the play has more edge, greater drive, and sharper impact.

I doubt if Miller could have drawn Stockmann any other way, partly, perhaps, because he has more sympathy with commitment than Ibsen. This Stockmann is naturally Miller's hero, by temperament and intellect. Then the time at which he was writing probably influenced him at least as much as the reception of *Ghosts* influenced Ibsen. It is possible that during McCarthyism Miller had no wish to disguise his Stockmann.

Stockmann believed: "On the wreckage of all the civiliza-tions in the world there ought to be a big sign, 'They didn't dare!'" Ibsen's clash between the Individual and Authority was as pertinent when Miller adapted it as when it was writ-ten. Even in minor aspects it was alive. Miller's Stockmann, after being declared "an enemy of the people," says: "I bet if I walked down the street now not one of them would admit he ever met me!" That was real enough; seven years later, Miller wrote in his Preface: "Astounded, I watched men pass me by without a nod whom I had known rather well for years."

CHAPTER VI

Death of a Salesman

"I sensed a warmth in the world that had not been there before. . . . A success places one among friends. The world is friendly, the audience is friendly, and that is good." After *All My Sons* the sky seemed open to Miller.

Death of a Salesman is governed by the need to know, to know and understand Willy Loman. "I wished to create a form," said Miller in his Preface, "which in itself as a form would literally be the process of Willy Loman's way of mind." Here Miller explores a mind some distance from his own. Willy's mind is all confusion; a contradiction of fact, dream, and longing entangled and inescapable. Miller's is all clarity; his thinking is precise in detail and at the same time is wide-ranging as a searchlight. They share certain preoccupations, but the two are kept distinct and separate. Miller never confuses his insight with Willy's lack of it, his knowledge of Willy with Willy's ignorance of himself, or his seeing with Willy's blindness. He never imposes his logic on Willy's confusion, but shares an outside insight with the audience to balance Willy's extreme subjectivism.

It was over Willy Loman that Miller attacked the Aristo-
telean view of tragedy as something fit only for kings and
heroes, and counterbalanced it with his own view of tragedy
and the common man. This is a revaluation or reinterpreta-
tion and not, as often suggested, a claim that his own work
is "high tragedy or nothing." A more detached view is necessary for this method of judging contemporary plays, when
kings can no longer bargain with the gods for their peoples'
prosperity, and an Oedipus cannot end the plagues of Thebes
by expiating his personal sin.

Miller's argument began in *Theatre Arts*, March, 1951, and
foreshadows the later one in his Preface. He linked the older
tragedy to the new: "From Orestes to Hamlet, Medea to
Macbeth, the underlying struggle has been that of the individual attempting to gain his 'rightful' position in his society."
Now this struggle is at its greatest in the common man,
making him the natural protagonist for tragedy. The need
to preserve their views of themselves is both catalyst and moti-
vating force behind Miller's characters. They are all keenly
aware of "the disaster inherent in being torn away from our
chosen image of what and who we are in this world."

This dread lives with Willy, who in his panic turns fanatic, and in himself proves many of Miller's arguments. His
idea of himself is all Willy has, the root of his stability, the
touchstone of meaning for him. To the objective observers,
Charley and Willy's sons, the circle is closed for Willy only
to Willy. Willy Loman's problem is not and could never be
a problem for Charley. Charley is not a fanatic: "Equally,"
says Miller in his Preface, "he has learned how to live without that frenzy, that ecstasy of spirit which Willy chases to
his end." The headlong search for fulfillment by the com-

mitted makes them treat the man who can walk away with
an exasperation bordering on envy. Brand, who by the light
of his fanaticism persuaded his parishioners to follow him, and
who was killed by an avalanche while seeking his God, might
have regarded a tranquil village priest in something of the
way that Hamlet regards Horatio, Chris at times regards
Keller, and Willy Loman regards Charley. Intensity is the
measure of tragic stature for Miller; he says in his Preface:
"If the intensity, the human passion to surpass his given
bounds, the fanatic insistence upon his self-conceived role . . .
are not present there can only be an outline of tragedy and no
living thing." And through Willy's intensity Miller recognized the tragedy in him, as Epstein recognized the nobility
in the faces he sculpted.

In defining the making of a tragic hero in his Preface, Miller divorces stature from rank, so often confused with it.
Since now it would be idle to pretend that without princes
plays fall short of tragedy, Miller points out that the corner
grocer can outdistance the President of the United States as
a tragic figure—"providing, of course, that the grocer's career
engages the issues of, for instance, the survival of the race,
the relationships of man to God—the questions, in short,
whose answers define humanity and the right way to live so
that the world is a home, instead of a battleground or a fog
in which disembodied spirits pass each other in an endless
twilight." This is fundamental in Miller, the end to which
all his plays are built.

I cannot understand the confusion Miller's theory has
caused, because as I write I find his arguments already proved.
There is nothing to add, unless the problem is other than it

appears and has more to do with the audience watching the tragic hero than with the hero himself.

There is, for instance, the question of the suddenness of tragedy. *Oedipus Rex* will make a greater impact on an audience than a more leisurely paced tragedy like *Agamemnon*. The impact of the original one-act version of *A View From the Bridge* is greater, I think, than *Death of a Salesman*. This is not because the play is more tragic intrinsically, but because its form is more compact and therefore more dynamic. Where you grow with *Death of a Salesman*, you react to *A View From the Bridge*. It is altogether a more direct and less complex response.

Add to this question of the elevation. As to *A View From the Bridge* Miller protested: "I am not any smarter than what my plays seem to say. I don't know any more. I really don't. That's as much as I know at any one time. I mean the assumption is that I'm writing about people who are very far below me. And I'm really not."[1] Again, is it only a question of rank that causes the complaint that modern tragedy is like the Smithfield Meat Market? Ancient tragedy is remote for an audience. They do not get involved in it, nor do they identify themselves with it. They cannot. Distance and detachment enhance its nobility. Nobody expects to walk out of the theatre and meet someone with the same story. Also, when a play deals directly with man vs. the gods its cosmic implications are guaranteed to be above and beyond any member of the audience. We do not think of Apollo as a sparring partner. I wonder whether an ancient Greek audience would be as detached and whether uncles looked nervously at their nephews after *Hamlet*. There can be no question

[1] "Cause Without a Rebel," *Encore*, June–July, 1957.

of detachment for us at a contemporary tragedy; instead there is involvement, identification, and it is possible to find Eddie Carbone outside the theatre.

Miller's view is valid in pointing out other times, other heroes, and other tragedies. According to his theory it is no wonder that he could not deny tragedy to Willy Loman, who fulfills it.

"Nobody dast blame this man. You don't understand: Willy was a salesman. And for a salesman, there is no rock bottom to the life. He don't put a bolt to a nut, he don't tell you the law or give you medicine. He's a man way out there in the blue, riding on a smile and a shoeshine. And when they start not smiling back—that's an earthquake. And then you get yourself a couple of spots on your hat, and you're finished. Nobody dast blame this man. A salesman is got to dream, boy. It comes with the territory."

We first meet Willy Loman as he returns home weighed down by suitcases too heavy for him to carry with ease. "We see a solid vault of apartment houses around the small, fragile-seeming home. An air of the dream clings to the place, a dream rising out of reality." This distinction is both characteristic of Miller and symbolic of the play.

Willy is exhausted—tired to death and terrified that he will not be able to drive a car again. He cannot keep his mind on it and keeps going off the road. He simply forgets he was driving. He knows he is failing and battles against a physical weakness and a time when things grow meaningless that once had a deal of meaning. In an attempt to justify his life, the pressure of Willy's thoughts has broken the barrier between the past and present in his mind. In this confusion he founders, unable to find solid ground. He is completely self-absorbed, and at one point is told: "You are the saddest, self-centredest soul I ever did see-saw." Almost as though Miller took one look at his creation and gave up.

There are always two stories for Willy—the one he tells and the one he confesses to, the one that happened. His protests are real, small, and ineffective. "There's not a breath of fresh air in the neighborhood. The grass don't grow any more, you can't raise a carrot in the back yard. They should've had a law against apartment houses." The protest grows into a general complaint about increasing population and competition, and in the face of it all dies on a personal complaint about cheese. Everything is difficult for Willy; even eating is hedged round with facts he never mastered and should know to do it successfully. He accuses his neighbor Charley of not knowing how to eat because he is too ignorant to know about vitamins.

All the people in the play are seen with a double vision: through Willy's mind and as they are. His love and his involvement soften hard outlines, like a landscape seen when the light is right; for instance, Biff lives heroic in Willy's mind, and only there is Linda that gentle, believing, and unknowing. In fact, Linda is practical, knows Willy as far as he can be known, understands him, appreciates him, and protects him by trying to take the edge off his confusion. Had Linda been as Willy saw her, she would not have known how to explain him to his two sons: "The man is exhausted. . . . A small man can be just as exhausted as a great man. He works for a company thirty-six years this March, opens up unheard-of territories to their trade-mark, and now in his old age they take his salary away. . . . He drives seven hundred miles, and when he gets there no one knows him any more, no one welcomes him. And what goes through a man's mind, driving seven hundred miles home without having earned a cent? Why shouldn't he talk to himself? Why? When he has to go to Charley and borrow fifty dollars a week and pretend to me that it's his pay? How long can that go on? How long? . . . And you tell me he has no character? The man who never worked a day but for your benefit? When does he get a medal for that?"

Willy has been trying to kill himself.

Apart from loneliness and disappointment on the road when business is bad and there's nobody to talk to, there is the overriding fear that he will never sell anything again, and the overbearing fact that he will not be able to make a living. All his life Willy describes himself as being "in a race with the junkyard." Miller etches in the facts: The struggle for existence is against insurance premiums, installment payments, car repairs, mortgages. When Willy makes $70, he has to find $120. He admits that he has to be at it ten to twelve hours a day, while other men do it easier. At the end of his struggle and effort he is faced with irony: "Work a life-time to pay off a house. You finally own it and there's nobody to live in it."

Willy put everything into his belief that selling is the greatest career a man could want. It breaks in his hands and he is fired. He is forced to borrow money from Charley, saving his respect with the reminder that he is keeping strict account and will pay back every penny. Charley, the man he despises too much to work for, is his only friend. Willy's hurt is so stamped upon him that it seems tangible. At the end of his terrible day his two sons walk out on him in a restaurant where they were going to dine together. "He was so humiliated he nearly limped when he came in," says Linda. After a painful reconciliation with Biff, the circle closes for Willy, and he kills himself.

Willy, like Miller's other heroes, is driven by Miller's healthy idea that nothing has to be accepted. It is the unspoken demand behind the plays and is a deafening reminder for Willy. Once the encouragement of Miller's belief is accepted, the next question is inevitable: "What are you going to do about it?" Willy admits to his sons that he hasn't a story left in his head. Stumble away from the question and he stumbles away from the hope that backs it to an escapism that escapes nothing and a meaninglessness that is both painful and negative. Nor is the question for him alone; the challenge is for everybody. To paraphrase Chris's line from *All My Sons*, Willy Loman didn't kill himself just so that the audience could be sorry.

Some of Willy's critics saw him as too insensitive to realize his situation; had this been true, there would have been no reason for his suicide. Linda's belief that he only needed a little salary has been taken too literally. Had it been possible to pay off Willy's house, buy him a new refrigerator, and pay him that salary, he still would not have peace of mind. Miller explains why in his Preface and traces the root cause of Willy's frustration. "Had Willy been unaware of his separation from values that endure he would have died contentedly while polishing his car, probably on a Sunday afternoon with a ball game coming over the radio. But he was agonized by his awareness of being in a false position, so constantly haunted by the hollowness of all he had placed his faith in, so aware, in short, that he must somehow be

filled in spirit or fly apart that he staked his life on the ultimate assertion." (Later, in *After The Fall*, Quentin is to be
driven by the same agony as he watches a succession of
breaking faiths.)

Miller went on to draw a distinction between consciousness
of a situation and an ability to express it: "That he had not
the intellectual fluency to verbalize his situation is not the
same thing as saying that he lacked awareness." In fact, it is
precisely Willy's sheer inability to explain his situation that
makes it impossible for him. He does not understand sufficiently, and through this debility is forced to turn in upon
himself, a separate and isolated entity. There is no lonelier
position to be in; because Willy does not know why his life
has disintegrated, he shoulders all the blame and all the guilt.
And all because he does not know. A knowledge of the social forces working upon him might have saved him. It
would at least have given him an objective viewpoint, and
that might have forestalled or even prevented his ultimate
collapse. But this lack of knowledge on Willy's part has little
to do with his awareness of his painful situation. It is not
necessary to know why you are in pain to feel it. Miller
here sets limits to the consciousness of a character and suggests that he is conscious up to the point at which guilt begins. That is probably as far as consciousness goes in most
of us.

To know is seen as a pure salvation in *Death of a Salesman*. In *After the Fall*, for the first time it is seen as double-
edged, a realization that in no way alters Miller's belief. He
wrote to me: "The only struggle which can draw together
any thematic order from this human chaos is precisely the
struggle to know. Not to suppress, not to ultimately end up

with heartless and efficient servants of some 'knowledge,' but to know in order to obey the human requirements of a truly human condition." The need to know is far more open in the later play. It is explored in depth, and the whole play is geared to that end. "For this reason, *After the Fall* sets forth the dichotomy, the split between what a man finds himself doing and what he would like to do; between what he sees is happening and his illusions about what is happening. Indeed, the moral of the play can be put thus: Given the evidence of such uncontrollable chaos, of such self-deception and deception of others, how is it possible to sensibly lay up against it any desired rule of order whatever? The answer is that the heart, while it lives, requires the effort to impose an order, and that this evidence, as muted as it is, as wordless and inexpressible, is the first thing that must be respected. Despite everything."

The view in *Salesman* is much simpler and more direct. The question of consciousness was with Miller then, as it had been in *All My Sons*, and is through the plays. In a letter, he traced it back dramatically. "Critics often cite Greek drama to show how low we have fallen—our characters are not self-aware enough, they say. Our naturalists, on the other hand, make a point of almost totally unaware characters. (Self-awareness.) First, I believe a re-reading of the Greeks will show how little the heroes know of their own motives. What puts people off, I think, is that they openly say what they do know, but what they do know is most often very little. On the other hand, my argument is that too many of our plays refuse to ask the simplest causative questions at all. Second, the audience has *always* 'known' more than any hero could because it is not acting but observing. Third, the vast majority of Greek plays do not conform to Aristotle's dicta concerning even the tragic flaw or fault, or the question of misjudgment. What misjudgment is there in Oedipus? The thing was determined from his very birth. I see the process, essentially as this: the hero is one, unlike most men, who quite unknowingly or with a certain degree of foreknowledge, *acts* at a moment when others would go silent or retire. In so acting he causes the scheme of things to react with retributive violence against him. It is a question of pressing the mechanism beyond its ability to exist in quiet. At bottom it is a questing after knowledge, a knowledge which is forbidden. Note the consistent Greek—and Hebrew—emphasis upon this. Oedipus, even before his catastrophic insistence upon knowing who is the cursed murderer, was the one who forced an answer out of the Sphinx. The idea is that regardless of the superficial or profound friendliness of the environment, the universe is basically prepared to destroy man *at the moment it is forced to give up its secrets.* The hero is the sacrifice we make for new understanding. His 'fault' is that he lacks wisdom—he cannot let well enough alone, he cannot respect danger sufficiently. There is a certain revulsion against Willy; in truth we feel revolted by all tragic heroes in part. It is because they are demanding that we too follow them, that we break the bounds of good sense which are also the bounds of the false life; false in the sense that it is incompletely aware."

It is this ignorance of personal danger, this unwisdom, this lack of "practicality" that make Miller's heroes heroic. They all share it, and because of it their demands on the audience, as Miller points out, are particularly high. Oedipus, the ancient archetypal hero, defies the oracle and in the face of danger insists on knowledge. All because he cannot support mystery. He cannot bear not to *know*. Willy Loman's challenge is a rebellion against a meaningless way of life and, by the illustration of his not knowing, against a lack of knowledge. For Miller, the man who can remain passive, who can settle for half, is the flawed character, and the tragic flaw is no fault. Oedipus has no "fault," Creon has. The blemished character in *Death of a Salesman* is not Willy; it is Charley. In Miller the fault is compromise. He wrote of Dr. Stockmann in *An Enemy of the People:* "He will not compromise for less than God's own share of the world while they have settled for less than Man's." These lines are so characteristic of Miller that he signs his name with every word.

In his letter, he went on to discuss the question of awareness, the hero's or the audience's: "The answer varies from play to play, but in itself the question cannot be the only or the main measure of the play's tragic import. All I wish to convey is that the tragic question is always 'Why?' Without it there is only the helpless, pathetic victim. I would add that Willy hardly lives a moment without asking it of everything he does and everything that happens to him. The very asking of it presupposes that one is not satisfied with conventional answers. It is rebellion. Pressed far enough, it leads far out into the cold lunar reaches of one's relationship to everything that exists in and out of the mind."

Let us get back to Willy, tormented by his situation; in particular, he cannot walk away from his relationship with his son Biff, which broke down when Biff found his father with a woman in a Boston hotel room. From that time he could never see Willy as anything but "a phony little fake," and never stopped trying to prove it. When Biff loses faith, so does Willy. The disillusionment is brisk and brutal, not the least of it being the humiliation of the woman; everything in their lives falls after it. Willy spends the rest of his life trying to rehabilitate himself in Biff's eyes, and Biff is lost. It is as though he never grew beyond the seventeen-year-old who flunked math. He defines himself to his brother Happy: "I'm like a boy. I'm not married, I'm not in business, I just—I'm like a boy." His life has stopped.

Willy cannot understand it: "Not finding yourself at the age of thirty-four is a disgrace." Then, apart from Biff seeing through Willy, he embodies a way of life that contradicts Willy's standards of success; standards that Biff can neither accept nor wholly reject. If Willy thinks Biff sees him only as a fake, Biff is convinced that to Willy he is only a failure.

For seventeen years Willy has been tearing himself apart over this dead-end relationship. He cannot do anything about it. It is elusive on the concrete, graspable level and he has nothing to give Biff. Miller's classic situation, difficult enough to be seen as impossible by everybody except Willy, who battles on regardless. His position prompts the sane, practical advice to leave things alone. He explains to Charley:

WILLY I can't understand it. He's going back to Texas again. What the hell is that?

CHARLEY Let him go.

WILLY I got nothin' to give him, Charley. I'm clean. I'm clean.

CHARLEY He won't starve. None of them starve. Forget about him.

WILLY Then what have I got to remember?

CHARLEY You take it too hard. To hell with it. When a deposit bottle is broken you don't get your nickel back.

Willy's preoccupation is just another thing that Charley will never understand about him.

Willy, dragged along behind his dream, judges people by the distance they are from attaining it. The most sudden change is in his relationship with Bernard, Charley's son. It moves from "You want him [Biff] to be a worm like Bernard?" to seeing Bernard in his father's office, when he seems to revere the boy he once despised. Bernard is on his way to argue a case in the Supreme Court, and never mentions it to Willy. Charley's forthright comment is: "He don't have to—he's gonna do it." Miller's plays are full of these wry, perceptive, and often brutal insights.

In his defeat Willy lives on the crowds cheering Biff the day he captained the school football team. But now Biff steals Oliver's fountain pen and to meet this crisis insists on holding to facts; implacably he insists: "We've been talking in a dream for fifteen years. I was a shipping clerk. . . . I was never a salesman for Bill Oliver." They face it. It is a Miller play. And from this conflict of Biff's fact and Willy's dream the play moves toward Willy's inevitable suicide.

Death of a Salesman takes root deeper than Miller's other plays; for days, it seemed, I waited for Willy Loman to die. It's as though the play covers a life-span. You know the Lomans better than you do your neighbors. Just as there is no single, clear-cut reason for Biff's failure, there is no one reason for Willy's suicide. It would be gross oversimplification to suggest that one single action or event could explain a failure or prompt a suicide. Biff gave up his life out of spite, as Willy suggests. He failed because Willy brought him up to be a big shot and he could never take orders from anybody, as he himself admits. Equally, Biff could not give himself or his life to Willy's brand of success (as Miller sees) and by that standard he failed. All these are valid and contributing causes to Biff's failure; the answer does not lie in any one of them, and it is doubtful if the complete answer is to be found in all of them. Rightly, Biff's failure adds up to more than this and, rightly again, it cannot be completely explained. Once a character is fully created you can explain his actions no better or more satisfactorily than you can explain your own. In his Preface Miller warns: "A work of art is not handed down from Olympus from a creature with a vision as wide as the world."

Let us go on to Willy's suicide, mercifully mixed in motive. "Revenge was in it and a power of love, a victory in that it would bequeath a fortune to the living and a flight from emptiness." But before Willy dies, Biff tries to show him how he had lived.

BIFF Pop! I'm a dime a dozen, and so are you!

WILLY I am not a dime a dozen! I am Willy Loman, and you are Biff Loman.

BIFF I am not a leader of men, Willy, and neither are you. You were never anything but a hard-working drummer who landed in the ash can like the rest of them! I'm one dollar an hour, Willy! I tried in seven states and couldn't raise it. A buck an hour! Do you gather my meaning? I'm not bringing home any prizes any more, and you're going to stop waiting for me to bring them home! Pop, I'm nothing! I'm nothing, Pop. Can't you understand that? There's no spite in it any

more. I'm just what I am, that's all. . . . Will you let me go,
for Christ's sake? Will you take that phony dream and burn
it before something happens?

Willy's dream destroyed him and he died to turn it into
reality. During his showdown with Biff, Willy hesitantly realizes that he is loved by his son; confirmed in his belief, he
cries out his faith: "That boy—that boy is going to be
magnificent."

Miller said of Willy in his Preface: "My sense of his character dictated his joy, and even what I felt was exaltation. In
terms of his character, he had achieved a very powerful piece
of knowledge, which is that he is loved by his son and has
been embraced by him and forgiven. In this he is given his
existence, so to speak—his fatherhood, for which he has always striven and which until now he could not achieve. That
he is unable to take this victory thoroughly to his heart, that
it closes the circle for him and propels him to his death, is
the wage of his sin, which was to have committed himself
so completely to the counterfeits of dignity and false coin-
age embodied in his idea of success that he can prove his
existence only by bestowing 'power' on posterity, a power
deriving from the sale of his last asset, himself, for the price
of an insurance policy."

Willy's suicide remains affirmative in that, in his eyes, it
resolves everything for him. He wins by his death all that
he craved in life. Miller is convinced that the play is not a
document of pessimism, and I do not think that it is.

Still following the dream of greatness, Willy imagines the
size of his funeral. "They'll come from Maine, Massachusetts,
Vermont, New Hampshire! . . . That boy will be thunder-

struck." What an opportunity to dazzle Biff! But the funeral
is attended only by the family, Charley, and Bernard. Willy
dies as he has lived.

If this were the entire content of *Death of a Salesman* the
play would be too personal to please Miller. *Salesman* has
a greater depth and a wider vision, perhaps growing out of
Miller's boyhood. As an adolescent during the second national catastrophe in American history—the Great Depression
of the thirties, Miller learnt early to distrust success. In
"Shadows of the Gods," writing of that time, he wondered
whether success should be admired. "Or should one always
see through it as an illusion which only existed to be blown
up and its owner destroyed and humiliated?"[2]

Death of a Salesman is dominated by this law of success.
It is the force behind the play and Miller writes chillingly
about it in his Preface: "The confusion of some critics viewing *Death of a Salesman* . . . is that they do not see that
Willy Loman has broken a law without whose protection
life is insupportable if not incomprehensible to him and to
many others; it is the law which says that a failure in society
and in business has no right to live. Unlike the law against
incest, the law of success is not administered by statute or
church, but it is very nearly as powerful in its grip upon
men. The confusion increases because, while it is a law,
it is by no means a wholly agreeable one even as it is slav-
ishly obeyed, for to fail is no longer to belong to society
in his estimate. Therefore, the path is opened for those who
wish to call Willy merely a foolish man even as they themselves are living in obedience to the same law that killed
him."

[2] *Harper's*, August, 1958.

Unlike Miller's other characters, Willy desperately wants to conform to the way of life imposed upon him. A John Proctor, for instance, does not believe with the majority, will not conform to it, and is sustained by the fact that he is right, but Willy's enforced nonconformity brings him only shame. His sense of right is vague at best and certainly no match for the pressures against him. Pressures that, incidentally, he cannot fight on the principle that you cannot fight what you would join. In these plays Willy is probably Miller's only nonconformist through circumstances, not choice. In this religion he would never dare to be a heretic.

The religion of success, like any other, has its myths, and Ben embodies legendary success. "William, when I walked into the jungle, I was seventeen. When I walked out I was twenty-one. And, by God, I was rich." This is exactly the way Willy would see success. Ben is Willy's older brother; he is also his daydream, the kind of man he wanted to become—his ideal image. In their dialogues, remembered or imagined, he is trying to achieve the viewpoint he has always sought, as well as confirmation of his own actions and beliefs. For Willy, it is an "ideal" conversation, one in which he is extending himself and, at the last, seeing himself as the practical, successful man he wanted to be. It is almost as though Miller wrote the character from a legendary angle; fiction clings to Ben—fiction and a brutal realism that Willy could never reach: "Never fight fair with a stranger, boy. You'll never get out of the jungle that way."

Willy, on the other hand, puts all his faith in the individual, in the winning personality: "Be liked and you will never want" is the mainstream of his philosophy. The one line always remembered from *Salesman* is Willy's warning to his boys about Charley: "He's liked—but he's not well liked."

In Miller you always come back to the irrevocable fact, the unavoidable logic of a situation. "When a man gets old you fire him, you have to, he can't do the work."[3] For these practical and impersonal reasons Willy was fired; his failure and the pain it causes him are pinned down to fact. As far as possible in Miller the intangible must be made tangible.

In Willy's sorry interview with Howard, he is too pushed and preoccupied with his own problems to choose his time; he interrupts Howard while he is absorbed in a wire recorder, a new toy he has bought for $150. Howard is fascinated by the machine and the breaking of the man goes unnoticed. He barely listens to Willy's plea: "You can't eat an orange and throw the peel away—a man is not a piece of fruit!" Undoubtedly Howard is bored with Willy, who seems to be doing no more than wasting his time. He has no use for him and sees him not as an individual but as an economic unit. One American critic saw this scene as party-line writing. Arthur Miller's name does not at once suggest politics to me, and the idea never entered my head. I believe that Miller's protest is directed toward the cutting down of the individual.

Death of a Salesman is of wide scope and great change covering Willy's life, but all that happens to Willy and Biff is implicit in it from the beginning. This dictates the audiences' reaction of "Oh God, of course."

"Willy is working on two logics which often collide," says Miller, explaining the play's structure in his Preface; "subsequent imitations of the form had to collapse for this particular reason. It is not possible, in my opinion, to graft it

[3] Preface to the *Collected Plays*.

onto a character whose psychology it does not reflect, and I have not used it since because it would be false to a more integrated—or less disintegrating—personality to pretend that the past and the present are so openly and vocally intertwined in his mind. . . . There are no flashbacks in this play but only a mobile concurrency of past and present, and this again, because in his desperation to justify his life Willy Loman has destroyed the boundaries between now and then." While following Willy's mind, Miller has discovered a new and flexible way of explaining the reasons behind the present situation, one that again emphasizes his wholeness.

Technically the play is intricate, complex, and only apparently formless. Beneath its casual flow and fall it is as precisely constructed as the more obviously dramatic one-act *A View From the Bridge*, which is the most skillfully timed play I know. One example of the precision of *Salesman* is the switchback over the fountain pen in Willy's mind to the basic cause of his trouble with Biff. While hearing about the pen, Willy seizes on Biff's flunking math. Had Biff gotten his credit he would never have come to Boston and seen the tart. He would not have thrown up his life. He would not have seen through and broken with his father. If this were not enough, Willy's memory of Boston is played alongside Happy's pick-ups for himself and Biff in the restaurant. Not only is the construction exact in incident, but also in dialogue, which Miller writes definitively in summing-up, expository lines.

 In *Salesman* the past elm-shades the present. The earlier, happier days stay with Willy, consoling him from time to time. The play is built of images; outlines are soft, taking on something of the quality of a dream. When Miller later used the mind's eye in *After the Fall,* his whole purpose had hardened; where the first play dreamed the second analyzed, at whatever cost, in a headlong search for definition. Quentin grapples directly with what kills him, seeking it out. Willy, while he can, evades it—it comes to him.

Death of a Salesman remains Miller's most comprehensive play: through its delicate shadings of mood and multiple meanings it lays itself open to flaws in production and to misunderstanding. This is another aspect it shares with *After the Fall*. Both plays need an Elia Kazan to woo performances from actors as complete as the plays themselves. I am uncertain whether either play, or any play, reaches Miller's own definition of great drama: "Balance is all. It will evade us until we can once again see man as whole, until sensitivity and power, justice and necessity are utterly face to face, until authority's justifications and rebellions too are tracked even to those heights where breath fails, where—because the largest point of view as well as the smaller has spoken—truly the rest is silence."[4]

A last question remains: Has Miller created tragedy in *Death of a Salesman?* It is questionable whether it is necessarily more tragic to fall from an achieved height than from one imagined. It is undoubtedly more dramatic to write about a giant dispossessed rather than a would-be giant. The Tamburlaines have the cards stacked for them, but this does not inevitably make them tragic. *Salesman* remains a daily tragedy, a tragedy of illusion. Willy fell only from an imagined height. Miller's search since his adolescence has been for "the rock upon which one may stand without illusion, a free man."[5]

[4] *Harper's*, August, 1958.
[5] *Ibid.*

CHAPTER VII

The Crucible

Cry *witch!* The Salem witch-hunt marked a time when "long-held hatreds of neighbors could now be openly expressed, and vengeance taken, despite the Bible's charitable injunctions. Land-lust . . . could now be elevated to the arena of morality; one could cry witch against one's neighbor and feel perfectly justified in the bargain. Old scores could be settled on a plane of heavenly combat between Lucifer and the Lord."

Its climate of terror is the first we know of this play. The slave Tituba's initial fright is followed by the Reverend Parris' fear—and the fear is of witchcraft. He has discovered some girls "dancing like heathen in the forest," and, shaken, he tells his niece Abigail (who led them) what he saw: "I saw Tituba . . . and I heard a screeching and gibberish coming from her mouth. She were swaying like a dumb beast over that fire!" In the shock of discovery a child has fallen sick, and the town leaps to cry witchcraft. Abigail, to escape whipping, embraces the excuse, and in the general hysteria vengeance breaks out.

Fear and guilt were in the air of Salem, heightened by the prim order of life. Children were regarded as young adults. "They never conceived that the children were anything but thankful for being permitted to walk straight, eyes slightly lowered, arms at the sides, and mouths shut until bidden to speak." Once this rigidity was broken the people found themselves prey to fantastic terrors never felt before. Ann Putnam, "a twisted soul of forty-five, a death-ridden woman, haunted by dreams," chillingly confesses to sending her young daughter Ruth to conjure up the dead and discover who murdered her brothers and sisters—all of whom had died at birth. Avidly the neighbors gather to inquire into Betty Parris' strange illness. "How high did she fly?" Complacently they assure one another that "the Devil's touch is heavier than sick." The fear in the Reverend Parris is greater than in all the rest. He will be hounded out of Salem for the witchcraft discovered in his house. He always feared for something, and now he fears his neighbors. It is as though a people suddenly turned savage. He expects to be turned out, and believes the people would be justified, since in his own eyes he is already tainted with the Devil.

The superstitions of the townspeople breed greater terror, and Abigail, quick to take advantage, warns her friends: "Let either of you breathe a word, or the edge of a word . . . and I will come to you in the black of some terrible night and I will bring a pointy reckoning that will shudder you. And you know I can do it; I saw the Indians smash my dear parents' heads on the pillow next to mine, and I have seen some reddish work done at night, and I can make you wish you had never seen the sun go down!" Abigail has been drinking blood, a charm to kill John Proctor's wife.

Abigail was a servant in the Proctors' house and loved John,
until Elizabeth found them out and dismissed her. Now
Abigail admits to him that Betty's sickness has nothing to do
with witchcraft. Proctor is one of Miller's ten-feet-tall indi-
vidualists, a farmer of unshakable integrity and dangerous
directness. "I may speak my heart, I think." Putnam accuses
him at once of being against Parris and against all authority.
Proctor has no patience with Parris and complains that he
preaches only hell-fire and forgets to mention God. He sees
the man's weakness—a vacillation based on fear that makes
it impossible for him to tell his parishioners they are wrong
about witchcraft. Instead, he goes along with the mounting
superstition and sends for Reverend Hale to discover whether
or not there are witches in Salem. This opens the way for
demonology to replace law.

For Hale, diabolism is a precise science that has nothing to
do with superstition. But by the nature of his belief he could
not be immune to the cry of "Spirits!" The shock of
Abigail's attack on Tituba releases the hysteria and convinces
Hale. Tituba is accused of conspiring with the Devil and a
desperate bewilderment breaks upon her. She knows nothing
but the terror, and understands nothing but that she will hang.
Panic prompts a confession she does not know how to make.
She gropes for a placating answer and out of this recounts
promises made to her by the Devil: "You work for me,
Tituba, and I make you free! I give you pretty dress to wear,
and put you way high up in the air, and you gone fly back
to Barbados!" It will not serve. Almost hypnotized, she gives
names suggested by Putnam. Startlingly, Abigail joins Tituba's
confession with her own and in an orgy of relief Betty fever-
ishly joins in the random calling out of names. Blasted with

ecstasy, the children cry out as if possessed, and the climate is created that makes witch-hunting possible.

Against this background Miller etches the Proctors' bleak relationship. Proctor describes Elizabeth as having an everlasting funeral marching round her heart. They live in isolation, while above them both tower the tremendous values by which they live.

In Salem a court has been set up to try and hang those accused of witchcraft, if they will not confess. Abigail has been elevated to sainthood. "Where she walks the crowd will part like the sea for Israel. And folks are brought before them, and if they scream and howl and fall to the floor—the person's clapped in jail for bewitchin' them." Proctor's servant, Mary Warren, returns with the news that the fourteen arrested have grown to thirty-nine, and that Goody Osburn will hang. Mary, a frightened, lonely girl, danced with the others and preens herself on being an official of the Court. Alarmed herself at its wonders, and alarming them, she explains how witchcraft is proved. "But then—then she sit there, denying and denying, and I feel a misty coldness climbin' up my back, and the skin on my skull begin to creep, and I feel a clamp around my neck and I cannot breathe air; and then— I hear a voice, a screamin' voice, and it were my voice—and all at once I remembered everything she done to me!"

Proctor is about to whip her when she yells that she saved Elizabeth's life that day. While Mary strives precariously for self-respect, Elizabeth realizes that Abigail wants her dead, and will cry out her name until she is taken.

The Reverend Hale interrupts this conflict. He has come to test the Proctors' Christianity. Elizabeth cannot wait to convince him, but Proctor's guilt over Abigail makes him falter.

Instead, he tells Hale of Abigail's confession that the children's sickness has nothing to do with witchcraft. Hale reminds him of confessions made to the Court. "And why not, if they must hang for denyin' it?" Those confessions prove nothing.

Intimations of Elizabeth's arrest that began with Mary Warren's outburst are taken further when Proctor's neighbors, Corey and Nurse, come with the news that Martha and Rebecca have been taken. Rebecca is charged with the supernatural murder of Goody Putnam's babies. If she is guilty, Hale insists, "then nothing is left to stop the whole green world from burning."

They come for Elizabeth. When, in spite of her proved innocence, she still leaves Hale questioning, Proctor can bear it no longer. "Why do you never wonder if Parris be innocent, or Abigail? Is the accuser always holy now? Were they born this morning as clean as God's fingers? I'll tell you what's walking Salem—vengeance is walking Salem . . . now the little crazy children are jangling the keys of the kingdom, and common vengeance writes the law!" But Elizabeth is taken and chained, while they watch, helpless.

Proctor insists that Mary testify in court and as her fear mounts so does his conviction. "Make your peace with it! Now Hell and Heaven grapple on our backs, and all our old pretense is ripped away—make your peace! Peace. It is a providence, and no great change; we are only what we always were, but naked now. Aye, naked! And the wind, God's icy wind, will blow!"

On this surge of feeling, attention turns back to the Court. Here other charges are brought. Giles Corey insists that Putnam is killing his neighbors for their land. A man whose pigs die swears that Martha Corey is bewitching them. But primarily, Mary Warren tremblingly admits that she never saw spirits. Judge Danforth cannot believe it. "I have seen marvels in this Court. I have seen people choked before my eyes by spirits; I have seen them stuck by pins and slashed by daggers." He refuses to believe that people fear this Court; if they do there is only one explanation: "There is fear in the country because there is a moving plot to topple Christ in the country!"

Proctor insists that he has not come to overthrow the Court, but to save his wife. In that case, Danforth urges him to drop the charge; Elizabeth will not be hanged because she is pregnant. Proctor finds he cannot; Corey and Nurse are his friends, and their wives are also accused. Danforth agrees to hear Mary Warren. Falteringly she insists that she is with God now and is confronted with the other children and with Abigail's denial. To prove her story, Mary is ordered to faint at will, but lacking the hysteria she cannot. Doubt rises, and out of it the children create terror. They are about to cry out Mary Warren as a witch when Proctor checks them with the truth about Abigail: "A man will not cast away his good name. You surely know that . . . I have made a bell of my honor! I have rung the doom of my good name." Elizabeth is called to confirm his accusation; she lies to save his name.

Danforth believes her. Abigail cries out Mary Warren as a witch: Mary has assumed the shape of a bird and high on a beam she stretches her claws, about to swoop down on the children and tear their faces. Only Proctor and Hale do not share in this horror. The girls scream and Mary finds herself screaming with them. She goes wild and accuses Proctor of being the Devil's man. Danforth clamors for confession.

In the midst of these wild and whirling words that seem to

presage a reeling universe, Proctor warns the Judge: "For them that quail to bring men out of ignorance, as I have quailed, and as you quail now when you know in all your black hearts that this be fraud—God damns our kind especially, and we will burn, we will burn together!" Reverend Hale quits the Court.

It is the morning of Proctor's execution. Meanwhile in Salem: "There are orphans wandering from house to house; abandoned cattle bellow on the highroads, the stink of rotting crops hangs everywhere, and no man knows when the harlots' cry will end his life." Abigail has stolen all Parris' savings and disappeared. Mr. Hale has come to urge those accused to confess, as if they die he counts himself their murderer. And still Danforth refuses to postpone the hangings. "While I speak God's law, I will not crack its voice with whimpering."

Elizabeth is fetched in the hope that she will persuade Proctor to confess. Hale tries to warn her by his own example. "The very crowns of holy law I brought, and what I touched with my bright confidence, it died; and where I turned the eye of my great faith, blood flowed up. Beware, Goody Proctor—cleave to no faith when faith brings blood." To her, this remains the Devil's argument.

Now this whole issue turns on the integrity of John Proctor, on his judgment or Danforth's. Elizabeth tells him how Giles Corey died. "Great stones they lay upon his chest until he plead Aye or Nay. They say he gave them but two words. 'More weight,' he says. And died." Proctor's guilt prompts him to confess, almost as a kind of expiation. He believes that it would be fraud for him to die like a saint and besmirch the honor of those that hang. It is as though his death has to be earned.

He looks to Elizabeth for absolution, but she reminds him that her forgiveness means nothing if he cannot forgive himself. All she can do is take her share of the guilt. "Do what you will. But let none be your judge. There be no higher judge under Heaven than Proctor is!" And there is no shedding of this particular responsibility. He decides to confess, but refuses to implicate others. "Then it is proved. Why must I say it? . . . I speak my own sins; I cannot judge another. I have no tongue for it."

But Proctor cannot turn so against himself. Painfully he recants because—"I have three children—how may I teach them to walk like men in the world, and I sold my friends? . . . Because it is my name! Because I cannot have another in my life! Because I lie and sign myself to lies! Because I am not worth the dust on the feet of them that hang! How may I live without my name? I have given you my soul; leave me my name!" In Miller, a man's name is his conscience, his immortal soul, and without it there is no person left.

Proctor recants, and in the wonder that he is capable of letting himself be hanged finds self-respect. Hale begs Elizabeth: "Be his helper!—What profit him to bleed? Shall the dust praise him? Shall the worms declare his truth? Go to him, take his shame away!" Indeed it is a longed-for absolution. But the fact remains that only Proctor can absolve Proctor. "And the drums rattle like bones in the morning air."

Given the plot of the Salem witch hunt, and knowing nothing of the history books, I suspect that one would try to trace it in *The Collected Works of Edgar Allan Poe*. But where Poe would have been content with the dramatic story of a witch-hunt—sanguinary forest orgies, charms of chicken blood, the marvelous murder of babies, a destructive yellow bird, crying out and confession, torture and hangings—for Arthur Miller, it is necessary to explain why these things take place and how, in fact, people come to believe in witches.

In a commentary written for the text Miller explores the background of his play and relates it to the present. He writes that no one can know what the people's lives were like, adding definitively: "They had no novelists—and would not have permitted anyone to read a novel if one were handy." Their hard life rather than their faith protected their morals, and their passion for minding each other's business created suspicions. Their lives were rigid, and with reason because— "To the best of their knowledge the American forest was the last place on earth that was not paying homage to God. . . . They believed, in short, that they held in their steady hands the candle that would light the world. We have inherited this belief, and it has helped and hurt us."

Since they believed they were living according to God's law, they saw in change a total disruption. The theocracy had been developed to keep the people together for their better protection materially and ideologically; but the time came when the imposed order outweighed the dangers. Miller sees the witch-hunt as "a perverse manifestation of the panic which set in among all classes when the balance began to turn toward greater individual freedom." The rest of the cause is in the temperament of the people: tightly reined, fear-driven, and deeply sin-conscious. But they had no means of absolution. The witch-hunt was an opportunity for mammoth public confession, by way of accusation. Miller points out: "Social disorder in any age breeds such mystical suspicions, and when, as in Salem, wonders are brought forth from below the social surface, it is too much to expect people to hold back very long from laying on the victims with all the force of their frustrations."

The scope of *The Crucible* is wide; a general illustration of a witch-hunt and an explanation of how and why they break out. To limit it to one particular twentieth-century witch-hunt is to wear blinkers. Miller's comment is for yesterday as well as for the day after tomorrow, and not merely the here-and-now of American politics. It is surely a kind of vanity to corner-off a section of a large work, identify with it, and claim that as the subject of the whole. It cannot be overlooked that *The Crucible* is applicable to any situation that allows the accuser to be always holy, as it also is to any conflict between the individual and authority. Timeless as *An Enemy of the People*, it symbolizes all forms of heresy-hunting, religious and political.

Miller himself covers the whole field by discussing contemporary diabolism alongside Hale's belief in the Devil. He writes of the necessity of the Devil: "A weapon designed and used time and time again in every age to whip men into a surrender to a particular church or church-state." He traces the Devil's progress, from Lucifer of the Spanish Inquisition to current politics. "A political policy is equated with moral right, and opposition to it with diabolical malevolence. Once such an equation is effectively made, society becomes a congerie of plots and counterplots, and the main role of government changes from that of the arbiter to that of the scourge of God."

In answer to the criticism, and much has been made of it, that witches are an impossibility whereas Communists are a fact, Miller writes that he has no doubt people were communing with the devil in Salem. He cites as evidence Tituba's

confession and the behavior of the children who were known
to have indulged in sorceries. It was, incidentally, a cardinal
fault in Sartre's film of the play, *Les Sorciers de Salem*, that,
not believing in witches himself, he allowed none of his characters to believe in them. This uncompromising twentieth-
century attitude not only robbed the film of conviction, but
of an important seventeenth-century viewpoint that should
have been its concern.

It may be that I have a simple mind. But if a dramatist says
his play deals with the Salem witch-hunt and goes to the
length of writing about it, I am inclined to believe him. By
implication the play would be about general witch-hunting
and by inference about McCarthyism, which happened to be
the current witch-hunt. I believe the play has been distorted
by trying to link the two too closely. But some American
critics found the link not close enough, and charged Miller
with evasion. To ignore their objections would be evasive. I
admit that their greater involvement would make them more
sensitive to this aspect of the play; it might also lead them to
a greater prejudice.

Legendary Arthur Millers range from Lincoln figure to
Left-Wing Idol. He is the distinguished American dramatist
of theatrical textbooks—from Aeschylus to Arthur Miller. He
is the tough American dramatist of the gossip columnist in
search of a caption. He is the man whom everybody knows—
until you actually want to know something about him. Then
suddenly nobody knows him very well. Ken Tynan once
defined him as "someone you'd expect to find as a stonemason
instead of a playwright." Alongside these, set some American
critics' view of evader and fellow traveler. Conflicts surge
around him and controversy crowds in.

Having read Eric Bentley, and been directed by him to Robert Warshow's article, "The Liberal Conscience in *The Crucible*," in *Commentary* (March, 1953)—"the best analysis of Mr. Miller yet written"—I assumed, over-hastily, that American criticism of *The Crucible* had been political rather than dramatic. I was wrong. Of seven New York papers, three saw contemporary parallels, three did not, and one found the play just a melodrama. It is significant, perhaps, that all these critics but one mentioned parallels, whether they found them or not. At worst, this was a line on how Miller was regarded, what was expected of him, and what was uppermost in the critics' minds. By way of comparison, A. V. Cookman, critic of *The Times* (London) saw Miller's anger as being directed against human stupidity in general, and thought the play was provoked by contemporary happenings in the States.

To return to the *Commentary* article, couched in the vein of "Brutus is an honorable man," Robert Warshow found in Miller a steadfast, almost selfless refusal of complexity and an assured, simple view of human behavior. This, he believed, was Miller's trump card in captivating an educated audience. An audience which demanded of its artists—and in that case presumably found in Miller—"an intelligent narrowness of mind and vision and a generalized tone of affirmation, offering not any particular insights or any particular truths, but simply the assurance that insight and truth as qualities . . . reside somehow in the various signals by which the artist and the audience have learned to recognize each other." At this point I looked back at the title to check that we were, in fact, discussing the same playwright. Warshow admitted that

Mr. Miller speaks out. He did not know what Mr. Miller is speaking out about, but he is speaking out!

In short, he was being evasive, and on this point political criticism of *The Crucible* turned. Arthur Miller said that he doubted whether he should ever have tempted agony by writing a play on the subject of the Salem witch-hunt, which he knew about for many years before McCarthyism. In his own terms, could he have walked away from it? If you believe he is evasive—yes. I think this view of the play as evasive could only be taken by those who expected Miller to hold to the party line. The fellow-traveler, or at best fellow-sympathizer, angle was taken further by Eric Bentley in *The Dramatic Event* and *What Is Theatre?*; in both books he is concerned with Miller's "evasion."

In *The Dramatic Event* (1954) there is a chapter provocatively entitled, "The Innocence of Arthur Miller." It begins with lavish praise; then, while applause still sounds, Bentley conjures Kafkaesque images and reminds us that Miller's mentality is that of the "unreconstructed liberal." *The Crucible* is interpreted politically; Bentley points out that "communism" is a word used to cover the politics of Marx, the politics of the Soviet Union, and, finally, "the activities of all liberals as they seem to illiberal illiterates." The scope of Miller's argument was limited because it was concerned only with the third use. It was Bentley's argument that the analogy between red-baiting and witch-hunting was complete only to communists. "For only to them is the menace of communism as fictitious as the menace of witches. The non-communist will look for certain reservations and provisos. In *The Crucible* there are none."

It must not be thought that Bentley was actually accusing

Miller of being a Communist. Perish the thought. "Arthur
Miller is the playwright of American liberal folklore." But he
was accusing him of assuming a general innocence and there
was no doubt that this bothered him. What he seemed to want
from Miller was a sense of guilt. He took up the theme again
in *What Is Theatre?*, where he found that Miller stacked the
cards; that his progressivism was too close to Communism,
that *A View From the Bridge* should have been written by a
poet, and wasn't, and that he did not recognize any synthesis
in Miller. He claims that he could never know what a Miller
play is about, and in this suspects a sinister device to mislead
the audience. "Mr. Miller stands accused of no disingenuous-
ness—except when he denies the possibility of his plays meaning what at the moment he wishes them not to mean. If *The
Crucible* was set in the seventeenth century so that, on convenient occasions its twentieth-century reference could be
denied, then its author *was* disingenuous." Would it be in-
genuous of me to say that I cannot imagine Arthur Miller
doing such a thing?

Some explanation of Bentley's opinion was necessary, and
he gave it in the chapter (again provocatively titled) "The
Missing Communist." Lenin said: "We must be able to . . .
resort to various stratagems, artifices, illegal methods, to
evasion and subterfuges. . . ." Bentley takes it up—"Or was
Lenin really in favor of evasion, and did certain evasions
multiply in geometric progression, until for millions of men,
Communist or not, they became standard practice. I italicize
Communist or not because the ultimate triumph of Leninism
lies in the mystification of non-communists." The chapter was
not about Miller, but he was mentioned in it.

I kept returning to the fact that Bentley never directly

accused Miller of being a Communist. Instead, I found a cat's
cradle of words that never seemed to chime exactly with the
implication behind them. I was uncertain at this point who
exactly was being evasive. It seemed a reflex with Bentley
that whenever he wrote about Communism Miller's name
happened to occur. Bentley's view of Miller seemed to be of
someone who appeared to be innocent and was not. He
suggested a dualism that I would take to be outside Miller's
range: that while Miller was being dishonest, he had no
doubt of his own integrity. There was nothing wrong with
this—except its probability. Integrity is fundamental to Miller;
all his plays turn on it, and he is too aware to fool himself in
this fashion. This particular view of Bentley's is incredible;
it is based on a kind of double negative reasoning—nothing is
as it appears, and the only thing that is, is what is not. I was
reminded of the dragon Proctor said he might have in his
house but nobody had ever seen it.

Howard Fast, writing in the *Daily Worker*, found that *The
Crucible* was about the Rosenbergs. I suspect that critics, as
well as individuals, find what they seek and tend to line up a
play's meaning with their particular problem or preoccupation. The fault looms large beside the ideal of an impartial
critic, who is supposed to shed his prejudices with his coat.
The difficulty of living up to the old ideal has called the ideal
itself into question. It has been argued, and with truth, that
dynamic critics were always thoroughly prejudiced—set
Hazlitt beside Lamb, or Shaw beside Max Beerbohm. The
argument runs that without opinion, prejudice, and preoccupation there is no person left watching the play. Just as the play
was not created in a vacuum, it cannot be judged in one. The
admission follows that a criticism of a play is a personal statement from a particular individual. For this reason, then, it is

likely that the best judge of a play's meaning is the man who wrote it. He is the only person in the world who can know what he started with and what his intentions were.

The Crucible's reception was as contrary and two-headed as its criticism. On its first night, January 22, 1953, it took nineteen curtain calls, and was lightly picketed during its run.

In the general controversy roused by the play, audiences stopped short at the witch-hunt and McCarthyism and overlooked Miller's point. He explains in his Preface how the audience came to misunderstand him. Strong right-wing opinion on the first night inspired the initial confusion by making some people uneasy, afraid, and partisan. They were deflected from the play's inner theme—the handing over of conscience. Miller was concerned with the creation of terror in people, with fear cut off from reason. "The sin of public terror is that it divests man of conscience, of himself. . . . I saw accepted the notion that conscience was no longer a private matter but one of state administration. I saw men handing conscience to other men and thanking other men for the opportunity of doing so." Miller was seeing the witch-hunt from the inside and trying to increase awareness of why it had happened; what exactly prompted that terror that made the rest possible? The audience was looking at it from the outside, more eager to apply it generally to their lives than to understand the questions it raised.

"It was not only the rise of 'McCarthyism' that moved me," he wrote in his Preface, "but something which seemed much more weird and mysterious. It was the fact that a political, objective, knowledgeable campaign from the far Right was capable of creating not only a terror, but a new subjective reality, a veritable mystique which was gradually assuming even a holy resonance. . . . The terror in these people was being knowingly planned and consciously engineered, and yet . . . all they knew was terror. That so interior and subjective an emotion could have been so manifestly created from without was a marvel to me. It underlines every word in *The Crucible*."

It seemed to Miller that, apart from self-preservation and fear of being exiled by society, social compliance is the result of a sense of guilt that people conceal by conforming. Believing guilt to be the mainspring of terror, *The Crucible* goes further than *All My Sons* and *Death of a Salesman*, which stop at its discovery. In *The Crucible* Miller suggests that it is possible to be aware beyond the point at which guilt begins. Proctor's guilt over Abigail did not blind him to the play-acting of the children and his own innocence of witchcraft. For Miller, guilt has changed from something impenetrable to "a betrayer, possibly the most real of our illusions, but nevertheless a quality of mind capable of being overthrown."[1]

The Salem witch-hunt was a subject ready-made for Miller's preoccupations in the early fifties. The handing over of conscience seemed to be the central fact of the time in Salem. In addition, the individual's abdication in favor of a higher authority was prompted by guilt rampant.

Miller discovered from the Court records that Abigail Williams, a child of eleven, sometime a servant in Proctor's house, cried out Elizabeth as a witch. Uncharacteristically, the child refused to incriminate John Proctor. He was a liberal-minded farmer, ahead of his time in that he insisted the trials were a fake. Miller writes in his Preface: "The central impulse for writing . . . was not the social but the interior psychological question, which was the question of that guilt

[1] Preface to the *Collected Plays*.

residing in Salem which the hysteria merely unleashed, but did not create. . . ." Therefore, Miller says, "the structure reflects that understanding, and it centers on John, Elizabeth, and Abigail."[2]

Encouraged by the overpowering feeling of the time, part of the confusion over *The Crucible* arose through a general love of categories that opposed Miller's love of synthesis. Once again it proves that plays should not be categorized any more than people. Through the controversy his plays spark off the fact remains that Miller is a straightforward, factual, and direct dramatist. If I have made him seem tortuous, the fault is mine and not his. A playwright lives by the amount of thought and feeling he can inspire, and traceless plays are like faceless people.

Taking up the running battle of *The Crucible*, it seems as though nothing about it escaped conflict. In spite of the play's success, its every aspect brings Miller squarely up against his critics and his audience. The play was to center on John, Elizabeth, and Abigail. Critics found the character-drawing abstract and accused Miller of replacing people by types, the easier to prove his thesis. Walter Kerr protested unassailably: "It is better to make a man than to make a point." This was cited as the play's main dramatic fault. But Miller was drawn to the people of Salem by their moral size and overwhelming values. Theirs was a society that believed it had found the right way to live and to die. Both prosecution and defense could speak in the name of colossal life values which "often served to raise this swirling and ludicrous mysticism to a level of high moral debate; and it did this despite the fact that most of the participants were unlettered,

2 *Ibid.*

simple folk."[3] These values are something our society has lost, and a search for them is inherent in all Miller's work.

But the reasons for the disappointment of critics and audience alike is altogether more personal, based on habit and conditioned expectation. Miller says: "The society of Salem was 'morally' vocal. People then avowed principles, sought to live by them and die by them. . . . I believe that the very moral awareness of the play and its characters—which are historically correct—was repulsive to the audience."[4] Because of Miller's driving need to know *why*—his first and last question—the way people think is as important to him as the way they feel. It is this that dictates his move away from subjectivism to greater self-awareness in *The Crucible*. The flaw complained of in Willy Loman was corrected in John Proctor, and, for many reasons, prompted greater dissatisfaction. As Miller points out, audiences and critics alike are conditioned to subjectivism and for this reason found more common ground with Willy, regardless of the period of the play. The character was altogether more graspable to them. An audience will more readily accept a character governed by feeling, like Willy Loman, than one who cannot help thinking aloud, attracted to analysis, like John Proctor or Quentin. Their awareness seems to make them at once remote and detached. Audiences, for the present, tend to walk away from it, primarily because they are less interested in knowing *why* than is Arthur Miller.

Where Miller is interested in causes, the audience cares only for results. Rightly, Miller presupposes: "But certainly the passion of knowing is as powerful as the passion of feeling

[3] *Ibid.*
[4] *Ibid.*

alone." Only to find that there is nothing certain about it. His passion for awareness is not new. Shaw had it, so did Brecht. What *is* new is Miller's insistence that subjectivism's higher stage is not self-awareness, but a synthesis of feeling and awareness.

In *The Crucible* the synthesis Miller has in mind lies more in the play as a whole than in his characters. It is not achieved in a single character until Quentin in *After the Fall*. *The Crucible* counteracts etched characters with a text full to overflowing with passion. The play is written in a powerful, mounting prose, and the height and pitch of the dramatic scenes are found nowhere else in Miller's work. This particular balance held between play and character is necessary. Without it and with more subjective character-drawing the play could easily collapse into chaos. The second problem solved by this balance is that of "remoteness" in an aware character who, from the audience's point of view, thinks too much. Spare character-drawing is not new for Miller; with his minor characters he has always told you precisely what you need to know of them and nothing more. Here the technique extends from Giles and Rebecca to John and Elizabeth. But this leanness does not make the agony of John Proctor's outbursts any less real. A character does not become unreal because he speaks only those lines that will define him. To assume that he does is to confuse realism with naturalism. The width between the two is no more than a razor's edge, but the difference is basic.

Fortunately, this argument does not stop at theory. We do not need to guess at what *The Crucible* would become with more subjective characters. Sartre's film, a very free version of the play, proves Miller's argument. John Proctor did not become more "real" by being played as a guilt-torn neurotic. He did not have more feeling, but simply the wrong kind. I watched unmoved while Yves Montand twitched in time to his tormented soul, and came out murmuring that Miller would never have created such a character. Miller's John Proctor would fight the final holocaust. The earth could split and rocks could fall like hail, and still he would be there. When Proctor finds he can face hanging, he is discovering again, as have Miller's other heroes before him, what a man can do and how much he can support to keep his own integrity.

Basically the same idea drives both Proctor and Willy Loman, in that neither can break away from the unspoken demand behind the play. And again the belief is Miller's refusal to understand or accept passivity or placidity. When he was in London at a symposium arranged by *Encore*, he protested: "I don't understand why anything has to be accepted. I don't get it." The easygoing English found this laughable. They seemed a little embarrassed by all this high earnestness when everybody else had been playing at debate. Nothing half as serious had been thought on that panel, far less said. This rejection of compliance is fundamental in Miller; that once grasped, laughter changes to alarm. It is the attitude of a man who would smilingly send you out to change the world.

At a performance of the play in Bristol the atmosphere was so faithfully created that the audience reacted as if somebody had thrown a firecracker into the auditorium. If they could, they would have pushed back their chairs. One fragile old lady looked around the delicate eighteenth-century theatre as if in fear for its survival. The production, by Warren Jenkins, included an extra scene for John and Abigail that is not usually staged. Apt as the scene is, with the dark night almost tangible, I think the play stronger, of firmer line and more dramatic impact without it. After Elizabeth's arrest, John follows her request to see Abigail. He warns her that he will denounce her in Court next day unless she frees his wife and promises never to cry witch again. As Miller intended, the scene draws attention to John, Elizabeth, and Abigail, but primarily it explores Abigail's delusion.

Eerie, set in a wood and haunted by Abigail's strangeness, the scene still haunts the mind in Patrick Robertson's miraculous set. Abigail, to herself, has undergone great spiritual change, almost believing in her own martyrdom. How can others be blind to it? A miniature Saint Joan is come to Salem. "And God gave me strength to call them liars, and God made men to listen to me, and by God I will scrub the world clean for love of Him!" Suddenly the religious ecstasy breaks, to reveal the reason behind it. "Oh, John, I will make you such a wife when the world is white again! You will be amazed to see me every day, a light of heaven in your house."

In a London production at the Royal Court Theatre no attempt was made to create the atmosphere of a witch-hunt, and for this, as well as other reasons, the production failed. The mood of the play left unestablished made the soaring language seem out of place. Instead of dear old ladies thoroughly alarmed, there were tough gallery-goers complaining of melodrama and careful stall-holders uncertain what to praise.[5]

[5] But the important London production of this play came in January, 1965. It was the version directed by Laurence Olivier for the National Theatre's second season. The critics welcomed this performance with greater enthusiasm than any Miller play had yet received in England, and Miller himself said of Olivier's production: "It's the best production of *The Crucible* I've ever seen."

Two hurdles in the play's production seem to be the child-Iago in Abigail, who must persuade the audience of her "holiness" while they know of her deviltry, and the evil of Danforth. The text insists that Danforth is evil, and Miller (in his Preface) deplores our inability to face this fact. He protests that if he had the play to write again he would stress this evil and make it an open issue. "I should say that my own—and the critics'—unbelief in this depth of evil is concomitant with our unbelief in good, too."

He wrote to me: "Danforth was indeed dedicated to securing the status quo against such as Proctor. But I am equally interested in his *function* in the drama, which is that of the rule-bearer, the man who always guards the boundaries which, if you insist on breaking through them, have the power to destroy you. His 'evil' is more than personal, it is nearly mythical. He does more evil than he knows how to do; while merely following his nose he guards ignorance, he is man's limit. Sartre reduced him to an almost economic policeman. He is thus unrecognizable to us because he lacks his real ideology, i.e., the ideology which believes that evil is good, that man must be preserved from knowledge. Sartre's Danforth does not see beyond the deception, ever. He too, like Proctor, should come to a realization. He must see that he has in fact practised deception, and then proceed to incorporate it in his 'good' ideology. When I say I did not make him evil enough, it is that I did not clearly demarcate the point at which he knows what he has done, and profoundly accepts it as a good thing. This alone is evil. It is a counterpart to Proctor's ultimate realization that he cannot sell himself for his life. Hale goes the other way: on seeing the deception he rejects it as evil. One of the actual Salem judges drank himself to death after the hysteria was over. But only one. The others insisted they had done well. In a word, Sartre's conception lacks moral dimension. It precludes a certain aspect of will. Also it is dramatically useless because his Danforth from beginning to end is the same. This serves only to reduce the importance of the whole story, for if it is not horrible enough to force Danforth to know that he must decide how to strengthen himself against what he has done, then he has done very little."

Danforth is "man's limit"; even if he had not been a Salem judge, this would be sufficient for Miller to find him evil; it is a cardinal crime to keep man from knowledge. What, then, is to be said of the rule-bearer who makes this his function? Miller's complaint over Danforth is that he is incomplete. The knowledge of what he has done is vital in any Miller character, and this conclusion has not been forced upon Danforth. Hale is altogether more placid. He does not have the conflicts of Proctor, nor the conflicts Miller regrets not having brought out in Danforth. Hale is the balance between the two.

Sartre's film begins wishfully: "This is a true story." From this point onward it is truer to Sartre's opinion than it is to historical fact and Miller's intention. All Marx, no Miller. It crossed my mind that the film was roughly what the critics who accused Miller of evasion expected from the play. Here was the ideological conflict they, not Miller, had in mind. Crudely blocked, as if in a child's coloring book, we see the evil rich who have no need to fear, who describe the farmers as "rabble," and who deliberately use the witch-hunt to dominate the people, knowing it to be fraud. The farmers are all poor, all noble, and all political martyrs. Danforth warns Parris that unrest through the country is caused by "witches and men of the lower classes." Proctor grows from a guilty neurotic into a workers' hero first class. Instead of reminding Danforth that God damns those who refuse to bring men out of their ignorance, he is led away savagely to the shout of "Defend yourself! They mean to murder you!" I thought John Proctor died to achieve self-respect and in protest against a town run wild. Sartre has him die to save the workers. Throughout the film, contemporary politics cymbal-clashed with the authentic seventeenth-century atmosphere Miller has created.

Sartre could have made an unforgettable film of *The Crucible* with those actors had he been making a film of *The Crucible* in the first place, not merely using it as a basis for something else. Mylene Demongeot is the best Abigail I have seen. She has a face that can change instantly and alarmingly from angelic to apoplectic. Even if she cannot quite stand up and see visions, she is the only Abigail I have yet seen who cannot be older than seventeen. Her fits and her tantrums are those of a child who has been crossed, and so is her vengeance. In her, the original Abigail, the child of eleven, keeps breaking through. Savagely she stabs the poppet with a needle, banging at it relentlessly until the head falls off. The people accused will hang—but—

"I want the light of God, I want the sweet love of Jesus! I danced for the Devil! I saw him; I wrote in his book; I go back to Jesus; I kiss His hand. I saw Sarah Good with the Devil! I saw Goody Osburn with the Devil! I saw Bridget Bishop with the Devil!"

CHAPTER VIII

A View From the Bridge

Arthur Miller defined his social drama in an essay introducing *A View From the Bridge* and *A Memory of Two Mondays*. "On Social Plays" is, in effect, his Preface in miniature but for one thing: Miller looks back to the ancient world and restores an idea that has become debased. A play to a Greek of the classical period was "by definition a dramatic consideration of the way men ought to live." And this line keeps running through Miller's work, basic to his approach. It is, perhaps, the steadiest of his preoccupations.

The essay is written against the division of man, against an isolationist playwriting. Miller points out that the Greek dramatist's concern with the psychology of a character was always toward some larger end; "The relations of man as a social animal rather than his definition as a separate entity. . . . The preoccupation of the Greek drama with ultimate law, with the Grand Design, so to speak, was therefore an expression of a basic assumption of the people, who could not yet conceive, luckily, that any man could prosper unless his polis prospered."

Miller looks longingly back to a time of such clarity, when drama was the voice of a whole united people, not that of an isolated individual working out his private salvation. This is what he would like to bring back, and his plays reflect the synthesis of the social and the psychological toward this end. Drama, he says, "gains its weight as it deals with more and more of the whole man, not either his subjective or his social life alone, and the Greek was unable to conceive of man as anything except as a whole."

He has written with a kind of fine generalship that carefully defends his position from all that formerly destroyed it; for instance, the partisanship of the thirties and cipher heroes. Once the idea of wholeness is accepted, partisanship cannot survive. Nor is the escape from the cipher toward the frustrated egocentric valid, for the result is pathos and not tragedy.

Miller traces the decline of tragedy to the fragmentation of our society in which man's concern centers more and more on his private life. The decline of the tragic hero parallels the decline of man in an industrial society, where his value depends on the way he fits into a machine-made pattern of efficiency. The tragic victory is denied us because, at bottom, we no longer believe in it. "We no longer believe that some ultimate sense can in fact be made of social causation, or in the possibility that any individual can, by a heroic effort, make sense of it."

Miller realized that the problem was simpler for Ibsen, Chekhov, and Shaw, who had reforms to hand, and an answer in socialism. And yet there is some link. It is possible that Shavian drama is, in part, a revolt against the emotional swamp of melodrama and false conventionalized nineteenth-century feeling. Anyone anxious to continue the parallel could argue that Miller's wooing drama away from intense neuroticism, twentieth-century feeling, is attempting the equivalent.

In summing up, he defines the new social drama built on the Greek pattern, and glances, in passing, at the pathetic hero often on view when this was written, in 1955: "The social drama in this generation must do more than analyze and arraign the social network of relationships. It must delve into the nature of man as he exists to discover what his needs are, so that those needs may be amplified and exteriorized in terms of social concepts. Thus, the new social dramatist . . . must be an even deeper psychologist than those of the past, and he must be conscious at least of the futility of isolating the psychological life of man lest he fall always short of tragedy, and return, again and again and again, to the pathetic swampland where the waters are old tears and not the generative seas from which new kinds of life arise."

"We have finally come to serve the machine. The machine must not be stopped, marred, left dirty and outmoded. Only man can be left marred, stopped, dirty and alone." This was an aspect of *Death of a Salesman*; *A Memory of Two Mondays* is the detailed illustration. Set in a warehouse at the time of the Depression, it is as though the whole play were sketched in light pencil. The people doing routine work that is beneath them are half-drawn since they are half-alive. They spend robot-like days—filling orders, packing, and posting automobile parts. Nothing is new—not even the jokes. They have no alternatives and one precarious release in drink. A boy rejects this way of life and goes off to find something better.

Miller has a great affection for *Two Mondays*—a docu-

mentary play, simply and sympathetically written; in Bert he
has sketched a portrait of his younger self. The character is
seen mainly through the eyes of Kenneth, who tries to explain
him by contrasting his will with their tidal aimlessness. "You
can almost see it in him, y'know? He's holdin' on to some-
thin'." When Bert leaves after a couple of years to go to college, the well-wishing is remote. Routine swirls around him
and they barely notice his going. He leaves without sign or
trace.

The play is minor Miller and little gauge of his stature. In
the theatre it is difficult to grasp. Its insights stay elusive due
to the strict economy of the writing and the characters' slight
relationships. To be established they need to be played definitively to the precise limits Miller set for them. At Nottingham,
Val May gave *Two Mondays* the legendary Miller treatment.
The beginning sounded effectively like an Elia Kazan film on
the loose, on the waterfront. The characters were never so
happy as when brandishing axles at each other, and in Kenneth's fight it was accidental nobody got killed—later in the
run, perhaps? It was as though the director reminded his
actors before the performance that Miller is a tough American
dramatist, and they were taking advantage of it. In fact, *Two
Mondays* is not a tough play. Mr. May recognized that the
tone of the dialogue is tough, without taking into account the
feeling behind what is said. The fragile script could not survive Miller's legend, however dramatic the production. Violence took the place of an underlying tension and the characters reached only conventional limits. Gus never reached that
"enormous sadness," and Bert was never more than a nice kid.
The boy's character escaped the actor entirely. He was neither
committed nor questioning, and he replaced the young Miller's

search with a vague kind of poetic sensitivity—the stock-in-trade of any actor playing any adolescent.

Nothing remains of the Cambridge A.D.C. production except Derek Jacobi's excellent Kenneth, and Bert's question, which underlies the whole play; "I don't understand how they can come every morning, Every morning and every morning, And no end in sight."

In its simplicity and power the original *A View From the Bridge* seems hewn from rock and shaped with a chisel. The one-act play has the agelessness of myth. Eddie Carbone has brought up his niece, Catherine, as his daughter and over the years has come to love her too well. Working as a longshoreman, he connives at the illegal entry of his wife's two cousins from Sicily, and gives them lodging. Catherine is drawn to the younger, a blond youth with a talent for singing, cooking, and sewing—all highly suspect to Eddie. And Eddie's desperation begins. He is furiously helpless, driven by a passion he can neither accept nor understand. There is nothing he will not do to destroy Rodolpho. He suggests that the boy is homosexual. Finally, he betrays both immigrants to the authorities, incidentally involving two other immigrants in their arrest, and threatens the whole neighborhood. His destruction is as blundering as it is inevitable. He loses his life, killed by the boy's brother.

The play gains its perfection through its structure, which Miller has described in "On Social Plays": "But as many times as I have been led backward into Eddie's life, 'deeper' into the subjective forces that made him what he evidently is, a counter impulse drew me back." Miller realized that the qualities of the events were psychologically telling and that nothing must relax "that clear, clean line of Eddie's catastrophe. This play falls into a single act because I saw the characters purely in terms of action and because they are a kind of people who, when inactive, have no new significant definition as people. . . . The form of the play, finally, had a special attraction for me because once the decision was made to tell it without an excess line, the play took a harder, more objective shape. In effect the form announces in the first moments of the play that only that will be told which is cogent, and that this story is the only part of Eddie Carbone's life worth our notice and therefore no effort will be made to draw in elements of his life that are beneath these, the most tense and meaningful of his hours."

It would be tempting to draw a general rule; so dramatic, so breathtaking, so perfect—so should all plays be constructed. But the fact remains that Miller has found the perfect form for *A View From the Bridge;* this structure is necessarily geared to a simple myth. It could not encompass a wider ranging and less clearly defined story. The play is built in a series of brief, mounting climaxes that are interspersed with half-spoken, fully hinted danger warnings. Miller can make dramatic points in seconds where other playwrights mull over them by the act, and these climaxes use the shock of definition, and break on their crest.

The flaw in the play was thought to be the Narrator, Alfieri. He suggested a Greek chorus to the critics and in him *hubris* reared its head—did Miller imagine himself a Sophocles? The real reason is at once more practical and more human. Alfieri, central to the play's construction, is a method of placing the mood and getting over information without loss of time. He is also the effect of the audience's reaction to *The Crucible.* Miller was discouraged by their failure to grasp the play's central theme. To prevent this—*you hear me, but don't know what I am saying*—over *A View From the Bridge,* Alfieri voices Miller's meaning. "I could write what had happened, why it had happened, and to one side express as much as I knew of my sense of its meaning for me," he said in his Preface. "Yet I wished to leave the action intact so that the onlooker could seize the right to interpret it entirely for himself and accept or reject my reading of its significance." Alfieri is Miller's insurance that the audience will at least know the playwright's interpretation.

"The awesomeness of a passion which, despite its contradicting the self-interest of the individual it inhabits, despite every kind of warning, despite even its destruction of the moral beliefs of the individual, proceeds to magnify its power over him until it destroys him."[1] Eddie's commitment is personal, which is the hardest kind of fanaticism to defend because nothing can be said for it. Eddie's only vice is his love for Catherine, but that is also the mainspring of his integrity and his defense. Eddie has no "cause" and his case is slight, in that his justifications can in no way balance the betrayal. This remains true however articulate you make him. By making Eddie a docker, Miller stripped the situation down to what is fundamental in it. You can add to it and embellish it, but the rest is gloss.

To some English critics Eddie was too complex for a docker, but his credibility does not depend on his job status. He could have had greater self-understanding with which to save or damn himself, and that is the cardinal difference between a docker and a don. Miller took up this aspect when interviewed by John Wain for *The Observer:* "You can see

[1] Preface to the *Collected Plays.*

how differently the play would have turned out if the central character had been, say, a professor instead of a dock labourer. The difference in psychology would be enormous. The labouring man has so few choices open to him. His life hems him in among his circumstances far more effectively than an educated man can be hemmed in." The absence of alternatives forces Eddie's situation. Again Miller is exploring a life cut off from choice, the same kind of determinism that moves through *A Memory of Two Mondays*.

However lucid Miller's viewpoint, the presence of the Narrator did not prevent some audiences and some critics from interpreting the play as being "about" informing. This was expected from Miller. An aspect of the play certainly is, but Miller uses the aspects of a situation to emphasize its wholeness. *A View From the Bridge* is about informing, as *Macbeth* is about Macduff's revenge. Eddie's informing comes as a particular and important infringement of the social law by which the Italian community of longshoremen live. No more than Joe Keller can Eddie live separate and isolated.

"In facts I find all the poetry, all the wonder, all the amazement of Spring. . . . I love what happened, instead of what might or ought to have happened." Alfieri's lines set the mood for both *Two Mondays* and *A View From the Bridge*. They also prompt me to admit that my preference for the original play is personal. It was a relative failure in New York, and because of this, as well as for other reasons, Miller rewrote it for the London production. His original detachment had broken; he saw his personal and psychological connection with what he had written and wanted to trace it further.

At first, Miller had kept a distance from Eddie's self-justifications. "In revising the play it became possible to accept for

myself the implication I had sought to make clear in the original version, which was that however one might dislike this
man . . . he possesses or exemplifies a wondrous and humane
fact, that he too can be driven to what in the last analysis is a
sacrifice of himself for his conception, however misguided, of
right, dignity and justice."[2]

But the truth that your life creates what you write, the
more detailed and wider exploration, the greater realism, did
not, I think, improve *A View From the Bridge*. They could
not. The original was clearer than the morning, which is perhaps why the rewritten version holds repetition and not revelation for me. In themselves some of the additions are vintage
Miller. "She likes people. What's wrong with that?" "Because
most people ain't people." And Eddie's complaint: "It's a
shootin' gallery in here and I'm the pigeon." Then the resounding Eddie Carbones echoing around the theatre is
Miller's name preoccupation made flesh.

Peter Brook's set for the London production constructed a
whole neighborhood built vertically. There was a steady flow
of strangers in the street and up and down the fire escapes;
and here the play did gain in Miller's intention. "The maturing
of Eddie's need to destroy Rodolpho was consequently seen in
the context which will make it of real moment, for the betrayal achieves its true proportions as it flies in the face of the
mores administered by Eddie's conscience—which is also the
conscience of his friends, co-workers and neighbors and not
just his own autonomous creation."[3]

It seemed to me that now the play's wonder was blurred by
detail. In developing the roles of the women Miller exposed all

[2] *Ibid.*
[3] *Ibid.*

that was implied, with stronger and more imaginative effect, in the original. In action their emotions, however genuine, seemed melodramatic. The play is too intrinsically dramatic to stand it. It is like a display of crystal alongside diamonds. Then Miller, in an attempt at greater clarity, explained relationships and distributed blame for them in a fashion quite new and alien to him. He underlined Eddie's love for his niece through Beatrice, and sacrificed one of the most moving scenes in modern drama. In its place the wife shrieked: "And you can never have her!" His myth was made ordinary, its quality put down. Before, one did not say *A View From the Bridge* and have O'Neill or Odets jack-in-the-box into mind. In England it was often compared. Miller's new design altered the ending. In the original, Eddie dies at Catherine's feet on the question: "Catherine—Why?" This is psychologically true; at his death no more harm can be done. In the new version he dies in his wife's arms. This last-minute clouding is false to all that has gone before, and the whole play would need to be rewritten to make it true.

And what of that carved structure, majestic in simplicity? Miller knew before he started—he knew in "On Social Plays." The focus was destroyed and the rewriting laid the play open to that "empathic flood" from which he had tried to protect the original. Its proportion was shattered.

At the Comedy Theatre I felt I was watching a street accident, with the playwright as casualty. I could only wonder why Miller had (in my opinion) ruined his own work. This gigantic Why is as pertinent as "the reasons for which a man will endanger and risk and lose his very life." Eddie Carbone's motives are complex; I still find Miller's simple to the point of naïveté. He did not see what he had created. Ibsen's Rubeck

in *When We Dead Awaken,* tempted by its quality, destroyed
his finest work. The destruction of *A View From the Bridge*
is all the more painful because it is unwitting. One of the
reasons for a man destroying his own work is accident. Another is the highest imaginable, that destructiveness in groping
after perfection that blinds one to quality even when it stares
from the text.

I am probably in a minority of one in damning the London
version of this play. Peter Brook put the case for it with concrete logic. In direct opposition—here it is. He said that Miller
wrote the play as a Brechtian experiment. Miller was fasci-
nated by Brecht's technique of removing people from the
naturalistic detail surrounding them and recording only the
climaxes of their lives, of cutting scenes short instead of elabo-
rating them with detail and of working with strict economy.
But Miller stems from a naturalistic tradition, Brook reasoned,
and because of this there was a discrepancy between his written play and his tragic intention. He had fallen between
Brechtian technique and his own bent for creating people in
the tradition descending from O'Neill.

In revising the play Miller lengthened the first scene and
made it richer in naturalistic detail; the original did not set the
family and their traditions completely. The worst problem,
both for Miller and for Peter Brook, was the new ending. The
last scene was elaborated so that a showdown was forced on
Eddie by Beatrice's accusation. Miller saw his death tragically
as the moment of truth, when he realized and accepted his
situation.

The London production reflected this concept of greater
naturalism. Mr. Brook tried to draw out all the warmth in the
play, increasing its naturalism by creating an entire Brooklyn

neighborhood. The immigrants come not to the New York of bright lights and dollars lining the gutters they had imagined, but to a steel trap, an iron cage. They come to a nineteenth-century red-brick tenement not economically worth rebuilding. The bright lights are there, even in view, but just across the water, and a world away. Then the steel cage opens and you find the warmth of the family, warmth that Latin groups create and hold to all over the world. For this reason it had to be a worker's home, warm and comfortable, not bleak—a home where Eddie would spend his evenings and that Beatrice would cling to and protect. This center is all they have, which makes its destruction the more poignant. In this way Peter Brook brings out the sense of family that is always strong in Miller.

The Paris production created new problems. One of Miller's intentions was to show what an innate puritanism does to people. Eddie cannot recognize his love for Catherine or admit it, even to himself. Catherine cannot recognize that Eddie attracts her. And Beatrice cannot admit to recognizing anything. This Anglo-American concept, Peter Brook was told, is one that no French audience would accept. It was insisted that Eddie become an aware man, however deeply ashamed. Catherine, in turn, could be played realistically, as Mary Ure wanted to play her. She was forced to assume over-innocence for fear of misleading the audience, which prefers ideals to people. They would assume that if she wasn't totally innocent, she was totally guilty. The French simply refused to accept as fact that a girl of seventeen could be completely unaware of Eddie's feelings or of her own.

Again the main problem was the ending. Since Eddie knew his situation, he could not suddenly go back into a state of know-nothing. Marcel Aymé, the French translator, wanted to leave Eddie alone and unkilled on the stage. Peter Brook could not allow it. He was custodian of the play on Miller's behalf, and the playwright's intentions had to be carried out. Further support came from Raf Vallone. He refused to be done out of his death-scene.

The play reached the point where Eddie Carbone goes out to die, his only solution. After goading, Marco refuses to kill him and, one by one, so do his neighbors. Picking up the thread Miller had given in Eddie's demand for his "name," they make him realize that he himself is responsible for the "name" given him—Informer. And as they turn away, with full realization he kills himself.

The French production is the only one that has had a general as opposed to a "highbrow" success. Peter Brook said: "It attracted the audiences of *My Fair Lady*, as well as those of *A Long Day's Journey Into Night*." He sees the French version as the final and culminating point of the play that began life as a one-act experiment in New York. He adds that he believed it would do Arthur Miller no service to present his play exactly as he wrote it, in the knowledge that it would not appeal to a French audience. What does Miller say about it? "Well, it's not the play I wrote, but . . ." Fine, he's delighted with it. Mr. Brook swept on.

On this basis, then, there is little point in presenting the original one-act play when it is found that audiences prefer its revision. Miller does himself; he says in his Preface that it is the better play, but not that much better. Still, a regret remains, and a lasting irony when you realize that the one person capable of directing the original *View From the*

Bridge is Peter Brook. It is as though a step had not been
taken: had the play kept its disciplined form, its subtlety,
and been directed with the naturalism of the Paris production—Peter Brook would have brought out the humanity
latent in the original version and succeeded with it as Arthur
Miller had done before him. I can imagine there are logical
reasons against this apparent contradiction; but the original
play is held in this balance. I think there could be theatrical
life in this friction, as there is in the text.

What Arthur Miller did say about it in a letter was: "*View*
is still quite spare as a piece of playwriting, but I can understand your reservations about the revision. The fact is,
though, that we have no tradition at all in this kind of play.
And I do not know where one finds actors trained to convey
the kind of emotion in that play. Brook is right in saying
it was revised toward naturalism. He is wrong in believing
that my tradition is so naturalistic as to make it impossible
for me to write in another way. In fact, most of my unpro-
duced plays are in the opposite tradition. *Salesman*, in fact,
is a much more stylized play than anyone has realized. I
succeeded too well, I suppose, in making it seem 'real.' Which
is fine with me. One style is as good as another provided
the truth comes out of it."

This kind of play is one where the choice of words is
exact and dialogue spare. The characters precisely reveal
themselves. It requires an actor of perception and insight so
acute that he can bring out all the undercurrents and meanings of a pared-down line so that the audience can get it. He
must make plain not only Eddie's character, but Miller's intention. In the original version the actor needs to be as

lucid, as restrained, as meaningful as the dialogue—and at the same time have the character's depth of feeling.

Comedy Theatre, London, October 11, 1956: The booming first night of *A View From the Bridge*. Marilyn Monroe a living legend in cherry-red satin, an army of photographers invading the stalls, and the audience hectic. Anthony Quayle's Eddie, in accordance with Miller's text, stressed the father and the breaking of Eddie's family life. His important relationship was with Beatrice.

In Paris, Theatre Antoine: The audience was completely dedicated, even breathing was hushed lest attention be distracted from the play. The production, tense as a well-timed fight, had the advantage of Raf Vallone's Eddie: each gesture had ten tons behind it and his strength was heightened by Evelyne Dandry's lyrical Catherine. Their relationship governed the play.

The New Shakespeare, Liverpool (November, 1957) was packed with an audience that seemed proud of their theatre and equally proud of themselves for having come. But Sam Wanamaker's production seemed to me too much of an actor's and director's interpretation. Marc Lawrence played Eddie mainly as a tortured neurotic; by making his performance too detailed, he made Eddie too nervously sensitive, too vulnerable, and that particular vulnerability is not part of Miller's intention.

Alfieri's epilogues sum up the difference between the New York and London versions of *A View From the Bridge:*

> And yet, when the tide is right
> And the green smell of the sea

Floats in through my window,
The waves of this bay
Are the waves against Siracusa,
And I see a face that suddenly seems carved;
The eyes look like tunnels
Leading back toward some ancestral beach
Where all of us once lived.

And I wonder at those times
How much of all of us
Really lives there yet,
And when we will truly have moved on,
On and away from that dark place,
That world that has fallen to stones.

This is Miller's myth, his "hallowed tale."

In the second version, it is Eddie's lack of compromise that is stressed and his likeness to Miller's other heroes underlined.

Most of the time now we settle for half and I like it better. But the truth is holy, and even as I know how wrong he was, and his death useless, I tremble, for I confess that something perversely pure calls to me from his memory—not purely good, but himself purely, for he allowed himself to be wholly known and for that I think I will love him more than all my sensible clients. And yet, it is better to settle for half, it must be! And so I mourn him—I admit it—with a certain . . . alarm.

CHAPTER IX

The Misfits

If *A View From the Bridge* seems based on a Greek myth; *The Misfits* is naturally American and particularly Arthur Miller's. The preoccupations of the earlier plays take on the scale of myth. Gigantic in concept and desolate, he has a whole stripped world here, bleak to point his meaning. Miller places his story in Reno, in a hectic town and in the desert. The American West offers him a dying myth, taken by many to be a live reality, and within this framework he finds a way of life that defines the rootless and the vagrant. Not sentiment, but the logic of Miller's design demands this background, and that it should be peopled by a shattered divorcée, two shiftless cowboys, and an introspective ex-pilot, now a widower. Threatened with isolation, personal and social, these people and this way of life define instability. This film script is like a city built on shifting sand; through it a search is going on for something stable in the face of change, for a way to live, and for a way out of chaos. One almost expects the sun to flicker.

Miller has never reached a greater synthesis. In each instance the people connect with their background, which mir-
rors their situations and their minds. Roslyn, Guido, and
Gay meet in Reno, and the place itself is symbolic of their
conflict and their loss. The first woman who speaks, a casual
passer-by, establishes this theme at once:

> THE WOMAN Am I headed right for the courthouse, mister?
> DRIVER'S VOICE Straight on one block and then two left.
> THE WOMAN Thank you kindly. It's awfully confusin' here.

(*There is a rural pathos in her eyes, an uprooted quality in
the intense mistrust with which she walks.*) Then Roslyn
and Gay find a lyrical, temporary refuge in the desert,
where— "The land seems undisturbed in its silence, a silence
that grows in the mind until it becomes a wordless voice."
But Miller's characters are never allowed so easy an escape.
The main theme makes its initial impact and, as if driven
by it, Gay, Roslyn, Guido, and Perce plunge into a raucous,
compressed town, in itself definitive. As though a city were
imprisoned within a narrow street, all is heightened to a kind
of forced life. Finally they return to the desert to follow
the only free and meaningful way of life left to them, one
that really ended long ago, until that too is rejected. On
the widest possible level the pieces of the fable fit together—
a precise jigsaw made for titans and barely graspable on any
smaller scale.

It seems a pity to reduce Miller's concept to a few explanatory sentences, but this has not been better done than in
The Times, London, May 30, 1961. The critic finds the film
one of blackest despair: "Despair that modern life makes true

virility—equated with the frontier values of the man without ties who must be his own master and for whom anything is better than wages—impossible. Despair that whatever one's intentions life makes a mockery of them and soils everything. Despair, particularly, at the inevitable incompatibility of man and woman, their desperate need for each other and their total inability to communicate or reconcile their utterly opposed ways of life and scales of value." This is a solid-ground view of *The Misfits*. This is what the film is about—this and more.

It must be admitted at the outset that, by many, Miller's vision splendid has been seen as common day. *The Misfits* has been misunderstood, both as a book and a film. In a sense, by sheer flattery, Miller led his reader and his audience to be wrong. He hoped for too much from them. He chose an obvious myth and allied it to a simple story in the hope that people would see into and beyond it. He could not know that the surface of his story would hold the audience fast—they would see a Western. On the other hand, he could not guess that the intellectual, rushing hot-foot for its meaning, would leap at once to the allegory; this man literally cannot wait; he is eager to fix conventional symbols to people and situations. Such symbols are death masks, and the intellectual sits in the wreckage he has made and complains pettishly that he has been here before. But thus it is that the audience, and the reader, has not realized that the conflicts in *The Misfits* are their conflicts, and that the characters' checks and limitations are also theirs. For these reasons *The Misfits* remains distant to them; they do not recognize the world it reflects.

Then, through a sentimental lushness in some of the writ-

ing, Miller has blurred his strong outlines and firm basic
structure. I missed the fundamental solidity of the original
story, which was like sandpapering the varnish off wood
until the wood has been stripped down to bare board without stain or gloss.

I am not concerned here with bread-and-circuses criticism—
the kind that feeds someone to the lions. Instead, let us probe
further into the confusion that haloes this film. It could be
caused by the fact that there are two films in *The Misfits*—
John Huston's and Arthur Miller's. They are not the same
and they remain unreconciled. Since there is not space for
two divergent visions in a single film they outcrowd each
other and each man has half his say. This compromise is
doomed. Basically, Miller is concerned with the inward loss
of his people, and shows you how it comes about through
a series of images in a world created for this purpose. Huston
is altogether more direct. He seizes on externals and tends to
oversimplify. Wherever possible he narrows Miller's breadth
of vision and reduces its scope.

He focuses on people, but cuts their background, which
shrinks Miller's world to the dimensions of a close-up. Miller's synthesis is lost, and with it that connection between
places and people that helps define them. They are no longer
a part of their background, because the constant close-up
reduces them to isolation. They could be anywhere, or nowhere in particular, except in the mustang sequence, where
all things meet, the balance of the design is redressed, and
Huston achieves the synthesis he could have had throughout
the film.

Then this cutting of background almost excised one of
Miller's main themes. In the text, Guido drives through Reno

to establish the town and give a context to the search for stability that runs through the book. Our attention is drawn to the gambling palaces, to the woman asking her way to the courthouse, to the juxtaposition of bridal gowns and a sign advertising divorce actions. Divorce figures and jazz come over the radio, while the commercial is for "Dream E-Zee Sleep." But in the film this background is never firmly established and, robbed of context, the theme is all but lost. It survives only in stray lines that could pass unnoticed because the audience has no fixed image with which to link them. Proof of its diminishing is that it was found possible to cut Roslyn's final question: "What is there that stays?" in which it all comes together.

This divergence of viewpoint is all the more tragic because of the imagination, powerful and strong, often beautiful, cinematic storytelling that John Huston brings to *The Misfits*. He showed exactly how the concept of the book could have been realized by his filming of the mustang sequence. Here the core of Miller's myth is translated unforgettably into visual terms. Black and blazing white, it lives in the mind. Freedom is defined in a galloping stallion. The agony of the plunging horses is pitiful; trapped, they surge against the ropes as though a single leap will free them. It is useless. In spite of all that power and strength and energy can do, the frail-looking ropes hold. Finally one man tames a wild stallion, then frees him. The essence of *The Misfits* is defined here.

It could be argued that Huston has compensated for blurring Miller's synthesis by his detailed filming of the people, that one is the price for the other. The camera pries into their faces as if to catch their thoughts. The balance of their relationships is delicate, and Miller's observation is precise, minute in detail. Detached, he records every blink and every flicker, the separation of a hair's breadth, and each slide toward disillusion. So far as actors are able and camera can record, this is seen in the film. Because nothing stays the same, the images Roslyn, Gay, Guido, and Perce have of each other are constantly changing, breaking, and re-forming. They are as fluid and unstable as if seen through water; *The Misfits* is made up of these shifting images.

Miller, when speaking of his people, said that they were never committed to anything; there was nothing in their lives they could not leave behind, until the relationship between Gay and Roslyn became too valid to walk away from. But commitment is an aspect of all Miller's plays, and *The Misfits* is no exception. He drew a distinction between Guido and Gay. "Because Guido could never give himself to anything, he could not give himself to Roslyn. Gay gave himself entirely to his concept of freedom, so he could give himself to her." There is a temperamental difference between compromise and totality that runs through all Miller's work, as well as through all drama. Where there is Oedipus there is Creon. Where there is Hamlet, Horatio. "The uncommitted do not get things changed," said Miller, "because they do not probe to the heart of a thing. Horatio does not, and would not, come all out for justice." Nor would Guido, nor would Charley in *Death of a Salesman*.

In Roslyn Taber, Miller has drawn a deeply perceptive portrait of Marilyn Monroe, with true insight into her fear and a great awareness of her need for tenderness and protection. The character is built on the bedrock of his understanding. She has an overwhelming depth of feeling, as though whatever might insulate her from what she sees has broken down. All that is left to withstand her complete involvement is a raw nervousness. She is totally vulnerable, identifying herself with anything being hurt. This depth of feeling informs all she does. Roslyn is committed to an ideal of relationship that makes compromise impossible. Miller says of her: "She approaches them with such spiritual nakedness that they cannot keep on with their casual relationships."

Miller sums up the lonely, the searching, and the lost in Roslyn. But because he is drawing her, she is not all waif. Roslyn is the most pitiful of fanatics. She is gently drawn with an unmatched sensitivity; but together with the knowledge that she is fragile goes an awareness that she is also resilient. In her, you keep coming up against a totality, both of demand and involvement. Her refusal to compromise is absolute; self-destructive and self-preserving, this is her strength. The character would crack without it. It is the indestructible thing in a person verging, superficially, on disintegration. It is the intractable in a person otherwise wholly tractable. Nothing prepares the cowboys for Roslyn's singleness of purpose, strong enough to change a way of life.

Marilyn Monroe played her with an almost tangible vulnerability. A person all but lost, a pale waif with a hushed and hesitant voice; but she never let you forget Roslyn's remorseless drive that will be maintained at whatever cost. It was a delicate balance to hold. There was a conflict within the character, a determination both trembling and buoyant. The performance was touching, but it was also realistic. Admirably, pathos was rejected in favor of a searing, nerve-wracked desperation, which made Roslyn as disturbing as a cry for help.

When we first meet her, Roslyn's life has newly disintegrated through her divorce. Unable to escape from her loneliness in her marriage, she accuses her baffled husband: "You aren't *there*, Raymond! If I'm going to be alone, I want to be by myself."

She explains to Isabelle that she is always back where she started. Later they face the dread that there is no solution.

ISABELLE You're too believing, dear. Cowboys are the last real men in the world, but they're as reliable as jack rabbits.

ROSLYN But what if that's all there is? Really and truly, I mean.

ISABELLE I guess a person just doesn't want to believe that . . .

ROSLYN I don't know any more. Maybe you're not supposed to believe anything people say. Maybe it's not even fair to them.

It is the tormented Roslyn who is able to face the situation, while Isabelle, sympathetically played by Thelma Ritter, evades it. Roslyn's conflict does not exist for her; she has come to terms Roslyn would find impossible.

After Roslyn's search with its undercurrent of despair, we switch to Gay and Guido, and to Gay's "Yeah. She's real prime." That ends the sequence.

The original story of *The Misfits* was based on Miller's own experience of mustanging with three cowboys. "The striking thing about my companions was that they were internally drifting without its being painful to them. They had a wonderful independence, and at the same time they weren't tough." (*Saturday Review*, February 4, 1961.) This freedom is summed up in Gay Langland who lives by the belief that "anything's better than wages." It's a kind of shorthand for the cowboys' protest against a loss of their identity; by conforming, by being regimented, by "having to sell their lives." Miller sums up by saying: "These men will not die in an industrial society."

Gay is the mainstay of *The Misfits*. His basic common sense, easy outlook, and untrammeled certainty were defined in the original story, published fully in *Armchair Esquire:*[1] "He did not know that anything could be undone that was done, any more than falling rain could be stopped in mid-air." In the film script Miller describes Gay in greater detail: "One senses that he does not expect very much, but that he sets the rhythm for whoever he walks with because he cannot follow. And he has no desire to lead. It is always a question of arranging for the next few days, maybe two weeks; beyond that there is only the state, and he knows people all over it. . . . He needs no guile because he has never required himself to promise anything, so his betrayals are minor and do not cling. 'If you have to you will,' he seems to believe."

This is Miller's natural man, as basic a character as a subtle mind could reach. The character changes as more questions, more doubts, are forced upon him. At the outset Gay is not lost. He lives self-contained, content with a way of life that rolls and goes nowhere. This certainty attracts Roslyn: "A calm seems to exude from him, an absence of uncertainty which has the quality of kindness, a serious concern for which she is grateful."

Gay was Clark Gable's last role, and the character was stamped with his own film personality, particularly in the early scenes. His Gay was, I think, more basic than Miller's. He had a certain ruthlessness that often goes with a lack of

[1] London: Heinemann & Co., 1959.

doubt, but out of this Gable drew the changes in the character and developed it with genuine insight. Gay grew before you, and you came to know and sympathize with him as if you had met him, then gradually came to know him.

Miller sees Guido as a certain kind of intellectual who knows a thing is destructive, is detached enough to know what it is, but still does it. Guido is a widower, once a bomber-pilot, who now puts his experience to use by driving mustangs out of the mountains with a low-flying, battered plane and a gun. Guido has chosen, and Guido's choice determines Miller's view of him, which is merciless. The man is anatomized. He is built on self-pity—moody, intense, and full of regret. He cannot help capitalizing on sympathy, and this opportunism is enlarged toward villainy. In a sense, Guido has given up before he began. He accepts because he does not care enough to do anything else. He speaks longingly to Roslyn: "You really want to live, don't you? Most of us are just looking for a place to hide and watch it all go by."

The small but deadly indictment continues, as though Miller has concentrated his dislike for certain intellectuals in the pilot. Guido thinks more than the others, but has the least insight. Because of this, his concepts of Roslyn keep breaking down with each new fact he learns. It seems that because he cannot categorize her, he cannot meet her on any ground whatever. In an effort to reach her, he begs: "How do you get to know somebody, kid? I can't make a landing. And I can't get up to God, either. Help me. I never said 'help me' in my life. I don't *know* anybody. Will you give me a little time? Say yes. At least say hello, Guido." And all they can say to each other is "hello." Guido is lost between earth and heaven.

Eli Wallach played him with an unwavering concentration. Nothing deflected the intensity of his gaze. The man was ever calculating, ever anxious, and ever tormented. It was as though he were tied to the stake before an invisible fire. Rightly playing Guido from his own point of view, Wallach drew the maximum in sympathy for Miller's petty intellectual. This made it seem as though Miller had changed his mind about Guido and let him down. In fact, Miller's view is consistent. The audience was beguiled by the sympathy of the actor and so could not accept that Guido could be likeable and a "villain." A bewildered reaction was: "I *liked* Guido. What happened?" Nothing would have happened had the audience found it possible to accept Miller's and Eli Wallach's views of Guido both together, instead of trying to make one cancel the other.

Perce, the rodeo rider, is just beginning. His life is not yet formed. When we meet him he is running from a betrayal. His mother remarried after his father's death and, "I don't know; she don't *hear* me. She's all *changed around*. You know what I mean? It's like she don't remember me any more." This background links with Roslyn's, who admits to Isabelle that her mother was never there. Perce, again like Roslyn, is trying to find where he belongs, but their original search has been simplified. "What the hell do you depend on? Do you know?" becomes "Who do you depend on, who?" Perce left home when his stepfather offered him wages on the farm that should have been his, and in explaining this to Roslyn, Montgomery Clift dredged up each word in pain.

Perce believes with the others, "Hell, anything's better than wages." Like them, he draws his pride from his way of life, and for this reason could never admit that their courage was destructive. He is flamboyant, as if to live up to his image of himself, but this holiday humor has the edge of hysteria. He shares Roslyn's values in that what he does must be total or it is meaningless. Hear him tell her of his refusal to fake. "I've broke this arm twice in the same place. You don't do that fakin' a fall, y'know. I don't fake anything. Some of these riders'll drop off and lay there like they're stone-dead. Just putting on a show, y'know. I don't fake it, do I, Gay?" "That's right. You're just a natural-born damn fool." Roslyn understands him. "Why! That's wonderful . . . to be that way! I know what you mean. I used to dance in places . . . and everybody said I was crazy. I mean I really tried, you know? Whereas people don't know the difference."

Perce reveals how deeply these people are shadowed by their legend. The more involved they are with it, the less they are without it. It defines them. Gay without his horses loses half himself. One of Miller's purposes in *The Misfits* was to penetrate the haze that surrounds certain kinds of work. He was drawing the distinction between, What do you do? and What are you? that applies to any way of life trailing romance with it. "The people in *The Misfits*," he said, "are people stripped of their romance, a romance connected with a way of life. They are forced to come to terms with what they are in themselves—apart from that."

Nothing is stable. Gay and Roslyn take over Guido's half-finished house and build up a frail relationship that, startlingly, all but shatters a moment after it seems to establish itself. In a kind of reconciliation prompted by relief at acceptance—Roslyn's view of Gay abruptly changes. The lyrical sequence ends as Roslyn's refusal to compromise on destruction makes its first impact. Tense and adamant, she tries to dissuade Gay from killing a rabbit:

"Please, Gay! I know how hard you worked—"

"Damned right I worked hard!" He points angrily at the garden and tries to laugh. "I never done that in my life for anybody! And I didn't do it for some bug-eyed rabbit!"

"Gay, please listen."

"You go in the house now and stop bein' silly!"

"I am not silly! You have no respect for me!" (Gay turns, suddenly furious.) "Gay, I don't care about the lettuce!"

"Well, *I* care about it! How about some respect for me?"

The quarrel is deflected by the arrival of Guido and Isabelle, and the promise of mustanging the next day, catching and roping wild horses, which is Gay's profession. They meet Perce Howland on the way to the Dayton Rodeo, and agree to put up his entrance money in return for his help with the mustangs.

After the silence of the desert, after the chaos of the town, it seems as though, tentatively, religion is offered as a solution. It is subtly rejected. A sweet old lady shakes her collection box for the Church Ladies' Auxiliary. Hear her speak to Roslyn: "Sinner! I can tell you want to make a big donation. You got it in the middle of your pretty eyes. You're lookin' for the light, sinner. I know you and I love you for your life of pain and sin. Give it to the one that understands, the only one that loves you in your lonely desert!" She is harmless, and yet beneath her rambling the plea is specially, almost cruelly, designed for Roslyn. The promise of the last sentence is, in the circumstances, tantamount to a bribe. Roslyn is all but reached by it, and starts giving the old lady all the money she has just won in the bar. But Gay intercepts: "She ain't sinned that much." And Roslyn is back on earth. This did not make its impact, partly through a restless camera and partly because Estelle Winwood played the woman as a complete fake. The incident came over as comedy of no significance whatever.

In fact it is the beginning of a theme that Miller develops in the text. From the rodeo arena, "the only visible building is a small church . . . its cross of boards twisting under the weight of weather into the form of an X." It is perhaps unjust to raise so small a point. I do so merely to place the significance of the Church Lady, and to link Gay's last word on death with what has gone before.

Perce has been thrown twice and half killed by a wild bull. Roslyn, in a distraught effort to understand Gay, asks: "But if he'd died . . . you'd feel terrible, wouldn't you? I mean, for no reason like that?" "Honey . . . we all got to go sometime, reason or no reason. Dyin's as natural as livin'; man who's too afraid to die is too afraid to live, far as I've ever seen. So there's nothin' to do but forget it, that's all. Seems to me." Gay's lack of concern completes the sequence.

The violence of the rodeo brings Roslyn's fear to the surface. It was muted before, in her encounter with Raymond, in the argument with Gay over the rabbit. Now, because of her values, she finds herself totally isolated from Gay and Guido. Perce is thrown and Roslyn, upset by Gay's casualness, tries to help. She is rejected. Unable to bear the thought of Perce having to go back and ride a wild bull, she urges him to take the money they have just won. Helplessly she asks: "But why're you doing it?" "Why, I put in for it, Roslyn. I'm entered."

Guido finds her concern unreasonable, and Gay encourages Perce, which again changes Roslyn's image of him. It seems that their day-to-day living is like a trap of a private nightmare to her. Miller's dialogue was pared to the adequate here, where the original was memorable. On the page Roslyn says: "It's like you scream and there's nothing coming out of your mouth, and everybody's going around, 'Hello, how are you, what a nice day,' and it's all great—and you're dying!" It borders on a dream remembered with shock on waking.

Throughout this Dayton sequence Miller uses an indifferent, near-savage crowd to underline painful events. They are a brutal chorus to the action. By chance, in a bar, Gay meets his children of a former marriage. He goes off in delight to fetch Roslyn to meet them, all the while boasting of their welcome, only to find that they've walked out on him. He climbs onto the hood of a car. "He is very drunk, and shaken. . . . His hat askew, his eyes perplexed, and his need blazing on his face, he roars out, 'Gaylord! *I know you hear me!*' . . . He suddenly slips on the hood and rolls off onto the ground. . . . Roslyn screams and runs to him, as the crowd roars with laughter."

After this searing climax to the painful day, Gay and Roslyn again try to secure their relationship. Gay promises that tomorrow, when they go mustanging, "I'll show you what I can do. You'll see what living is." She agrees, not realizing that to her it will look more like dying. But what Roslyn does know is that their reconciliation of a moment before is no more than a mutual isolation.

The conflicts in *The Misfits* are forced irrepressibly to

their full height over the mustanging. Carefully Miller prepares for the hunt, laying out the issues as if placing soldiers before a battle. In the stillness Guido uses metaphor to describe the coming situation: "That star is so far away that by the time its light hits the earth, it might not even be up there any more. In other words, we can see only what something was, never what it is now." In the film the metaphor is left, but Miller's definition is cut. This is precisely the cowboys' condition over the mustanging; a necessary blindness needed to keep a dead myth alive.

In herself, Roslyn embodies Miller's plea for connection, first made in *All My Sons*. As Guido praises her involvement, she protests: "People say I'm just nervous." "If there hadn't been nervous people in the world," he reassures her, "we'd still be eating each other."

Suddenly the known fact that everybody accepts is brought home to the unknowing Roslyn. The wild horses are to be sold to the dealer and killed for dog food. Gay explains with complete neutrality: "They're what they call chicken-feed horses—turn them into dog food. You know—what you buy in the store for the dog or the cat? I thought you knew that. Everybody . . . knows that." Everybody but Roslyn, and the knowledge appalls her, as well as her inability to face this fundamental change in Gay.

Gay protests that she is looking at him like a stranger—in effect what he has become. Desperately, to avoid losing her, he tries to explain, and Roslyn begins to know Gay. Part defensive and part explanatory, he tells her how it was, and tries to share his vision: "When I started, they used a lot of them I caught. There was mustang blood pullin' all the ploughs in the West; they couldn't have settled here without somebody caught mustangs for them. It . . . it just got changed around, see? I'm doin' the same thing I ever did . . . It's just that they . . . they changed it around. There was no such thing as a can of dog food in those days. It . . . it was a good thing to do, honey."

Roslyn is adamant. "But they kill them now." Gay cannot believe that this is as bad as she sees it. He explains that they are only misfit horses, too small for riding, and protests: "A kind man can kill." "No he can't!" There is no middle course for Roslyn. She knows there is no compromise. Finally, Gay has to admit: "Well, if it's bad, maybe you gotta take a little bad with the good or you'll go on the rest of your life runnin'!"

"What's there to stop for? You're just the same as everybody!" With this realization Roslyn is again adrift, and Gay's make-and-mend logic can have little meaning. Miller's committed people are Shylocks of the spirit, who would sooner have nothing than settle for less than all. It is as though there must be somebody left to make these high demands. They are, perhaps, a kind of reminder, as one sets a flag to mark a position. It does not matter that Gay's logic is impeccable. There is a gulf fixed by temperament between admitting it— and accepting it. Gay almost succeeds in bridging this gulf for Roslyn. He draws her and her experience into his explanation, and persuades her, at least to the point of an uneasy truce. Neither has won, but she has to accept his reasoning: "I can't run the world any more than you could. I hunt these horses to keep myself free. That's all."

John Huston, when interviewed by Bill Weatherby for *The Guardian* (February 25, 1960), said that *The Misfits* is about "people that aren't willing to sell their lives. They will sell their work but they won't sell their lives and for that reason they're misfits." Willy Loman is the only leading Miller character who literally sold his life. Chris Keller, John Proctor, Eddie Carbone, and Quentin all fit precisely into John Huston's definition. In this the misfits are not flawed. It is the same kind of reasoning that finds a tragic flaw in Creon, but none in Oedipus.

The mustang hunt is a powerfully driven sequence that moves as though a gale blows through it. I could never have imagined it being so perfectly filmed. The horses are hunted down across a prehistoric lake bed: "It is a floor of clay, entirely bare, white, and flat as a table. . . . The silence is absolute. There is no wind. . . . Set between mountain ranges the lake bed stretches about twenty-five miles wide and as long as the eye can see. Not a blade of grass or stone mars its absolutely flat surface, from which heat waves rise. In the distance it glistens like ice."

This is Gay's country, but it is here his isolation begins. Even on the edge of his main thematic conflict, Miller has time for Gay. Perce and Roslyn are joined by their view of mustanging as they wait for Guido to drive the horses out of the mountains. They are the first to see the plane, and at once Gay's pride begins to chafe. "He never worked this fast before. I'd've seen him but I didn't expect him so soon." He cannot help insisting: "I've sat here waitin' two-three hours before he come out. That's why I didn't see him." This is a detail, the kind of detail not found in a symbol. For a moment we might almost be listening to Willy Loman.

Gay offers the binoculars to Roslyn to see the oncoming horses that are to be killed—six and a colt. "The image shakes, as her hands lose their steadiness, then flows out crazily as the

strength goes out of her hands." This is a visual image showing what has been happening to her image of Gay. It is a
state of mind made actual, and we are able to see something
intangible change. Then, by linking Roslyn's reaction to the
solid earth that shakes and loses its form, Miller tells you and
instantaneously shows you what instability is. Deeper than
definition this illustrates and sums up one of his main themes.
I now know how Coleridge felt when he lost Xanadu. In the
film the image stayed firm as a rock.

The mustang hunt becomes a challenge for Perce, who for
the first time realizes the price of their freedom.

PERCE Don't make much sense for six, does it?

GAY Six is six. Better'n wages, ain't it? . . . I said it's better than
wages, ain't it?

PERCE (*with damaged conviction*) I guess anything's better'n
wages.

In the face of Perce's doubt Gay asserts his position for the
last time.

GAY I'm beginnin' to smell wages all over you, boy.

PERCE I sure wish my old man hadn't of died. You never saw a
prettier ranch.

GAY Fella, when you through wishin', all there is is doin' a
man's work. And there ain't much of that left in this country.

The second Guido lands his plane, they roar across the
desert in a truck to rope the mustangs. There is Gay's joy in
real work beside Roslyn's terror, Guido's excitement, and
Perce's uncertainty. Roslyn weeps in fright and agony as
the horses are cruelly roped. Finally Gay, embarrassed by the

concession and guilt-struck over the horses, suggests to Perce
and Guido that they give Roslyn the herd. Ironically, she
cancels this by offering to buy the horses for two hundred
dollars. Gay's offer dies. "I sell to dealers only. All they're
lookin' to buy is the horse." The price they could expect
from the dealer was a hundred and ten, hundred and twenty
dollars.

This total disruption of understanding is followed immediately by Roslyn's contempt for Guido when he tries
to buy her, as she tried to buy Gay. Guido uses the herd as a
bribe and offers to stop the hunt:

GUIDO You're through with Gay now, right? Well, tell me.
He doesn't know what you're all about, Roslyn, he'll never
know. Come back with me; give me a week, two weeks. I'll
teach you things you never knew. Let me show you what
I am. You don't know me. What do you say? Give me a
reason and I'll stop it. There'll be hell to pay, but you give
me a reason and I'll do it!

ROSLYN A *reason!* You! Sensitive fella? So full of feelings? So
sad about your wife, and crying to me about the bombs you
dropped and the people you killed. You have to get something to be human? You were never sad for anybody in your
life, Guido! You only know the sad words! You could blow
up the whole world, and all you'd ever feel is sorry for *yourself!*

It is a shattering indictment.

From his not being able to hear the plane, the mustang
hunt is a trial of Gay's pride, and of the way of life he represents. At last Roslyn, past the limit of endurance, screams an
attack defining this pride: "*Liars!* Killers! Murderers! *Liars!!*
You're only living when you can watch something die! Kill

everything, that's all you want! Why don't you just kill
yourselves and be happy? . . . You know everything except
what it feels like to be alive. You're three dear, sweet dead
men."

The sequence surges from Roslyn's agony at the destruction to Guido's personal outburst. The character is torn apart
by anger, frustration, and revenge. Painfully Guido cries out
against Roslyn's drive for perfection. It is the frustrated protest of nonunderstanding; at the same time, it could be a
distorted longing for the complete involvement that he can
never reach.

While Gay is helping Guido get his plane started, Perce
frees the horses. Gay finds the truck gone and himself helpless. "The headlights of the truck are impossibly distant now.
He runs toward them. Tears are on his cheeks and angry calls
come from his throat, but more than anger is his clear frustration, as though, above all, his hand had been forced from
its grip on his life and he had been made smaller." And it is
this he redeems by first subduing and then freeing the
stallion.

He cuts the rope, to Guido's mounting panic and bewilderment. "What the hell'd you catch him for?" "Just . . . done
it. Don't like nobody makin' up my mind for me, that's all."
Gay explains his reasons with no clouding whatever, and with
this again takes charge of his own life. "God damn them all!
They changed it. Changed it all around. They smeared it all
over with blood, turned it into shit and money just like
everything else. You know that. I know that. It's just ropin'
a dream now. Find some other way to know you're alive . . .
if they got another way, any more."

Only Miller could have created Gay Langland. His reasons

for walking away from his once meaningful way of life recall
Chris Keller: "What you have is really loot, and there's blood
on it." Gay's vision of Western freedom parallels Willy's
dream of the good-fellowship on the road. Was and is; it is
something like reading O. Henry before seeing *The Asphalt
Jungle*. But in *The Misfits* Miller goes further and adds an
extra dimension to his hero. Gay is strong enough to survive
the breaking of his illusion, his myth. Ibsen would call it the
"life lie." Gay is able to walk away, where Willy Loman
could not. With a degree of courage Miller forces Gay to
accept that once a way of life is over, once it loses its validity,
there is nothing left but to walk away from it. "If you have
to, you will."

Gay's world changed around him. Roslyn comes in time
for Gay and forces him to recognize it, where Biff comes too
late for Willy, who even at the end evades the fact, and dies
happy in his illusion. He dies, you remember, believing that
he has found the solution, both for Biff and himself. Miller
does not allow us to share Willy's illusion. In *The Misfits* he
does not allow this escape to either his characters or his
audience. Neither is allowed to live by the past, however
attractive. Miller knows our, and perhaps his own, ambivalence toward the Western legend. To find *The Misfits* desolate or despairing tells us more about ourselves than it does
about Miller or the film.

As if to point the present application of his fable from
another angle, Miller drew an analogy between the cowboys'
situation and a bureaucracy, or any condition in which people keep doing things as they have always done them *because*
they have always done them—until somebody asks Why?
"And when it is asked it can be volcanic"—as Roslyn proves.

"Gay was brought to a realization through her, that he was a supplier of dog food. That's what his freedom and bravery amounted to; his pride, his manhood, his bravery, just that. They take his horses away from him, and he himself frees the last one. It would have been too silly to do anything else."

Gay is strong enough to try and find some other way to be alive, but at the same time giving up mustanging is a real loss to him. It was not only real work, but the basis of his self-respect. Gay has found a foothold in this search for meaning, but together with this goes the uncertainty of ever finding it again. For the first time in his life, Gay is lost. Instead of being able to go anywhere, he has nowhere to go. It is significant that Guido alone does not understand. "Where'll you be? Some gas station, polishing windshields? Or making change in the supermarket! Try the laundromat—they might need a fella to load the machines!" He points up Gay's conflict by yelling, "Gay! Where you goin'?"

Guido stays on the side of death and fights a battle for his way of life, which he must eventually lose. Gay's abdication is a serious threat to him, particularly since Perce has decided to return to farming. In the film Perce's line of explanation is cut, which leaves the character unresolved. Meanwhile the myth hangs in the balance.

Through Gay's exhaustion, we return to Roslyn's sense of loss. Huston rightly has taken the axe to Miller's sentimental dialogue in this scene. In the text Roslyn explains: "But you know something? For a minute, when those horses galloped away, it was almost like I gave them back their life. And all of a sudden I got a feeling—it's crazy!—I suddenly thought, 'He must love me, or how would I dare do this?' Because I always just ran away when I couldn't stand it. Gay—for a minute you made me not afraid. And it was like my life flew into my body. For the first time."

Miller's strength lies in logic, in seeing through and into and beyond situations. It is a power of mind. His searing dramatic scenes usually stem from a clash between illusion and reality, which, again, is basically a perceptive power of mind. In Roslyn's speech genuine insight wars with a heightened romanticism that must elude him. Miller is so little a sentimentalist that he cannot write in this vein. The key is pitched too high, and romance curdles into melodrama.

Alan Seager, in *Esquire* (October, 1959), quotes extracts from Miller's notebooks. In one of them Miller warns himself to keep his sympathy for one of his characters, and actually goes on to explain why he should. "Remember the nature of his work. Remember pity. The erosion of the tentative commitment to a particular job for sixteen years." This seems to me to be characteristic.

Unfortunately, Roslyn's basic question was also cut: "What is there that stays?" Through the deceptive simplicity of Miller's setting, behind the complexity of his superficially simple people, we reach bedrock in this. The answer can be no more than tentative, and Miller offers a Forster-like solution: "God knows. Everything I ever see was comin' or goin' away. Same as you. Maybe the only thing is . . . the knowin'. 'Cause I know you now, Roslyn. I do know you. Maybe that's all the peace there is or can be."

The film and the text end in Hollywood style with stars and three alien-sounding lines of dialogue. "How do you find your way back in the dark?" "Just head for that big star straight on. The highway's under it, take us right home."

Miller usually signs his name between the lines of his dialogue. You can recognize it. The sheer height of *The Crucible*, the driving force of *Death of a Salesman*, or the kind of humor that is basically serious, followed by a sudden deflating insight. In fact, Miller did speak of a more ironic ending, in which Roslyn hits out at Gay in a way that cannot be repaired. He takes this passionate concern for living things from her, but, through a misunderstanding, loses her. This ending was never written.

The biggest hurdle in writing this chapter was getting to see *The Misfits* in the first place. Released in New York in February, 1961, by United Artists. Released in London— when? United Artists seemed to know the answer to this just about as well as I did. Miller's book was published by Secker and Warburg, then by Penguin. A hopeful spur? Time passed. I grew frantic. They consulted horoscopes. The crystal ball stayed dark. At last word came, not from United Artists at all, but from Ion Trewin, a young journalist in Plymouth: *The Misfits* was to be shown there in a week's time. For me this was beacon-lighting news. *The Misfits* was finally press-shown at the London Pavilion on May 29, 1961, and released there on June 2, 1961.

English press reaction to the film was, on the whole, more favorable than the American, which reached its most damning in *Time*, February 3, 1961: "*The Misfits* is a dozen pictures rolled into one. Most of them, unfortunately, are terrible. . . . It is a routine gland opera, an honest but clumsy western, a pseudosociological study of the American cowboy in the last disgusting stages of obsolescence, a raucous ode to Reno and the horrors of divorce, a ponderous disquisition on man's inhumanity to man, woman, and various other animals, an obtuse attempt to write sophisticated comedy, a woolly lament for the loss of innocence in American life and, above all, a glum, long (2 hr. 5 min.), fatuously embarrassing psychoanalysis of Marilyn Monroe, Arthur Miller, and what went wrong with their famous marriage."

In the New York *Herald Tribune* (February 5, 1961), on the other hand, we find: "It has a vitality so rich that I dare say it can scarcely be taken in at one viewing. It gives that sense of warm, almost fleshly contact with reality that one never experiences except where a film has grown out of somebody's direct response to life."

Roslyn Taber was Marilyn Monroe's last role. On Sunday, August 5, 1962, the shock of her death held the world. The stunned day followed; a claustrophobic awareness that something appalling had just happened. Miller is reported to have said: "If she was simple it would have been easy to help her. She could have made it with a little luck. She needed a blessing."

The Misfits is Arthur Miller's myth. Writing about it is like climbing from valleys to hills and back again. It lives on both levels. On the practical, social level Gay has lost his way of life in a society grown alien. On the mythic level, by liberating the horses, he has liberated himself, and reconciled man and nature.

CHAPTER X

After the Fall

After the Fall is the testimony of a life—a mind made visual.
In swirls of light image cuts to image, the one enlarging and
defining the other. It traces connection through the forming
and reforming of pattern, as a means of understanding and
explanation. It is as though the technique of a Resnais/Robbe-
Grillet film were purposefully used to find "a moral biology
—a morality based on human nature."[1] Miller's simple definition of moral: "You tell the truth, even against yourself."

In its first production at the Lincoln Center, Quentin and
his people emerge through a grey wash of light. This is
Miller's inevitable play, perhaps the one that most closely
follows his cast of mind and the greater part of his experience.
He gives Quentin the facts to prompt the questions, and the
answers drawn from them enable him to go on. "Quentin at
the beginning of the play is innocent—a man without insight
into himself: a man without remorse," Miller defines him.

[1] "Arthur Miller's Quest for Truth," by William Goyen. New
York *Herald Tribune*, January 19, 1964.

"He is unaware of the destruction in himself. He feels his life is pointless, except that he does have this hope that he is not entirely purposeless."[2] The progress of the play is Quentin's recognition. His driven need to discover his guilt takes him into every aspect of his life. Miller's awareness is a gift from hell or heaven, and the search is to its limit. He is an unsparing guide; his leaping mind links each situation to the principle behind it, and the principle to its myth. Central to the play is man's power to choose either destruction or survival. "It is also the basis of Christianity," said Miller. "Man needs to recognize and be aware of the destructive elements in himself. Once he stays innocent of these, he is unaware and cannot belong to a civilization. That is why Cain and Abel is the first story in the Bible."[3]

Miller uses the concentration camp as an image of destruction, and waits for Quentin to recognize that he is not alien to it. He realizes more than an unexplained, and haltingly admitted, complicity when he knows his share in his father's destruction. "The mother made him her favorite," Miller said. "He benefits from that destruction, gaining the love his father loses. As the father goes down, Quentin comes up." This is an early guilt to him, and it links with the Camp when Quentin says: "But who would not rather be the sole survivor of this place than all its finest victims?"

Quentin is intimately involved, but *After the Fall* needs multi-vision, and Miller's truth is far less personal than is imagined. Writing about the Auschwitz trials in the *Daily Express* (March 16, 1964), he said: "The question in the Frankfurt courtroom spreads out beyond the defendants and

[2] *The Stage*, February 13, 1964.
[3] *Ibid*.

Elia Kazan and Arthur Miller on the pre-
Broadway tour of *Death of a Salesman*.

Inge Morath/Magnum

Arthur Miller.

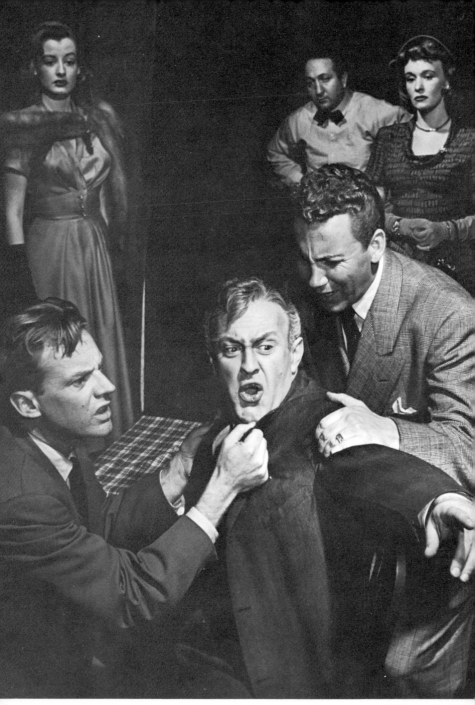

W. Eugene Smith

DEATH OF A SALESMAN: Arthur Kennedy (Biff);
Lee J. Cobb, the definitive Willy Loman; and
Cameron Mitchell (Happy).

Eugene Smith

DEATH OF A SALESMAN:
Mildred Dunnock as Linda Loman.

Gjon Mili

THE CRUCIBLE: Beatrice Straight (Elizabeth) faces

Walter Hampden (Danforth). In the foreground, Madeleine
Sherwood (Abigail) and Arthur Kennedy (John Proctor).

THE MISFITS: Clark Gable (Gay)
and Marilyn Monroe (Roslyn).

THE MISFITS: Clark Gable (Gay),
Marilyn Monroe (Roslyn), Eli Wallach
(Guido), and Montgomery Clift (Perce).

INCIDENT AT VICHY: Stanley Beck (Bayard) warns about the sealed trains. Left to right, Ira Lewis (the Boy), Joseph Wiseman (LeDuc), Will Lee (old Jew) David Wayne (Von Berg), David J. Stewart (Monceau), Michael Strong (LeBeau), Jack Waltzer (the Waiter), and Harold Scott (Gypsy).

AFTER THE FALL: Jason Robards
(Quentin) and Barbara Loden (Maggie).

spirals around the world and into the heart of every man. It
is his own complicity with murder, even the murders he did
not perform himself with his own hands. The murders, however, from which he profited if only by having survived."
Holga catches this in a kind of shorthand when she says:
"Quentin . . . no one they didn't kill can be innocent again."

After the Fall insists on leaving light blazing that most
people hope to douse. It is part of a general need to know, to
remember. Out of this the Camp also stands for the impossibility of evading the past, as Quentin and Maggie had tried
to do. Holga brings him there. As a German she has come to
terms with guilt and comes back to the Camp almost as a kind
of expiation—"perhaps because I didn't die here." Her acceptance is complete and she urges Quentin toward his inescapable end. "I had the same dream each night—that I had
a child, and even in the dream I saw that the child was my
life; and it was an idiot. And I wept, and a hundred times I
ran away, but each time I came back it had the same dreadful
face. Until I thought, if I could kiss it, whatever in it was
my own, perhaps I could rest. And I bent to its broken face,
and it was horrible . . . but I kissed it. . . . I think one must
finally take one's life in one's arms, Quentin."

It seems that however different their experience, Quentin
and Holga take similar things from it. Quentin crystallizes
Holga's dream when he tells Maggie: "Only what you've
done will save you." Miller said that it was physically harder
for Holga, but emotionally easier. "The issues were forced
on her, where Quentin had to look for them."

Holga is freedom for Quentin. Independent, she is less
subjective than Louise, who says: "I am not all that un-
interesting, Quentin." In a twist of the line, Holga is il-

lumined; "But I may not be all that interesting." The fault could be hers, and suddenly there was no blame. This is new for Quentin, to whom responsibility comes naturally.

The difference with Holga is that Quentin will never "have to feel guilty for her face." Like all the characters in *After the Fall*, she has her role in Quentin's life, as well as her place in Miller's argument. She links Quentin's own awareness of destruction with the greater mass destruction; and she always appears when he is at his most desperate. In effect she comes to save him. The psychological insight behind the linking and webbing of themes is acute. Holga talks of dying, Quentin of dying for the dead—and Maggie appears.

Beyond pathos and blinding agony, Maggie brings with her the whole question of salvation through other people, and the myth defining it is Lazarus. She asks total love: "That is," says Miller, "love without limits, total acceptance by the world. But if you love without limit, you are prepared to die for other people and we are not. We want to survive."[4] The play is built on this fact, and it is more than depth of pity for Maggie that makes this aspect hard to face. We all look to other people for salvation, whether through love, through security, or through knowledge. One of the terrors between the lines of *After the Fall* is its certain isolation—and this against all longing, all right, and all hoped-for good.

Maggie brings Miller back directly to his main theme and to a general truth behind a character that has been seen in purely personal terms. He contradicted Rumor "painted full of tongues" in *Life*, February 7, 1964: "Maggie . . . is not in fact Marilyn Monroe. Maggie is a character in a play about the human animal's unwillingness or inability to discover in

4 *Ibid.*

himself the seeds of his own destruction. Maggie is in this play because she most perfectly exemplifies the self-destructiveness which finally comes when one views oneself as pure victim. And she most perfectly exemplifies this view because she comes so close to being a pure victim—of parents, of a Puritanical sexual code and of her exploitation as an entertainer."

The fundamental need to know, the spine in Miller, is inevitable in Quentin: "You ever felt you once saw yourself —absolutely true? I may have dreamed it, but I swear, I feel that somewhere along the line—with Maggie, I think—for one split second I saw my life; what I had done, what had been done to me, and even what I ought to do. And that vision sometimes hangs behind my head, blind now, bleached out like the moon in the morning; and if I could only let in some necessary darkness it would shine again."

This is the beginning of a searing awareness. I don't know whether Miller realized the height of his challenge and deliberately couched fighting words in flawless prose. The fact is that Quentin's need to discover his guilt exposes ours. The reaction to the play turns on how much awareness the audience is willing to share. "Of course I understood, but it is what you allow yourself to admit! To admit what you see endangers principles!" You cannot admit to recognizing Quentin's guilts without sharing them. And each time that you would, like Maggie, cry out: "Not me! Not me!"—your own voice comes back to you, "Yes, you!" No wonder the cry going up here is "I don't want to *know*," and innocence is paraded like an Easter bonnet.

Miller watched the dying of the light with patience, and a kind of fulfilled expectation. The gage had not been taken

up, that was all. "It is an intricate play," he explained mildly.
"I have tried to relate the subjective to the objective truth. I
don't think this has been done before, which is why it seems
strange."[5] Carelessly Miller gave me the key to all his work
and, particularly, to *After the Fall*. In his thinking he has always related the two truths—it is his strength. But he has
never done so as freely or as openly as here. Quentin cannot
begin a speech but it slides from the personal to the general,
from the incident to the principle governing the action. "I
don't think I feel very sure of myself any more. I feel sometimes that I don't see reality at all. I'm glad I took on Lou,
but it only hit me lately that no respectable lawyer would
touch him. It's like some unseen web of connection between
people is simply not there. And I always relied on it somehow: I never quite believed that people could be so easily
disposed of. And it's larger than the political question. I
think it's got me a little scared."

Quentin makes these links because Miller knows there is
salvation in them. He knows the value of a detached insight
that enables him to see the facts apart from the people involved and to set both in context, as one would draw a map.
There is no way out of chaos without this balance. There is
no understanding otherwise. A pervading subjectivism will
wreck you here; a life could be wasted in that wilderness.
The tragedy and the irony is that Miller is right—and that
his insight was largely useless. Just as Quentin's knowledge
was useless to the people he wanted to help since they could
neither see what it was nor save themselves by it. To them,
he simply could not give them the kind of help they needed.
Quentin realizes that all they see is the detachment, and he

[5] *Ibid.*

turns it to self-accusation. In truth, he could not give the
linking mind or that insight that sees into a situation and so
comes through it.

Miller's method is not needed through the even-running
days—only when dying, and the audience largely shares the
characters' bewilderment. Quentin's detachment has been
seen as an Olympian self-absorption. Naturally Quentin is
concerned with his search, with his truth; the whole agony
of the play is to discover it. More waywardly, his detachment is seen as something reached apart from his experience.
This is impossible, as the pain in the play, strong enough at
times to drive you from it, proves. The insights in *After the
Fall* are barred from the mere spectator.

In Quentin, both truths—subjective and objective—are
taken to their limits, which again calls for intellectual agility
on the part of the audience. But audiences are not used to
Miller's cross-country ambles and tend to sink back into
subjectivism. This is proved if only the subjective side of
Quentin can be seen. It is rightly impossible not to react to
Maggie, which tends to put the audience in her position—
someone drowning who cannot see the rope. Her desolation,
however perfect, ends in a heart-splitting image. The audience is left mourning, equally for her and itself. But in all
Miller's plays the question behind agony is Why? He asks
it here and, for the Maggies as well as ourselves, survival
hangs on the answer.

Jason Robards, in the Lincoln Center production, comes
close to being an ideal Quentin. He has the right kind of
tension and, above all, he knows what it means to be committed. It is a question of temperament, and not purely
American, as people suppose. Robards has a straightforward

casualness, a simplicity ingrained. He can think his way through Miller's argument, and speaks testing each word as though it were a quicksand of infinite depth. He remains alone; a distance between him and his people that underlines his struggle to reach them. Robards spares us none of Quentin's self-laceration. Self-justification and self-pity are elements of all true despair—they remain in *Hamlet*, but are usually cut to flatter a character and heighten his tragedy. *After the Fall* makes no compromises; the lines of Quentin's agony are etched on his face, and his restlessness reflects his tossing mind.

Quentin is an unwilling moralist, one who feels himself not good enough to judge others. The ideal way to write of the moralist would be in brass; to speak as a resounding gong, self-accusation ringing loud. To do this is to move away from Quentin's personal agony and make his sins abstract, to turn from tragedy to a Greek tragic mask. The moralist in Quentin strains ever toward the perfect face; but let us move back toward intimacy, toward the man.

The mere fact of judging troubles Quentin, and for this reason he puts his life on trial. To be judged. To be known. The search is his. He had been sustained by a belief that he was moving toward a point of resolution: "Where . . . God knows what . . . I would be justified, or even condemned. A verdict, anyway. I think now that my disaster really began when I looked up one day . . . and the bench was empty. No judge in sight. All that remained was the endless argument with oneself. . . ." He is alone—judged the only way possible in a Miller play: "By his own conscience, his own values, his own deeds."[6] But his need is to be justified rather than absolved. The best he can hope is that this mountain of guilt will not all be his. There is no absolution in Miller, only a desperate fight to an uncertain and precarious victory.

When the trial begins, Quentin is isolated with his experience. He has lost all sense of necessity: "With me, whether I open a book or think of marrying again, it is so damned clear that I've chosen what I do—it cuts the strings between my hands and heaven. It sounds foolish, but I feel . . . unblessed." In this grey drift of chaos he is living meaninglessly, and for nothing—and this is nearer to a kind of dying. It is a hand-to-mind existence, a sickly clutching at straws of interest that breaks all connection between people and things.

He has lived through all his hopes, and guilt has eroded his promises. He protests, "I'm a stranger to my life," and this is new in Miller. Quentin is looking for what else there is; Miller's other heroes knew already, because Miller did. Looking back to those earlier plays there is an underlying certainty in them, loud as laughter, that there isn't here. Some inner vision has collapsed like a body with the bones taken out. Quentin thinks back to what he believed was a more hopeful time, with issues clear-cut and certain, but finds it flawed. His beliefs failed him even as he believed in them—"socialism once, then love." The belief was there, but it did not save.

He cannot help finding: "The evidence is bad for promises. But how do you touch the world without a promise? And yet I mustn't forget the way I wake each morning like a boy, even now, even now! But where's the evidence? Or is it simply that my heart still beats?" This outcast longing prompts his overriding question, Is he entitled to take up his life again? Apart from *can* he, *should* he? After two divorces he feels that he cannot face marriage with Holga until he

knows who and what he'd be bringing her. This steep condition implies total awareness, a razor-sharp double-edge ter-
rifying in itself. Quentin is the only one who cannot afford
not to know. Louise can be without insight, Maggie ill-
equipped, the mother unknowing. These excuses are in
themselves a kind of absolution.

Quentin, like Miller's other heroes, sets up Brand-like
absolutes for himself and this totality cannot help but breed
guilt for him. He tries to live on an all-or-nothing basis, and
ever equates compromise with fraud. "Grief isn't grief unless
it kills you. Love without limits." Other claims spiral beyond
his: from birth his mother hoped he would be "a light in the
world" that would somehow continue and justify her own
life. The last spiral is Maggie's, who sees in him the power
and salvation of a personal god.

Quentin is back on high. A moralist who takes the world's
conscience as well as his own. His glass ever magnifies sins
and his responsibility for them. There is a certain guilt in
him for all that he cannot rightly resolve. In Quentin, Miller
brings the two faces of the moralist together, and tries to
reconcile the one of flesh with the one of bronze.

"I can still hear her voice in the street sometimes, loud and
real, calling my name." This memory of a voice defines the
mother, and Miller's writing in these early family scenes is
penetratingly real. "Did they pass a law that kid can't get a
haircut?" You can hear the direct questions of the small boy
punctuating the mother's longing. The collapse of this warm
security with the Depression takes the world with it: "I been
to every bank in New York, I can't get a bill paid, how the
hell they going to lend me money? No—no, there's no money
in London, there's no money in Hamburg, there's no money in Hamburg, there's no money in Hamburg, there's no money in Hamburg, there's no money in Hamburg, there ain't a cargo

moving in the world, the ocean's empty, Billy. . . ." The
father speaks the language of Willy Loman. This kind Atlas
of a man, as he must have appeared to Quentin, is destroyed
by the mother's contempt.

Quentin watches them become separate, and he lives with
this image. Miller points out that, psychologically, this was
the beginning of Quentin's demand of Louise not to become a
Separate Person: "To wipe out his parents' separation, he
wanted to run the train backwards, to make it not have
happened." That was also Quentin's first encounter with a
determined innocence, as the mother protested that she didn't
say anything—a kind of mental color-blindness. The realization is just not there. She would have been astounded by
Quentin's later accusation that she was making him an
accomplice in his father's destruction.

As though following a strand in some inescapable web,
both innocence and the determination to stay a separate
person are taken up by Louise, Quentin's first wife. This is
the intimate working out of a wider theme that has been with
Miller through the plays—the impossibility and the guilt of
living as a separate person. Here he traces it through the
political relationship that links Quentin, Lou, and Mickey,
and develops it, mathematically almost, to its logical conclusion in the Camp.

Louise takes it up in a protest fervent as his belief:
"Quentin, I am not a praise machine! I am not a blur and I
am not your mother! I am a separate person!" Quentin "stares
at her, and what lies beyond her." Then he speaks: "I see
that now. . . . But it bewilders me. In fact, I got the same
idea when I realized that Lou had gone from one of his
former students to another and none would take him—"

Louise interrupts: "What's Lou got to do with it? I think it's admirable that you—"

As far as Quentin is concerned, Lou has everything to do with it. Hopefully, he traces the general principle: "Yes, but I am doing what you call an admirable thing because I can't bear to be a separate person! I think so. I really don't want to be known as a Red lawyer; and I really don't want the newspapers to eat me alive; and if it came down to it, Lou could defend himself. But when that decent, broken man who never wanted anything but the good of the world, sits across my desk . . . I don't know how to say that my interests are no longer the same as his, and that if he doesn't change I consign him to hell because we are separate persons."

The principle is impeccable, but it is meaningless to Louise, who is preoccupied with her own uncertainty. She feels that Quentin is blind to her, that she doesn't exist for him—"I don't know what I am to you!" The real conflict here is between her dependence and his independence, and it is one that stays through his marriage with Maggie. Quentin cannot bring his meaning home to her for similar reasons. "Honey, it always comes down to the same thing, don't you see? Now listen to me. You're still proceeding on the basis that you're alone. That you can be disposed of. And the slightest contradiction of your wishes makes the earth tremble." When Maggie's failure to believe it helps to kill her, the private development of this theme reaches its limit.

(I cannot help feeling that it is a kind of vandalism to unravel the intricacies and complexities of this play; fortunately it can only be partial. This chapter is no more than a glimpse at it.)

Louise, dominated by her sense of injury, lives in an armed

innocence that leaves all guilt to Quentin. She cannot be persuaded from her merciful refuge: her deadly choosing not to see that can shed all responsibility. "But I swear, Louise," Quentin says, "if you just once, and of your own will, and right as you are—if you would come to me and say that something important was your fault and that you were sorry . . . it would help."

They are like two people who no longer speak the same language, but each can, by an effort, understand piercingly what the other is saying. Louise's insight, when she does have it, is acute. She realizes the need for Quentin to make his own decision over Lou's case, and sees it as a first step toward certainty, if nothing else. She can sum up Quentin's need for connection, and she knows that he tries to live by a standard that is largely abandoned. "You tend to make relatives out of people. Max is not your father, or your brother, or anything but a very important lawyer with his own interests. He's not going to endanger his whole firm to defend a Communist. I don't know how you got that illusion."

The marriage breaks—as Louise sees it through Quentin's withdrawal; as Quentin sees it through Louise's walled-in innocence that makes it impossible for her even to recognize the struggle going on. "Then what are you doing here? . . . What the hell are you compromising yourself for if you're so goddamned honest?" Miller notes in a stage direction that neither can let down his demand for apology, for grace. It is as though Louise and Quentin looked for absolution from each other; where Maggie and Quentin looked for a blessing.

Quentin realized: "Everything is one thing. You see? I don't know what we are to one another! Or rather what we ought to be!" The links between people have broken. Lou

is a professor of law, whose undoing is his own kindness. He
does not know how to hurt, and a state could be built on an
integrity so perfect. The Lous come as a blessing, but are
usually made a sacrifice. This gentle man is being investigated
by the Committee, which enters every aspect of his life and
threatens to wreck it. His position alarms Elsie, who tries to
prevent his publishing his new book for fear of prompting
another attack. "And yet, if I put the book away, it's a kind
of suicide to me. Everything I know is in that book." Lou
needs to publish to reclaim himself—to undo an earlier book
in which he had lied, as he believed, in a good cause. Lou's
admission becomes for Quentin, "the day the world ended
. . . and no one was innocent again."

Lou's perplexity is set beside Mickey's assurance; the assurance of a man who has made his world as you build a
house. He is unhindered by Lou's doubt or Quentin's searching totality. Mickey would appear a victim only to the eye
of God, and even then would probably refute the definition.
He has come to terms—except for one thing: Mickey cannot
bear to be an outsider. He lives here and now and cannot
wait for McCarthyism to pass, or believe that it will. The
reaction of his partners on hearing that he had been a Communist for a few months appalled him. "Quent, I could feel
their backs turning on me. It was horrible! As though they
would let me die." His dread is not misplaced; they would.
As we let people die in the Camp; as Quentin would have
let Maggie die. Every walk away from destruction finds its
parallel image.

Mickey urges Lou along the road he was going, and speaks
out of his new conviction for both of them: "I think a man's
got to take the rap, Lou, for what he's done, for what he is.

I think what you hide poisons you." He goes on to justify
his own position, in that he no longer knows what he is
defending by keeping silent. "The Party? But I despise the
Party, and have for many years. Just like you. Yet there is
something, something that closes my throat when I think of
telling names. What am I defending? It's a dream, now, a
dream of solidarity, but hasn't that died a long time ago?"

He has come for Lou's permission to name him—in effect,
for permission to destroy him. But Lou reaches for the
answering principle that takes the argument beyond the limits
of current politics. "If everyone broke faith there would be
no civilization! That is why the Committee is the face of the
Philistine! And it astounds me that you can speak of truth
and justice in relation to that gang of cheap publicity hounds."

The two men are equal in guilt and each, in a brilliant
crystallization of the theme of *The Crucible*, accuses the
other of handing over conscience—Mickey to the Committee,
Lou to his wife. Lou tries to condemn Mickey, until Mickey
devastatingly exposes the ventriloquism involved: "But from
your conscience or from hers? Who is speaking to me, Lou?"

Around Quentin faith has been breaking like glass. Later in
the play, when he defends the Reverend Harley Barnes, he
wonders whether they would allow the Committe not to
answer. "I am not sure what we are upholding anymore—
are we good by merely saying No to evil? Even in a righteous
No there's some disguise. Isn't it necessary . . . to say . . . to
finally say Yes . . . to *something?*" Partly out of this need he
is drawn to Maggie.

Unable to live with guilt, Lou kills himself. "Maybe it's
not enough—to know yourself. Or maybe it's too much."
He dies alone, having seen through Quentin's unwilling faith-

fulness. In talking of his death, Miller quoted Camus: " 'We are in a state of suicide.' This has been through the plays, whether the death is actual or the people are killed in other ways. In the other plays, suicide relaxed tensions and resolved. Here it doesn't." It cannot: survival is so painful that Brand's avalanche would be a gentle death for Quentin; Lou's death again shows him his complicity with destruction. Now his link with the Camp has become positive, and his recognition, identity even, is too strong to be blinked. This knowledge is the working out of a pattern begun by his mother in childhood, carried on by Louise, and elaborated by Lou and Mickey.

The principle traced for Louise ends in: "This is not some crazy aberration of human nature to me. I can easily see the perfectly normal contractors and their cigars; the carpenters, plumbers, sitting at their ease over lunch pails, I can see them laying the pipes to run the blood out of this mansion; good fathers, devoted sons, grateful that someone else will die, not they. And how can one understand that, if one is innocent; if somewhere in the soul there is no accomplice . . . of that joy, that joy, that joy when a burden dies . . . and leaves you safe?"

Elia Kazan, whose direction leaves the play's image—Quentin surrounded by his life—etched on the mind, said that there is more moral ambivalence here than before in Miller. It is possible that an earlier Miller play would have given Quentin the overriding argument in these scenes to the reassurance of the audience, who would then have known what Miller wanted them to think. Although, as this book shows, he has never been happy about making up anybody's mind, nor is this mesh of motive new to him.

I can imagine that the play could seem too intricate, but this is fascination rather than flaw. It is a meandering masterpiece for its content and the passionate feeling inspiring it. All that mars it, for me, is Miller's occasional tendency to overwrite. Never at ease with sentimental writing, his imagery can turn florid; there are certain lines you long to cut and beg for a discipline more austere. The necessary linking means the constant use of the same images—say, the mother and the sailboat. The reason is always there, but it can appear a sailboat too frequent, especially when seen, not read.

Perhaps audiences and critics have been confused by *After the Fall* because its truth is kaleidoscopic. Miller has built his play on a constantly shifting pattern of truth, as well as on various kinds of truth. It depends on who is speaking; Quentin's truth is mainly objective, Louise's subjective, Maggie's instinctive. These truths merge, clash, and re-form like the images in the play itself.

Felice, for instance, is a dark mirror-image of Maggie in temperament and situation. She gives Quentin the same power for psychologically the same reason; her life has broken and in him she sees salvation. But this power is naked in Felice; there is nothing else, and it brings dread with it because the link between them is casual, accidental. "If you can save someone as unwittingly as Quentin does Felice, you can destroy them unwittingly," said Miller. "If you have this power how do you control it?" Unwillingly, Quentin feels responsible for Felice, even though responsibility for what people take from you is theirs, and cannot be controlled.

By a stroke of inspiration that highlights its irony, this whole situation has been turned inside out by the playing of Zohra Lampert. As a bright lining heightens a dark coat, she makes Maggie's tragedy her comedy. Exuberant as a brass band, this poster-paint "Maggie" moves through the play hopeful as a tattered flag.

And so to the miracle and the pain of Maggie. In her, feeling is as translucent as a lighted candle makes the glass that shields it, and at the beginning an almost dreamlike wonder surrounds her—"that wishing girl," "that victory in lace." She comes to Quentin as a release: "She wasn't defending anything, upholding anything, or accusing—she was just *there*, like a tree or a cat." But it is an unreachable freedom. Quentin will always look for the issues; he could change his skin easier than change this. Maggie's honesty is a touchstone for Quentin; she is not pretending to be innocent. But in fact Maggie cannot be anything but innocent. Her truth is purely subjective and instinctive, relating ever back to herself; an objective insight is beyond her. This underlines one of the play's ironies: the faster you run from something, the faster you move toward it. There is no escape—only a circular trap of circumstances.

As black balances white and holds its own, there is a double view of Maggie, painful for her to recognize and for Quentin to admit. No matter how high she climbs as a singer, she remains a joke to most people. Quentin reassures her and, at once, accuses himself of fraud. "I should have agreed that she was a beautiful piece trying to take herself seriously." While urging truth on Maggie, he, up to a point, protects her from it. It is impossible not to reassure the Maggies.

"But how can you speak of love, she had been chewed and spat out by a long line of grinning men! Her name floating in the stench of locker rooms and parlor-car cigar smoke! She had the truth that day I brought the lie that she had to be

'saved'! From what—except my own contempt?" This is guilt
to both of them. Maggie senses that Quentin is ashamed of
her, and when challenged he has to admit: "I wasn't ashamed.
But afraid. I wasn't sure if any of them . . . had had you."
This corroborates, for her, that he never gave her a chance.

From the beginning, Quentin is an interpreter for Maggie,
able to come between her and her fears. Spontaneous, striving,
lost, she has an open longing to learn from him. "But I don't
know if it's true what I see. But you do. You see it and you
know if it's true." At this early meeting Maggie is drawing on
his understanding, his insight, and his awareness of her. He
does "know." It is simple for Quentin to interpret for Maggie.
He keeps coming back to the fact that she is frightened. She
is—by a waking dream, a panic-reliving of the past when her
mother tried to kill her. Quentin persuades her to talk about
it and resolves her fears, even to the point of freeing her from
guilt. Maggie's love and trust are absolute; but anyone lost
giving absolute trust often gives equally absolute responsibility.

Maggie was looking for someone to steady the world. But
as one doubt is healed another grows in its place. She seems
to chase her own uncertainty as if only by peeling away layer
on layer of doubt can she ever reach a safe center. She
takes reassurance "like a child wanting some final embrace"—
but remains uneasy. Alone even at her wedding: "It's that
nobody's here . . . from me. I'm like a stranger here! If my
mother or my father or anybody who loved me—"

In writing of Maggie you write letter and comma of
Barbara Loden's performance. Here is a single and complete
identity. Barbara will see as Maggie sees, know as she knows.
"I'm telling you like Maggie," she said, and with a tangible

pity spoke her bewilderment. "She was looking for someone to give her life a purpose and make her better than she was; I guess that covers it. She wasn't equipped! She did try to make it work! Well, see, she's right! He did promise—and it didn't happen. Then he let her down by joining *them.* He'd told her to fight for her rights; then when she did he placated the people she was fighting. She's right! They do make a lot of money out of a performer; but they don't break their hearts and get their hands clammy."

Maggie is a star self-made, and with her success the star takes over. Quentin does stand between her and the Network, but Maggie expected a more ruthless fighter. When it contradicts his sense of right, she goads him by playing on the doubt that perhaps he is weak—only one weapon in this Who's-Afraid-of-Virginia-Woolf armory. This low-keyed, prosaic explanation bypasses her agony. The real question is the one tearing at Maggie: "Look. You don't want me. What the hell are you doing here?"

Quentin's promise not to walk out reflects tragically his early reassurance—when it was easy for him. Now: "You can't take pills on top of whiskey, dear. That's how it happened last time. And it's not going to happen again. Never. I'll be right back." Held by Maggie's agony, he cannot leave the house. It is all but impossible to watch the pain in this as her desperation engulfs the audience. I can still see Barbara Loden's broken dance circling him; the person gone and chilling as a wax doll, set moving disjointedly to music. He can't bear to watch her, and how to help her? He reaches toward the hope of limitless love, Quentin's last absolute. It's like watching the collapse of the world. A cry fights with a lump in the throat the size of a cancer. "In whose name? In

whose blood-covered name do you look into a face you
loved, and say, Now, you have been found wanting, and now
in your extremity you die!"

Quentin's nightmare-images of failure and death converge
and dissolve. The myth of Lazarus towers over them, solid
as sculpted, massive in its strength, half-shrouded still, but
straight leaning forward as if for flight.

Maggie looked to Quentin for salvation. She told him once:
"You like gave me my feelings to say." The very notion of a
spiritual Pygmalion would be bizarre to Quentin, who, himself independent, would not recognize the role. But through
Maggie's eyes it is natural, and she never changes in this. At
the height of her goading, when words could draw blood,
she can say; "I'm allowed to say what I see." This distant
echo of her longing to learn from him now becomes a kind
of challenge. "Allowed" leaves Quentin all-powerful, as
though she expects him to stop her. It is no longer a question
of his knowledge, but of her attitude. The relationship remains as between child and father, or devout adult and God.

Complete dependence equally destroys two people. It is
"My life on your head, all the responsibility, and all the
blame." Quentin, for instance, is to stop her taking pills; the
effort must be his. But Quentin knows that he cannot save
her, even at the cost of his own destruction. All that remains
is to persuade her to take back responsibility for her life: "I'm
not going to be the rescuer any more. It's only fair to tell
you, I just haven't got it any more. They're your pills and
your life; you keep count."

They struggle on the edge of exhaustion, and Maggie keeps
trying to give him her life by giving him the pills. To Quentin
she is merely trying to make him responsible for her death—

"setting me up for a murder." He explains: "A suicide kills two people, Maggie. That's what it's for. So I'm removing myself and perhaps it will lose its point."

Maggie, desperate, still looks for salvation through love. "But Jesus must have loved her. Right?"

QUENTIN Who?

MAGGIE Lazarus.

QUENTIN That's right, yes! He . . . loved her enough to raise her from the dead. But he's God, see . . . and God's power is love without limit. But when a man dares reach for that . . . he is only reaching for the power. Whoever goes to save another person with the lie of limitless love throws a shadow on the face of God. And God is what happened, God is what is. . . .

This definition of God as reality is characteristic. The myth breaks. And in telling what happened, Quentin interprets for Maggie for the last time: "Maggie, we . . . used one another."

MAGGIE Not me, not me!

QUENTIN Yes, you. And I. "To live," we cried, and "Now," we cried. And loved each other's innocence as though to love enough what was not there would cover up what was. But there is an angel, and night and day he brings back to us exactly what we want to lose. And no chemical can kill him, no blindness dark enough to make him lose his way; so you must love him, he keeps truth in the world."

Miller's Blakelike vision dissolves, as Quentin reaches to draw Maggie into it. "You eat those pills like power, but only what you've done will save you. If you could only say, I have been cruel, this frightening room would open! If you could say, I have been kicked around, but I have been just as inexcusably vicious to others; I have called my husband idiot in public, I have been utterly selfish despite my generosity, I have been hurt by a long line of men but I have co-operated with my persecutors. . . . And I am full of hatred, I, Maggie, the sweet lover of all life—I hate the world! . . . hate women, hate men, hate all who will not grovel at my feet proclaiming my limitless love for ever and ever!" He urges her: "Do the hardest thing of all—see your own hatred, and live!"

Quentin is striving for Maggie's acceptance of herself, an awareness of her own responsibility for her own destruction. All through Miller, insight saves, and here it is all there is left. Quentin faces Maggie with this truth in the all-or-nothing hope that she is still able to grasp it. But his hope is "a lightning before death"—he comes too late for Maggie. She wants to die, and does not care enough to fire-walk through this insight. "Her innocence killed her," said Miller. "She was all innocence. She could not see where her interest lay in recognizing her hatred."

Maggie protests Quentin's judgment. She cannot recognize his truth and opposes it with another. She faces him with her disillusionment and her injury. She had found a letter in his desk two months after they were married: "The only one I will ever love is my daughter. If I could only find an honorable way to die." And Maggie's new world collapsed. Now she does not even expect him to be able to tell truth. Quentin wrote it because Maggie had returned him to his beginning by accusing him of making her feel that she didn't exist—just as Louise had done. "That I could have brought two women so different to the same conclusion—it closed a circle for me. And I wanted to face the worst thing I could imagine—that I could not love. And I wrote it down, like a letter . . . from myself." Part of the dread behind these scenes is the way they are both brought back to their beginnings, as if the struggle and the hope were nothing. They are cancelled out like the overturning of a checkerboard.

At last there is the truce of Quentin's absolutes coming down: "Maggie, we've got to have some humility toward ourselves; we were born of many errors, a human being has to forgive himself!" But Maggie remains unreached—lost. She tries to go back to a happier time as if need alone could re-create it, and the impossibility warns Quentin of his certain disintegration. When Maggie begs: "But if Lazarus . . . ," he can only reply: "I am not the Saviour and I am not the help. . . . You are not going to kill me, Maggie, and that's all this is for!"

They struggle for the pills, and in the struggle he tries to kill her, and so takes her back to her beginning—when her mother had tried to kill her. As her terror rises, so does his at this final recognition of the murder in himself. It is open now. They both know.

I think that if I had to find a single, tangible image for *After the Fall* it would be Epstein's *Lazarus*—both in that Maggie looked to Quentin for salvation and that Quentin is able to come back from the "dead." It is characteristic of Miller, and of our time, that man can only look to himself for salvation. Miller's power of mind, his logic, here becomes "the strength to live unblessed."

Maggie asks what Lazarus was supposed to prove:

QUENTIN The power of faith.

MAGGIE What about those who have no faith?

QUENTIN They only have the will.

MAGGIE But how do you get the will?

QUENTIN You have faith.

Quentin has only the will. If, like Maggie, you literally cannot live without a blessing—then there is nothing left.

To know is all. Now all that remains is Quentin's acceptance of himself. We have been moving toward this through *After the Fall*. "What love, what wave of pity will ever reach this knowledge—I know how to kill . . ." Miller catches up all his themes in a great net at the last, and Quentin finds that: "Always in your own blood-covered name you turn your back!" His destruction again links with the Camp, and Miller's question spirals beyond him: "Who can be innocent again on this mountain of skulls? I tell you what I know! My brothers died . . . but my brothers built this place." Innocence is the illusion; the choice remains what it has always been—between Abel and Cain.

Miller's people always did face all he knew, and his search spares no one. It is as if someone took his life and tore it up in front of you, the while explaining why he was doing it. It seems incredible that any hope at all can be pulled out of such darkness. For this reason, people may see the pain, but not the point—see that every hope is blasted with insight, and yet that insight is all that will save you. To know is all.

Quentin survives with a tentative hope that "it does seem feasible not to be afraid." A more positive answer could neither be reached nor believed. There are no solutions in

Miller; but what there is—what can bring the characters and
the audience safe home—is a morale, an attitude of mind.
Quentin's discovery, however agonizing, is not in the least
remote from Miller's other characters. But it is much more
conscious now: "Is the knowing all? To know, and even
happily that we meet unblessed; not in some garden of wax
fruit and painted trees, that lie of Eden, but after, after the
Fall, after many, many deaths. Is the knowing all? And the
wish to kill is never killed, but with some gift of courage one
may look into its face when it appears, and with a stroke of
love—as to an idiot in the house—forgive it; again and
again . . . forever?"

CHAPTER XI

Incident at Vichy

"A 'moral' ounce is taken up to weigh down the otherwise too-light heart which contemplates uneasily its relative freedom from injustice's penalty, the guilt of having been spared."[1]

Incident at Vichy is a black pendant to *After the Fall*. It is as though Miller had taken the central theme of his larger work—man's need to recognize the destructive elements in himself before he can belong to a civilization—and made it unevadable. This is a line drawing of a play, written in three weeks and based on fact. Miller was told its story some ten years ago, even to the ending, when a Gentile gives a waiting Jew his pass and tells him to go. "The Jew had never before laid eyes on his savior. He never saw him again."[2] Miller has compressed a profound humanity into the play's simple frame, which must have seemed specially designed for his purpose—"the transformation of guilt into responsibility."

[1] "Our Guilt for the World's Evil," by Arthur Miller. *The New York Times*, January 3, 1965.
[2] *Ibid.*

The play takes the mind, and its compassion makes up for the fact that it hasn't Miller's complex welding of subjective and objective truth, which in *Death of a Salesman*, *The Crucible*, *A View From the Bridge*, and *After the Fall* took heart and mind and all. This depth of exploration is outside its design.

The lights go down and through the darkness a concertina plays "Lili Marlene." The insistent tune hangs in the air and lingers as the lights rise on a detention room in Vichy, September, 1942, where six men and a boy wait. "They are frightened and tend to make themselves small and unobtrusive." Summarily brought in off the street, the pitch of their uncertainty is high in Lebeau, an artist, whose fear keeps breaking his determination to stay calm. He watches the stoicism of Bayard, a Communist electrician; Monceau, an actor; a waiter—and a gypsy, the alien among them, denied both feeling and fellowship. Marchand, a businessman, is isolated by his security and alone in his belief that this is merely a document check. The others feel that it could be racial.

As if to confirm their fears, an old Jew is brought in, who sits among them. He says nothing, but in himself symbolizes both them and the play. Von Berg, an Austrian prince, and LeDuc are caught up in the same arrest. The characters are necessarily skeletal to keep the play's simple form, and you only know of them what you might have discovered had you been there that morning. The whole play is written in a kind of dramatist's shorthand; LeDuc is symbol for the "Miller" character—an authoritative questioner, a man of insight who is totally unable to accept passivity. He announces himself in the play's first clash with the major, a wounded German line officer on loan from the regular Army: "Sir, I must ask the reason for this. I am a combat officer of the French Army. There is no authority to arrest me in French territory. The Occupation has not revoked French law in Southern France."

There is no reaction. The Professor of Racial Anthropology and the Captain of Police tell the detectives how to maintain the secrecy of the arrests.

But because of LeDuc's authority, the terrified, bat-wing questions of Lebeau become serious and find their voice and measure. Why are they there? Has forced labor been applied in the Vichy zone? Amid this uncertainty Bayard tells them that a "30-car freight train pulled in yesterday. The engineer is Polish so I couldn't talk to him, but one of the switchmen says he heard people inside. . . . It came from Toulouse. I heard there's been a quiet round-up of Jews in Toulouse the last couple of weeks. And what's a Polish engineer doing on a train in Southern France?" They face, then evade, the prospect of a concentration camp, until Bayard quietly confirms: "The cars are locked on the outside. And they stink. You can smell the stench a hundred yards away. Babies are crying inside. And women. They don't lock volunteers in that way. I never heard of it." His insistence drowns the actor's disbelief, and he tells them how to escape: "There are four bolts halfway up the door on the inside. Try to pick up a nail or a screwdriver, even a sharp stone—you can chisel the wood out around those bolts and the doors will open. . . ."

If *After the Fall* was built in a series of images, *Incident at Vichy* is constructed of disintegrating beliefs. Prince Von Berg is civilization incarnate. His name is a thousand years old, and his title is his name, his family—just as every man has a name and a family. He sees Nazism as "an ocean of vulgarity," and this slight statement builds into his belief. "Can a people with respect for art go about hounding Jews? Making a prison of Europe, pushing themselves forward as a race of policemen and brutes?" He realizes that it is possible, that civilizing art is no defense. And so each man's defense dissolves under the pressure of opposing belief.

As the businessman is released and the gypsy taken, each looks for some protection against the coming interrogation. Monceau, the actor, believes in creating his own reality. "The important thing is not to look like a victim." His faith is in his talent, in his personality.

Bayard points out that to meet this on a personal basis is to be turned into an idiot. The only salvation is an objective viewpoint, like his own in a Communist future. This leads to an even clash between himself and Von Berg, which Miller argues like the two sides of a faith. Through the play, themes are repeated and balances are perfectly held.

BAYARD Is any of us an individual to them? Class interest makes history, not individuals.

VON BERG Yes, that seems to be the trouble.

BAYARD Facts are not trouble. A human being has to glory in the facts.

VON BERG But the facts . . . Dear sir, what if the facts are dreadful? And will always be dreadful?

BAYARD So is childbirth, so is—

VON BERG But a child comes of it. What if nothing comes of the facts but endless, endless disaster?

To bring home his point to Bayard that 99 per cent of the Nazis are ordinary working-class people, Von Berg describes how he saw Nazism take hold in his own house: "But they adore him! My cook, my gardeners, the people who work in my forests, the chauffeur, the gamekeeper—they are all *Nazis!* I saw it come over them, the love for this creature—my housekeeper dreams of him in her bed, she'd serve my breakfast like a god had slept with her, in a dream slicing my toast. I saw this adoration in my own house!—That, that is the dreadful fact."

The prince's belief that only a few individuals are immune to propaganda is meaningless to Bayard: "You mean the whole world is going to hang on that thread?"

The waiter's boss brings the captain's coffee, talks with the waiter, and their real situation emerges through the waiter's hushed: "It's not to work. . . . They have furnaces. . . . He heard the detectives! . . . People get burned up in furnaces. It's not to work. They burn you up in Poland."

MONCEAU That is the most fantastic idiocy I ever heard in my life.

LEBEAU As long as you have regular French papers though. . . .
There's nothing about Jew on *my* papers.

WAITER They're going to look at your penis.

As Bayard is taken, the town life outside invades the detention room. A concertina plays and the imprisoned waiter says: "That's the boss's son, Maurice. They're starting to serve lunch."

LeDuc urges escape; there is only one guard at the door. But he comes up against Monceau's passivity; he is the only other able-bodied man, and he will do nothing. Unshakable, he simply does not believe the waiter. The prince does, and also that the Nazis "have pointed the way to the future. What one used to conceive a human being to be, will have no room on this earth."

The play is punctuated by the official "Next!"—this time it's the waiter. The major, unnerved by the little man's terror and his own disgust, tries to walk out on the proceedings. He cannot. The best he can do is to enforce a ten-minute respite for himself.

Miller explores the irony of their being caught. It was all avoidable. They were caught over nothing. Only the boy had a real reason for being out that morning. He was on his way to the pawnshop with his mother's wedding ring, because there was nothing at home to eat. The others were in France because of things people cannot leave. The actor wanted to keep the lead in *Cyrano*, just as Lebeau's mother could not give up the furniture when they had a visa for America before the invasion. And they both left Paris for the safety of Vichy.

To avoid LeDuc's persistence, Monceau looks to the prince for reassurance that the perceptive German audience would surely not burn up actors in furnaces? Only to be told that the prince left Austria when the Germans murdered his musicians.

LeDuc makes a last attempt to understand the actor: "Would you mind telling me, are you religious?"

MONCEAU Not at all.

LEDUC Then why do you feel this passionate desire to be sacrificed?

In an exploration of guilt, he discovers that we have all been trained to die, "with illusions or without them, exhausted or fresh, Jew and Gentile both."

Monceau reminds LeDuc that the majority of mankind is condemned because of its race, and so prevents the audience from limiting the play to Nazism and Vichy. "It's the way the world is, so why don't you stop insulting others with romantic challenges?"

The argument is clinched by LeDuc in a line that could have come from *The Crucible*. "Your heart is conquered territory, mister."

The boy confirms their captivity by giving the prince the ring to return to his mother. Terrified, the boy is about to try and escape alone, but when he and LeDuc move toward the guard they are prevented by the major. Escape had been impossible: two sentries guard the corners.

In a drunken haze the major protests his feeling to LeDuc, but it is meaningless. LeDuc's only concern is that the major gets them out; in their clash the major proves to him that there cannot be persons any more.

MAJOR (*with manic amusement, yet deeply questioning*). Why do you deserve to live more than I do?

LeDuc Because I am incapable of doing what you are doing. I am better for the world than you.

He promises, to the major's contempt: "I will love you as long as I live—"

MAJOR That means so much to you? That someone loves you? It's amazing, you don't understand anything. Nothing of that kind is left; don't you understand that yet?

LeDuc It is left in me.

MAJOR (*more loudly*). There are no persons any more, don't
you see that? There will never be persons again. What do I
care if you love me? Are you out of your mind? What am I,
a dog, that I must be loved? You . . . goddamned Jews! . . .
(*He fires into the ceiling.*) Everything stops now . . . Now
it is all stopped. Now you tell me. You tell me. Now nothing
is moving. You tell me. Go ahead now.

LeDuc What shall I tell you?

MAJOR Tell me how . . . how there can be persons anymore. I
have you at the end of this revolver—(*indicates the professor*)—he has me—and somebody has him—and somebody
has somebody else. Now tell me. . . .

And in this stopped world he offers to let LeDuc go and keep
the rest. LeDuc tries to hide his trembling hands.

MAJOR Don't hide your hands. I am trying to understand why
you are better for the world than me. Why do you hide
your hands? Would you go out of that door with a light
heart, run to your woman, drink a toast to your skin? . . .
Why are you better than anybody else?

LeDuc I have no duty to make a gift of myself to your sadism.

MAJOR But I do? To others' sadism? Of myself? I have this
duty and you do not? To make a gift of myself?

LeDuc I have nothing to say.

MAJOR That's better.—Next!

That "Next!" comes rapidly now—the actor—the artist—
the boy. Then the old Jew, who will not leave his bundle; he
clings to it with soft cries. The police expect some treasure,
but in the struggle the sack explodes in a shock of feathers.

Now we are left with the question over-hanging the play,

an insight that Quentin tried to drive home. Here it is begun by Von Berg (when he suggests that the Nazis have created a new definition for man), carried on by the major, and concluded in the final scenes between LeDuc and the prince with an acceptance of responsibility and recognition.

VON BERG There is nothing, is that it? For you there is nothing? . . .

LEDUC Prince, in my profession one gets the habit of looking at people quite impersonally. It is not you I am angry with. In one part of my mind it is not even this Nazi. I am only angry that I should have been born before the day when man has accepted his own nature: that he is *not* reasonable, that he is full of murder, that his ideals are only the little tax he pays for the right to hate and kill with a clear conscience. I am only angry that I was not above this delusion myself. That there was not time to truly make part of myself what I know, and to teach others the truth.

VON BERG There are ideals, Doctor, of another kind. There are people who would find it easier to die than stain one finger with this murder. They exist. I swear it to you. People for whom everything is *not* permitted, foolish people and ineffectual, but we do exist and will not dishonor our tradition. I ask your friendship.

LEDUC I owe you the truth, Prince; you won't believe it now, but I wish you would think about it and what it means. I have never analyzed a gentile who did not have, somewhere hidden in his mind, a dislike if not a hatred for the Jews.

VON BERG That is impossible; it is not true of me.

LEDUC Until you know it is true of you, you will destroy whatever truth can come of this atrocity. Part of knowing who we are is knowing we are not someone else. And Jew is only the name we give to that stranger, that agony we cannot feel, that death we look at like a cold abstraction. Each man has his Jew; it is the other. And the Jews have their Jews. And now, above all, you must see that you have yours—the man whose death leaves you relieved that you are not him, despite your decency. And that is why there is nothing and will be nothing—until you face your own complicity with this . . . your own humanity.

Von Berg denies it entirely, and as proof of his good faith tells of attempting suicide. LeDuc proves that the prince had a shred of complicity by reminding him of his cousin, Baron Kessler, a Nazi who helped remove all Jewish doctors from the medical school in Vienna. The prince had surely known of it.

Von Berg Yes. I heard it. I . . . had forgotten it. You see, he was—

LeDuc Your cousin. I understand. (*They are quite joined, and LeDuc is mourning for the prince as well as for himself.*) And in any case it is only a small part of Baron Kessler to you. I do understand it. But it is all of Baron Kessler to me. When you said his name it was with love; and I'm sure he must be a man of some kindness, with whom you can see eye to eye on many things. But when I hear that name I see a knife. You see now why I say there is nothing and will be nothing, when even you cannot really put yourself in my place? Even you!? And that is why your thoughts of suicide do not move me. It is not your guilt I want, it's your responsibility—that might have helped. Yes, if you had understood that Baron Kessler was in part, in some part, in some small and frightful part—doing your will. You might have done something then, with your standing and your name and your decency, aside from shooting yourself!

The point of the scene is underlined by the half-hysterical laughter from the office where they have the old Jew. Von

Berg's question comes with full horror and awareness: "What can ever save us?!"

Only Miller could have stripped the play to such bleakness, and then drawn affirmation from it. The prince accepts LeDuc's challenge, by giving up his pass and taking LeDuc's place. He proves his faith by taking it to its limit. Even as he makes his proof, four new prisoners are brought in, anonymous, interchangeable. In this echo of the major's scene, the major and the prince outface each other as the light dies.

Harold Clurman's production is as spare as the form of the play, put together with a keen sense of its proportion and balance. To watch the play grow in performance through a series of previews is to move toward definition. Out of an early blur individuals stand out as each actor finds his character and sparks recognition—some only to lose it again. But by the first night shades of gray stand out in white and black.

I traced this progress through program notes while watching the Repertory Theater company of the Lincoln Center at the ANTA Washington Square Theater. The play had yet to find its heights at its first preview on November 18, 1964. Dollars had not yet become francs, and the men were "American" French. As they did each time, the audience applauded the drama of the major's scene (Hal Holbrook and Joseph Wiseman) and welcomed the play itself with enthusiasm. A distance had been traveled by the Saturday matinee, November 21. The audience was slightly restive at the beginning, perhaps due to the long pause that starts the play, and to Bayard (Stanley Beck) being too quiet to make an impact. Now all had been sharpened. The play strengthened with LeDuc's (Joseph Wiseman) entrance, which became, and remains, a highlight. "It's not to work" held the house breathless. At each performance Hal Holbrook's scene took both audience and play. Then it built to its key scene between LeDuc and the prince (David Wayne), and left the house cheering. That evening confirmed that a Saturday-night audience is the same in London or New York. It is a kind of irony, in which the house is packed with an audience come to cheer, not really to see the play. They were restless, slow, uncertain. Wanting a response in the early scenes, the playing was leaden, but the actors were steadily becoming less "American." Holbrook's scene was excellent that night, played in a gasping exhaustion and ending with the precision of a pistol shot.

Thanksgiving Day—and an audience looking for relaxation responded to the comedy with the artist, to Marchand's (Paul Mann) scene with the gypsy (Harold Scott); it by-passed Miller's irony and astringent wit. David Wayne's prince grew in gentleness, and Jack Waltzer's isolation as the waiter was more moving than before. It seemed to make no difference whether the audience was restless or attentive; whether they were held by the play or watched it with a wandering mind—the end was the same, and the reception enthusiastic. At the sixth preview Paul Mann's Marchand radiated rotund well-being—the complete Marchand, dangerous, even when laughing. He and Will Lee (the old Jew) found their characters early, and remained consistent. For me, this tended to be the actors' evening: a tension built up in David J. Stewart that I didn't see in him again. Stanley Beck found Bayard, who was neither too slow nor too heavy. The audience was restless over his scenes; at each performance they grew restive at this point. The scene between LeDuc and Monceau came into sharp focus, and Holbrook was particularly fine on the idiocy of being loved. Joseph Wiseman lapsed into intoning LeDuc's key speech, but all was well at the last preview (December 2), when the scene, spoken, came over in its original power.

Overheard walking toward Washington Square: "Well, they just sit there, and the audience just thinks."

First night, December 3, 1964: The play was defined in a flawlessly timed production before an audience even more attentive than a similar first-night audience in London. They were with the play earlier, in the main, than the preview audiences had been. Joseph Wiseman brought a new incisiveness to LeDuc; his performance was better timed and had gained in pace. It was as if he had found the character at last. At each performance the emotional artist (Michael Strong) found common ground with the audience—a sympathy, perhaps, in that his fear is open and both comic and pathetic? The house was pin-still at "It's not to work," and held, as always, by Holbrook's scene—"Why do you deserve to live more than I do?" The scene reached its climax, to be succeeded by the greater, the last exchange between LeDuc and the prince. David Wayne seemed to sum up Miller's prince in his gentle, urbane performance: a frail stability in chaos and yet too strong to be swept aside, a foil for LeDuc as well as opposition for the major. On LeDuc's blazing demand, "I want not your guilt but your responsibility," a wave of spontaneous applause swept the house and broke round the actors as they took their calls.

It seemed at the outset that *Incident at Vichy* was the play expected from Miller, particularly by those who see him primarily as a detached dramatist of ideas. In the main, the

human questions in the play were overlooked, and a superficial
view of it was taken. This does not apply to Howard
Taubman, of the *New York Times,* who speaks eloquently
for Miller, whether it is *After the Fall* or *Incident at Vichy:*
"Arthur Miller has written a moving play, a searching play,
one of the most important plays of our time. . . . *Incident at
Vichy* is a drama of towering moral passion. It is an inquest
into the sources of Nazi viciousness and into the evil that
corrodes the spirit of so much of mankind. It is a thundering
cry of anguish that might issue from the heart of a prophet."

He was closely followed by Norman Nadel, of the New
York *World-Telegram & Sun,* and John McClain in the
New York *Journal-American.* In a review celebrating the
resilience of Miller's idealism, Mr. Nadel found this "incident"
"for a while seemed to embrace everyone, everywhere."
John McClain found the play good, if not very theatrical;
but he also found it an example of Miller's best writing in
that he himself was held, even in the play's static moments.

In the New York *Post,* Richard Watts, Jr., felt that Miller
was getting back into his stride as a dramatist of ideas, and
gave him a reserved Welcome Home. He found the play
continually absorbing, though not one of Miller's major
works. Mr. Watts was one of the first to sound an argument
that was to be read again in the dissenting weeklies: that
Miller had found no new angle on his subject. He then went
on to praise the "earnest force of the writing."

Incident at Vichy roused almost as great a controversy as
After the Fall. Walter Kerr led the opposition in the New
York *Herald Tribune:* "The audience may feel guilty to find
two thirds of the occasion tedious. I did. The matter is so
recent and so serious, and we are all of us so engaged in it,

that we scarcely dare acknowledge our dissatisfaction with its theatrical cloaking. When the play proper is less than binding, when it is in fact less than a play, we are confronted with a kind of moral blackmail. We must attend and approve because we *are* guilty. But that leaves the theatre as theatre nonexistent."

The only other New York daily paper to oppose the play was the *Daily News;* Douglas Watt admitted the "flurries of strong language," found the theatricality of the play contrived, and dismissed its philosophy as "claptrap."

Saturday Review found the play a searching dramatic essay. Henry Hewes realized that Miller "seems to be digging down to the roots of all natural human behavior," and in this appreciated his larger purpose. This reaction was balanced by John McCarten, writing in *The New Yorker*, who found the play didactic and undramatic.

A review in *Time* raised the point that it was morally impermissible for the doctor to accept his life at the cost of the prince's. Also, that "Miller has written an equation with a missing term—power. Power precedes responsibility. One is not accountable for events that one is powerless to avert or effect." This opposes the play's view of total individual responsibility.

Newsweek found the play a "slight step up from the depths of *After the Fall*," but, linking the play only with the Nazis, found it derivative. (It was not, in fact, Miller's view that was narrow.) Its reviewer suggested that Miller would find the prince, in his opposition to Nazism, a deplorable ally, "just as the refined white liberal is for James Baldwin." But this limits Miller's prince, and LeDuc's "You see now why I say there is nothing and will be nothing, when even you cannot really put yourself in my place? "Even you" only makes sense if the prince is the finest man that Miller can imagine.

Hear Miller on the man on whom his prince is based, the Gentile who handed over his pass to the Jew in Vichy: "Whenever I felt the seemingly implacable tide of human drift and withering of will, in myself and in others, this faceless person came to mind. And he appears most clearly and imperatively amid the jumble of emotions surrounding the Negro in this country, and the whole unsettled moral problem of the destruction of the Jews in Europe."[3]

The prince discovered at Vichy the cause of his general sense of guilt, Miller said in the *New York Times*. It was "his own secret joy and relief that, after all, he is not a Jew and will not be destroyed." Quentin made a similar discovery over Lou's death in *After the Fall*. Miller drew his prince as a man of intense sympathy, who could have survived, "but at a price too great for him to pay—the authenticity of his own self-image and his pride. And here I stop; I do not know why any man actually sacrifices himself any more than I know why people commit suicide." And yet John Proctor could have survived on the same basis as the prince, and in both instances survival was rejected.

The most blistering attack came from Robert Brustein in the *New Republic*, both against the play, which he saw purely in terms of the Nazis, and against Arthur Miller. To bypass the sound and the fury and get to the point: he found the characters symbolic and that Miller had given us less a play than another solemn sermon on Human Responsibility. He saw the limits Miller himself imposed, but not how he transcended them. The gypsy, for instance, illustrates LeDuc's

[3] *Ibid.*

point that the Jews have *their* Jews, as well as standing for
the thirty thousand gypsies who were killed by the Nazis.
The actor symbolizes all men who seek safety by obeying
the law—any law—as well as the people who denounced as
lunatic those who warned them of the camps—precisely the
actor's response to the waiter's story.

Mr. Brustein cited Hannah Arendt's *Eichmann in Jerusalem*
as one of the sources of *Incident at Vichy:* "Miss Arendt
showed how all Europe was implicated in the fate of the Jews,
but she hardly exculpated the Germans. In *Incident at Vichy*,
however, Mr. Miller compares the treatment of the Jews by
the Nazis with the hounding of the middle classes by the
Russians, the exploitation of Africans and Indians by the
British, and the suppression of Negroes by the Americans—
and somehow manages to get the Germans off the hook."

I cannot see how following racialism to its logical conclusion lets anybody off the hook; nor does a universal guilt
lessen an individual guilt. Mr. Brustein raised the same argument that arose over Quentin, that LeDuc, the "Miller"
character, exonerates his own guilt. I should have thought
he'd have recognized it. How do you bring home to someone
else something you yourself don't know?

In an interview with Barbara Gelb (*New York Times*,
November 29), Arthur Miller said: "The play has a shape, a
form, a truth. It very successfully does what I want it to
do." *Incident at Vichy* forces recognition, even unwilling
recognition, of our complicity with evil. This was proved,
unconsciously, by a person stomping out of the theatre, saying, in the words of Miller's prince, and almost in Miller's
line: "It's not true of me! He can't make it true of me!" And
it is toward this end, I think, that *Vichy* takes its simple form.

Miller went on in the same interview to ensure that nobody could suppose that this play was only about Vichy,
and that its situation ended with the war. "The occasion of
the play is the occupation of France but it's about today. It
concerns the question of insight—of seeing in ourselves the
capacity for collaboration with the evil one condemns. It is
a question that exists for all of us—what, for example, is the
responsibility of each of us for allowing the slums of Harlem
to exist? Some perfectly exemplary citizens, considerate of
their families and friends, contributing to charities and so
forth, are directly profiting from conditions like that." This
recalls Baron Kessler as the prince sees him, and Quentin, in
After the Fall, visualizing the carpenters and plumbers who
laid the pipes in the concentration camp.

I first saw *Incident at Vichy* as a measure of loss. Its subject makes this inevitable. In choosing Nazi-occupied Europe,
Miller placed his people at the turning point of humanity,
when all the old values fell away. There is nothing left—the
fact has to be accepted, like a death. Miller takes us through
a maze of beliefs to discover if anything does remain. Each
man is alone; one by one each is stripped of everything that
supports him—reason, logic, faith in a political future, in the
effectiveness of the civilized individual, in art, in personality
or talent, even in the possibility that there can be persons
again. Not one has an ideal left in his head; in fact, the prince
is hoping for a money-loving cynic he can bribe. The definition of humanity itself has swung around to its opposite
meaning. Dr. Arendt states in her book: "The trouble with
Eichmann was precisely that so many were like him, and that
the many were neither perverted nor sadistic, but were and
still are, terribly and terrifyingly normal." Miller, after at-

tending the Nazi war criminals' trials in Frankfurt, recorded the respectable, good-citizen aspect of the men on trial.

This may have sparked the play and Miller's realization that the story he was told of Vichy made his point. In the *New York Times* (January 3) he tried to persuade the reader to make links he finds natural, even unavoidable: "If the hostility and aggression which lie hidden in every human being could be accepted as a fact rather than as a reprehensible sin, perhaps the race could begin to guard against its ravages, which always take us 'unawares,' as something from 'outside,' from the hands of 'others.'" He knew that this link would readily be made over the Germans, but wondered whether it would be made over the Vietnamese torturing Vietcong prisoners. "The Vietnamese are wearing United States equipment, are paid by us, and could not torture without us. There is no way around this—the prisoner crying out in agony is *our prisoner*."

Incident at Vichy carries further the question of guilt and innocence that takes root in Miller's plays, from David Beeves in *The Man Who Had All the Luck*, and grows through them. Joe Keller was aware of his guilt, but not of the need to do anything about it. Willy's guilt, in part, blinded him to his real situation, and Miller found then that we are conscious only up to the point at which guilt begins. This tends to make victims of us all. Prompted by the time, he realized in *The Crucible* that the crippling force of guilt prevents people from taking action. It became "the most real of our illusions, but nevertheless a quality of mind capable of being overthrown." The conflict reaches agony in the confusion of guilt and innocence, justice with injustice, in *After the Fall*. Here, and in *Incident at Vichy*, the last step is taken—

beyond acceptance to responsibility. The prince's action is reflected in that of the three young civil rights workers murdered in Mississippi. In writing of them, Miller said that by transforming guilt into responsibility, into action, they "opened the way to a vision that leapt the pit of remorse and helplessness."[4]

In the main, Miller's plays impelled a recognition that time has made easy. He says in his Preface that he was surprised to find the truth of *All My Sons* so rapidly accepted. Willy Loman found instant recognition and compassion. John Proctor's necessary stand against the witch-hunt took more time, but general approval of the play grows as we move further from the McCarthy era. Eddie Carbone's trap was too particular to himself to be generally upsetting, and *A Memory of Two Mondays* built into daily life long-past protest. The challenge of *The Misfits* with its shifting world passed virtually unnoticed. Miller's demands were always high, and the very reactions to these plays attest their relevance. Plays have been praised, in retrospect, for being ahead of our time—I wonder how many have been praised for striking its hour? Miller does this when he writes of the guilts of Quentin, the dependence of Maggie, and of open destruction in the image of *Incident at Vichy*. The prince finds Miller's answer to "What can ever save us?" He and the major stand face to face—a stumble into daylight with the major's darker, colder balance held as its parallel.

[4] *Ibid.*

Casts

ALL MY SONS
Coronet Theatre, New York   *January 29, 1947*

JOE KELLER	Ed Begley
DR. JOM BAYLISS	John McGovern
FRANK LUBEY	Dudley Sadler
SUE BAYLISS	Peggy Meredith
LYDIA LUBEY	Hope Cameron
CHRIS KELLER	Arthur Kennedy
BERT	Eugene Steiner
KATE KELLER	Beth Merrill
ANN DEEVER	Lois Wheeler
GEORGE DEEVER	Karl Malden

Directed by Elia Kazan
Designed and lighted by Mordecai Gorelik

ALL MY SONS
Lyric Theatre, Hammersmith   *May 11, 1948*
Globe Theatre, London   *June 16, 1948*

JOE KELLER	Joseph Calleia
DR. JOM BAYLISS	Hugh Pryse
FRANK LUBEY	Peter Hutton
SUE BAYLISS	Louise Lister
LYDIA LUBEY	Barbara Todd
CHRIS KELLER	Richard Leech
BERT	Robin Netscher
KATE KELLER	Margalo Gillmore
ANN DEEVER	Harriette Johns
GEORGE DEEVER	John McLaren

Directed by Warren Jenkins

237

ーター

238   *Arthur Miller: The Burning Glass*

DEATH OF A SALESMAN
Morosco Theatre, New York   *February 10, 1949*

WILLY LOMAN	Lee J. Cobb
LINDA	Mildred Dunnock
BIFF	Arthur Kennedy
HAPPY	Cameron Mitchell
BERNARD	Don Keefer
THE WOMAN	Winnifred Cushing
CHARLEY	Howard Smith
UNCLE BEN	Thomas Chalmers
HOWARD WAGNER	Alan Hewitt
JENNY	Ann Driscoll
STANLEY	Tom Pedi
MISS FORSYTHE	Constance Ford
LETTA	Hope Cameron

Directed by Elia Kazan
Setting and lighting by Jo Mielziner

DEATH OF A SALESMAN
Phoenix Theatre, London   *July 28, 1949*

WILLY LOMAN	Paul Muni
LINDA	Katharine Alexander
HAPPY	Frank Maxwell
BIFF	Kevin McCarthy
BERNARD	Sam Main
THE WOMAN	Bessie Love
CHARLEY	Ralph Theadore
UNCLE BEN	Henry Oscar
HOWARD WAGNER	J. Anthony La Penna
JENNY	Joan MacArthur
STANLEY	George Margo
MISS FORSYTHE	Mary Laura Wood
LETTA	Barbara Cummings
A WAITER	Ronald Frazer

Directed by Elia Kazan
Setting and lighting by Jo Mielziner

AN ENEMY OF THE PEOPLE
Broadhurst Theatre, New York   *December 28, 1950*

MORTEN KIIL	Art Smith
BILLING	Michael Strong
MRS. STOCKMANN	Florence Eldridge
PETER STOCKMANN	Morris Carnovsky
HOVSTAD	Martin Brooks
DR. STOCKMANN	Frederic March
MORTEN	Ralph Robertson
EJLIF	Richard Trask
CAPT. HORSTER	Ralph Dunn
PETRA	Anna Minot
ASLAKSEN	Fred Stewart
THE DRUNK	Lou Gilbert

Directed by Robert Lewis
Settings and costumes by Aline Bernstein
Play adapted by Arthur Miller from the original by Henrik Ibsen

AN ENEMY OF THE PEOPLE
Theatre Royal, Lincoln *February 24, 1958*

MORTEN KIIL	Colin Ellis
BILLING	Bryon Warden
CATHERINE STOCKMANN	Sheila Price
PETER STOCKMANN	Brian Hawksley
HOVSTAD	John Pickles
DR. STOCKMANN	George Coulouris
MORTEN	Keith Smith
EJLIF	Richard Hamill
CAPTAIN HORSTER	K. V. Moore
PETRA	Daphne Wetton
ASLAKSEN	David Perry
THE DRUNK	John Brittany

TOWNSPEOPLE
James Reid
Anne Heslop
Audrey Smith
Joan Kennedy
P. Robson
C. Farrar
A. Smith
Noel Makin
Mary Vaughan
Victoria Watts
R. Royle
K. R. Atkinson
A. J. Robinson

Directed by John Hale

THE CRUCIBLE
Martin Beck Theatre, New York   *January 22, 1953*

BETTY PARRIS	Janet Alexander
TITUBA	Jacqueline Andre
REV. SAMUEL PARRIS	Fred Stewart
ABIGAIL WILLIAMS	Madeleine Sherwood
SUSANNA WALCOTT	Barbara Stanton
MRS. ANN PUTNAM	Jane Hoffman
THOMAS PUTNAM	Raymond Bramley
MERCY LEWIS	Dorothy Jolliffe
MARY WARREN	Jenny Egan
JOHN PROCTOR	Arthur Kennedy
REBECCA NURSE	Jean Adair
GILES COREY	Joseph Sweeney
REV. JOHN HALE	E. G. Marshall
ELIZABETH PROCTOR	Beatrice Straight
FRANCIS NURSE	Graham Velsey
EZEKIEL CHEEVER	Don McHenry
JOHN WILLARD	George Mitchell
JUDGE HATHORNE	Philip Coolidge
DEPUTY-GOVERNOR DANFORTH	Walter Hampden
SARAH GOOD	Adele Fortin
HOPKINS	Donald Marye

Directed by Jed Harris
Settings by Boris Aronson

THE CRUCIBLE
Theatre Royal, Bristol   *November 9, 1954*

BETTY PARRIS	Annette Crosbie
REV. SAMUEL PARRIS	John Cairney
TITUBA	Barbara Assoon
ABIGAIL WILLIAMS	Pat Sandys
SUSANNA WALCOTT	Patricia Hesley
MRS. ANN PUTNAM	Phyllida Law
THOMAS PUTNAM	Ronald Hines
MERCY LEWIS	Gillian Lewis
MARY WARREN	Perlita Neilson
JOHN PROCTOR	Edgar Wreford
REBECCA NURSE	Mary Savidge
GILES COREY	Paul Lee
REV. JOHN HALE	Michael Allinson
ELIZABETH PROCTOR	Rosemary Harris
FRANCIS NURSE	Antony Tuckey
EZEKIEL CHEEVER	Bruce Sharman
JOHN WILLARD	Edward Hardwicke
JUDGE HATHORNE	Peter Wylde
DEPUTY-GOV. DANFORTH	John Kidd
SARAH GOOD	Phyllida Law

Directed by Warren Jenkins
Settings by Patrick Robertson

THE CRUCIBLE
Royal Court Theatre, London   *April 9, 1956*

BETTY PARRIS	Marcia Manolesceu
REV. SAMUEL PARRIS	John Welsh
TITUBA	Connie Smith
ABIGAIL WILLIAMS	Mary Ure
SUSANNA WALCOTT	Helena Hughes
MRS. ANN PUTNAM	Rachel Kempson
THOMAS PUTNAM	Nigel Davenport
MERCY LEWIS	Josee Richard
MARY WARREN	Joan Plowright
JOHN PROCTOR	Michael Gwynn
REBECCA NURSE	Agnes Lauchlan
REV. JOHN HALE	Kenneth Haig
ELIZABETH PROCTOR	Rosalie Crutchley
FRANCIS NURSE	Stephen Dartnell
EZEKIEL CHEEVER	Christopher Fettes
JOHN WILLARD	George Selway
HOPKINS	Alan Bates
DEPUTY-GOV. DANFORTH	George Devine
JUDGE HATHORNE	Robert Stephens
SARAH GOOD	Barbara Grimes

Directed by George Devine, assisted by Tony Richardson
Settings by Stephen Doncaster
Costumes by Motley

THE CRUCIBLE
The National Theatre, London   *January, 1965*

BETTY PARRIS	Janina Faye
REVEREND SAMUEL PARRIS	Kenneth Mackintosh
TITUBA	Pearl Prescod
ABIGAIL WILLIAMS	Sarah Miles
SUSANNA WALCOTT	Janie Booth
GOODWIFE ANN PUTNAM	Barbara Hicks
THOMAS PUTNAM	Trevor Martin
MERCY LEWIS	Sheila Reid
MARY WARREN	Jeanne Hepple
JOHN PROCTOR	Colin Blakely
GOODWIFE REBECCA NURSE	Wynne Clark
GILES COREY	Frank Finlay
REVEREND JOHN HALE	Robert Lang
GOODWIFE ELIZABETH PROCTOR	Joyce Redman
FRANCIS NURSE	Keith Marsh
EZEKIEL CHEEVER	Michael Turner
MARSHAL HERRICK	James Mellor
DEPUTIES }	Mike Gambon Robert Russell
JUDGE HATHORNE	Peter Cellier
DEPUTY-GOVERNOR DANFORTH	Anthony Nicholls

Production by Laurence Olivier
Scenery and costumes by Michael Annals
Lighting by Brian Freeland

245

A MEMORY OF TWO MONDAYS
Coronet Theatre, New York *September 29, 1955*

BERT	Leo Penn
RAYMOND	David Clarke
AGNES	Eileen Heckart
PATRICIA	Gloria Marlowe
GUS	J. Carrol Naish
JIM	Russell Collins
KENNETH	Biff McGuire
LARRY	Van Heflin
FRANK	Jack Warden
JERRY	Richard Davalos
WILLIAM	Antony Vorno
TOM	Curt Conway
MECHANIC	Tom Pedi
MISTER EAGLE	Ralph Bell

Directed by Martin Ritt
Designed by Boris Aronson

A VIEW FROM THE BRIDGE
Coronet Theatre, New York   *September 29, 1955*

LOUIS	David Clarke
MIKE	Tom Pedi
ALFIERI	J. Carrol Naish
EDDIE	Van Heflin
CATHERINE	Gloria Marlowe
BEATRICE	Eileen Heckart
MARCO	Jack Warden
TONY	Antony Vorno
RODOLPHO	Richard Davalos
FIRST IMMIGRATION OFFICER	Curt Conway
SECOND " "	Ralph Bell
MR. LIPARI	Russell Collins
MRS. LIPARI	Anne Driscoll
TWO "SUBMARINES"	Leo Penn, Milton Carny

Directed by Martin Ritt
Designed by Boris Aronson

A VIEW FROM THE BRIDGE
Comedy Theatre, London   *October 11, 1956*

LOUIS	Richard Harris
MIKE	Norman Mitchell
ALFIERI	Michael Gwynn
EDDIE	Anthony Quayle
CATHERINE	Mary Ure
BEATRICE	Megs Jenkins
MARCO	Ian Bannen
TONY	Ralph Nossek
RODOLPHO	Brian Bedford
FIRST IMMIGRATION OFFICER	John Stone
SECOND " "	Colin Rix
MR. LIPARI	Mervyn Blake
MRS. LIPARI	Catherine Willmer
A "SUBMARINE"	Peter James

Directed and Designed by Peter Brook

A VIEW FROM THE BRIDGE
Theatre Antoine, Paris   *March 11, 1958*

ALFIERI	Henri Nassiet
PETER	André Rousselet
MIKE	Jacques Ferrière
EDDIE	Raf Vallone
CATHERINE	Evelyne Dandry
BEATRICE	Lila Kedrova
TONY.	Serge Dubos
MARCO	Marcel Bozzufi
RODOLFO	José Varela
FIRST IMMIGRATION OFFICER	Jean Morel
SECOND " "	Pierre Pascal
THIRD " "	Edmond George
LIPARI'S NEPHEW	Ernest Varial
LIPARI'S WIFE	Maya Morani
LIPARI'S DAUGHTER	Clara Lerins
FIRST DOCKER	Philippe Chauveau
SECOND DOCKER	Alain Dal
THIRD DOCKER	Jean-Paul Ferrari

Directed and Designed by Peter Brook
Translated by Marcel Aymé

A VIEW FROM THE BRIDGE
New Shakespeare Theatre, Liverpool   *October 31, 1957*

LOUIS	Roy Pattison
MIKE	Roger Boston
MR. ALFIERI	Sam Wanamaker
EDDIE	Marc Lawrence
CATHERINE	Catherine Feller
BEATRICE	Vera Fusek
TONY	Robert Algar
MARCO	Ralph Nossek
RODOLPHO	Tim Seely
FIRST IMMIGRATION OFFICER	Michael O'Brien
SECOND " "	Stuart Allen
MR. LIPARI	Robert Quinn
MRS. LIPARI	Nancy Graham

Directed by Sam Wanamaker
Settings by Ellen Meyer

THE MISFITS
*A John Huston Production presented by Seven Arts Productions
and released by United Artists*

GAY LANGLAND	Clark Gable
ROSLYN TABER	Marilyn Monroe
PERCE HOWLAND	Montgomery Clift
ISABELLE STEERS	Thelma Ritter
GUIDO	Eli Wallach
THE OLD MAN IN THE BAR	James Barton
THE CHURCH LADY	Estelle Winwood
RAYMOND TABER	Kevin McCarthy
YOUNG BOY IN BAR (LESTER)	Dennis Shaw
CHARLES STEERS	Philip Mitchell
OLD GROOM	Walter Ramage
FRESH COWBOY IN BAR	J. Lewis Smith
SUSAN	Marietta Tree
BARTENDER	Bobby La Salle
MAN IN BAR	Ryall Bowker
AMBULANCE ATTENDANT	Ralph Roberts

Screenplay by Arthur Miller
Produced by Frank E. Taylor
Directed by John Huston

AFTER THE FALL
Repertory Theater of Lincoln Center, New York

January 23, 1965

QUENTIN	Jason Robards, Jr.
FELICE	Zohra Lampert
HOLGA	Salome Jens
DAN	Michael Strong
FATHER	Paul Mann
MOTHER	Virginia Kaye
NURSES	Faye Dunaway, Diane Shalet
MAGGIE	Barbara Loden
ELSIE	Patricia Roe
LOU	David J. Stewart
LOUISE	Mariclare Costello
MICKEY	Ralph Meeker
MAN IN PARK	Stanley Beck
CARRIE	Ruth Attaway
LUCAS	Harold Scott
CHAIRMAN	David Wayne
HARLEY BARNES	Hal Holbrook
PORTER	Jack Waltzer
MAGGIE'S SECRETARY	Crystal Field
PIANIST	Scott Cunningham
OTHERS	Clint Kimbrough John Phillip Law Barry Primus James Greene

Directed by Elia Kazan
Production and Lighting designed by Jo Mielziner

INCIDENT AT VICHY
Repertory Theater of Lincoln Center, New York
December 3, 1964

LeBeau, the Painter	Michael Strong
Bayard, the Electrician	Stanley Beck
Marchand, the Businessman	Paul Mann
Police Guard	C. Thomas Blackwell
Monceau, the Actor	David L. Stewart
Gypsy	Harold Scott
The Waiter	Jack Waltzer
The Boy	Ira Lewis
The Major	Hal Holbrook
First Detective	Alek Primrose
Old Jew	Will Lee
Second Detective	James Dukas
LeDuc, the Doctor	Joseph Wiseman
Police Captain	James Greene
Von Berg, the Prince	David Wayne
Professor Hoffman	Clinton Kimbrough
Ferrand, the Cafe Proprietor	Graham Jarvis
Four Prisoners	Pierre Epstein Stephan Peters Tony Lo Bianco John Vari

Directed by Harold Clurman
Designed by Boris Aronson
Lighting by Jean Rosenthal
Costumes by Jane Greenwood

Index